I0706043

BY: D.M. MEWHA

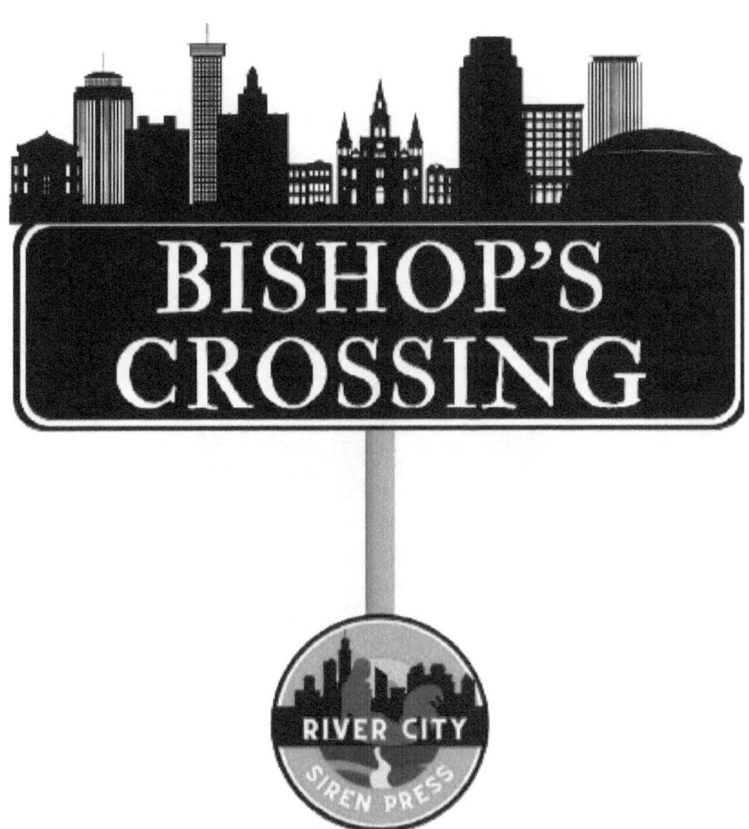

Copyright © 2024 by D.M. Mewha and River City Siren Press

Hardcover ISBN: 978-1-964989-00-6

Paperback ISBN: 978-1-964989-01-3

For Jodi, who taught me that love is like pi—natural, irrational, and very important.

"Love is like pi—natural, irrational, and very important."
- Lisa Hoffman

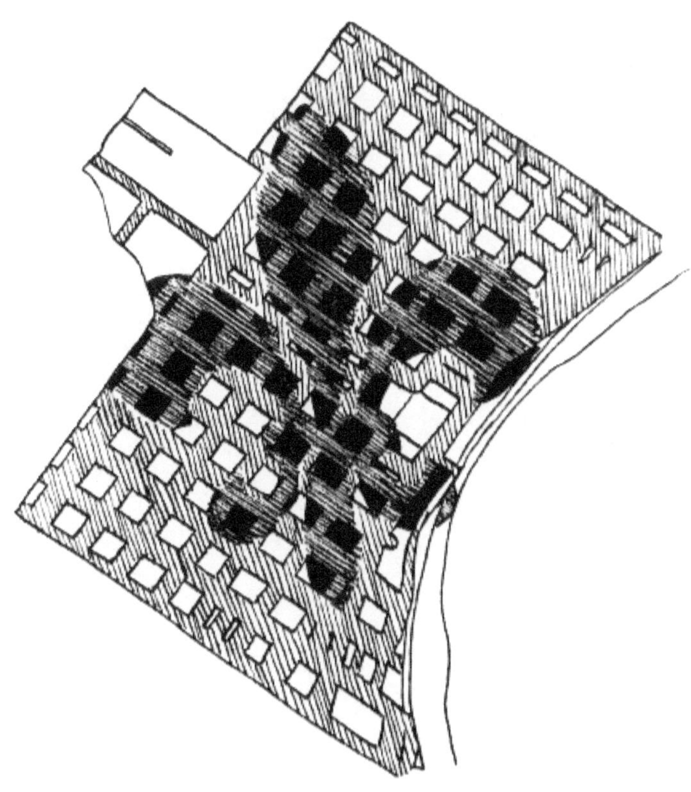

Original Artwork by Jodi Lea

Art Digitized by Anna Frassmann-Swadinsky

Chapter
ONE

S ome days it's easy to hate yourself.

This was gonna be one of those days.

"Mmmmm. You up, baby?"

Fucking finally.

"Yeah, in here," I called from the bathroom.

I clawed my way out of a deep sleep well over an hour ago, like a swimmer that had stayed under for too long trying to fight their way back to the surface, vaguely aware my mouth felt and tasted like the bathroom floor of a dive bar. I swallowed and instantly regretted it, so I relocated to brush my teeth.

Then I'd begun the process of trying to wake up the mystery woman in my bed, a process that had resulted in. . . well, an hour of her rolling over and mumbling.

The voice asking the question was thick with sleep, its owner's breath indicative of the copious amounts of booze she drank the night before. That *we* drank the night before. I glanced over her and stared in shock at the clock display.

Nearly noon.

Shit.

I swallowed, trying and failing to push down a sense of panic that was building in my gut while the smells and sounds of the French Quarter drifted in through the open window, a mixture of traffic, gumbo, and jazz drifting on the humid air. It did nothing to help the nausea.

"Yeah," I replied, shifting my gaze from the clock to the woman in my bed. Caramel skin, dark curly hair. Pretty. She deserved better than what was about to happen.

Looking around the room, I found a pair of sandals and a sundress. Even with the raging headache digging its claws into my brain, I was positive neither was mine. I hurried out of the bathroom, bent down, grabbed the dress, and tossed it to her, leaving a trail of her perfume in its wake.

"Sorry, but you gotta go."

"You're kidding, right?"

"Don't know if you had a bra, but see if you can find it, 'kay?"

"You're not? What the fuck, Bishop?"

I struggled to latch onto her name. I think she was a C. Christine? Claudine? Jesus, I'm such an asshole.

"Look, I promise I'm not normally like this. . . Cassie?"

I paused as she sat up, covering herself with her dress; she went from confused to angry. Her eyes were gorgeous. And hurt.

"Claudia, asshole. My name's Claudia. Jesus, I can't believe I fell for your bullshit!"

"That's sort of the thing, Claudia, and I really am sorry I couldn't remember, and you're right; I'm a total asshole and deserve you being pissed at me and calling me every name in the book. They're all on the money. It's just that I have something I've gotta do in about ten, no, five minutes now, and I'd rather keep that part of my life separate from. . ." I gestured at her vaguely.

"From your boozy, misogynistic womanizing?" she spat back.

I sighed. "Yeah. The audience wouldn't really appreciate it, and my good name's already taken enough hits on that front. I swear to you while I'm most assuredly an asshole and I deserve everything you're thinking about me right now, as well as quite a bit you're not, in this particular case, I'm on the side of the angels."

"You're so full of shit."

I heard the front door open, then close.

Fuuuuuuck.

"Who's that?" Claudia demanded. "Are you married or something?" She swung her feet out of bed and yanked up her red polka-dotted underwear. I think they were supposed to look like a ladybug. I remembered being amused by them last night. Right now, they spelled impending doom as she stormed toward the door of the bedroom. Coming to my feet, I tried to stop her.

"Look, Claudia, this isn't what you think. I—"

"Don't you *dare* touch me, you son of a bitch!" she shouted, holding her hands up in front of her.

I followed suit.

"Who is she? *Who*, you piece of shit? I can't believe I bought into the suave bullshit you pulled last night, but if some chick is just walking into your place, she's got a right to know what a total dick you are!" she screamed in my face, punctuating each obscenity with a poke in the middle of my chest.

I sighed. No way that hadn't been heard in the living room.

"That," I said, pointing over my shoulder, "is my daughter Mary. She visits on Saturdays at noon. My alarm didn't go off this morning to wake me up."

"Hello," Mary called from the living room. She was a precocious eight-year-old but still clearly sounded child-like.

Claudia's eyes went wide, and she put her hands in front of her mouth as she inhaled in horror.

"Oh my God, I am *so* sorry! Why didn't you—" Her voice was getting quieter and higher pitched as the conversation proceeded.

"Just get dressed," I muttered, walking over to retrieve my pants and grab a fresh shirt from my closet.

Claudia complied, stammering apologies as she slipped on her dress and scooped up her footwear from the bottom of my bed. I opened the bedroom door to find Mary sitting quietly on the couch, paging through one of her comic books.

I walked out and kissed her forehead; she wrinkled her nose.

"You smell like your ashtrays, Daddy. And the floor downstairs."

I smiled and leaned against the wall as Claudia exited the bedroom, sandals in hand.

"Hi, I'm—"

"Claudia. I heard. Nice to meet you. I'm Mary."

Unsure how to respond at this point, Claudia looked at Mary. My daughter's green eyes met Claudia's hazel ones, which only served to make Claudia all the more uncomfortable. After a moment, Claudia looked away from the skinny little girl, her eyes scanning the room and finding me hovering in the doorway, arms crossed over my chest.

"Hey Bishop, I'm gonna head out! I'll see you again soon."

I sighed.

Mind full of regret and self-recrimination, I nodded, then watched as she walked out the front door.

"She seems nice," Mary commented. "She cursed a lot less than the last one you had here."

The door closed, then my eyes followed suit. Taking a deep breath, I steeled myself for a conversation I'd hoped to avoid. Opening them, I looked out the window and caught my image staring back at me, my grey eyes locking onto their reflection and stared for a heartbeat, taking in the picture in front of me. Tousled dirty blonde hair sitting on top of a haggard face with too much stubble. A sad smile that sometimes turned into a smirk.

Basically, I saw a guy with no cards left to play. Taking a deep breath, I tried anyway.

"Look, Mare-bear—"

"Don't Mare-bear me, Daddy," Mary demanded, cutting me off. "I was by myself this time, but what if Mommy or even worse, what if Victor walked me up?"

"You're old enough that they don't really need to do that anymore," I protested.

"You live over a *bar*, Daddy," my child reasonably pointed out.

"I know, kiddo, I know. . ."

"Do you?" she asked. "Do you *really* know? Mommy and Victor are starting to talk about 'long term plans.' They're starting to talk about getting engaged, Daddy. Getting *married*. You keep saying that you love Mommy, and you want to be there for her. But you keep doing stupid stuff like this. You're running out of time to get your shit together."

I blinked.

"You're picking up some rough language, Daughter-o-mine," I replied. "But that aside, I promise you, I will take your sage words to heart."

Mary smiled at me. It was the kind of smile that breaks a parent's heart. The sort that says, 'I want to believe you, but you've let me down too often for it to carry much weight.'

I hated that smile. Probably because I'd earned it.

Officially speaking, I own a restaurant and bar in the New Orleans French Quarter. Bishop's Crossing. Charming little place complete with gas lights that date back to God-only-knows-when flickering in the endlessly muggy Big Easy air with two dozen dark wooden tables crammed into the interior and flowing out onto the street. There's a steady stream of tourists, seasoned with enough regulars that I never really need to worry about the money thing. I purchased the place years ago, after an abrupt change in careers brought about by an unexpected change in my family situation—namely, my dad going nuts and killing my mother and sister.

In front of me.

That's the sort of thing that leaves an impression. Made it so being a priest was less appealing than it had been. How could a just and loving God allow blah blah blah? You've heard that song and dance, so I'll spare you the rest.

Yeah, that's right, the guy leaning against the bar at Bishop's Crossing attended seminary. Notre Dame Seminary here in New Orleans, to be specific, from the time I finished college with a degree in theology until August 25, 2005. That's when things went a bit off the rails on me.

That's when I was introduced to The Gloaming, that place just at the edge of your vision, the spot that gives you chills when you're walking alone at night and come on a particularly dark alley.

That place where monsters live.

You see, what I do, or more specifically, what I *used* to do, is to stick my nose into The Gloaming and give it a good shake. I was an occultist. Got heavily into it after the incident with my father. I wanted it to make sense. I wanted a reason—an answer.

I don't do tarot, palm, or scalp readings. I'm not some sort of psychic, though if I concentrate hard enough, I can see what some people call 'auras,' which can be handy but tends to cause as much trouble as it solves. Has been since it showed up when I was a teenager. I don't have a crystal ball, and I sure as hell didn't want the same sort of drunken tourists who drink in my bar stopping in for a consultation.

For ten years, I was a demonologist, occult researcher, and sometimes investigator. It was ten years that left me a mess. Ten years that cost me a chance to be with the woman I love and the disapproving daughter we had together. Ten years of wading through the worst shit in the world, somehow coming out the other side of it and realizing it didn't make me deeper, more intelligent, or happy. It didn't seem to help anyone else or make any sort of difference.

It just ruined lives.

It certainly ruined mine.

It nearly destroyed me, so I left it behind. I locked up the back room with the dusty tomes and the objects I'd gathered over the years. I ignored the strange auras I saw around figures as they came and went. I ignored the anguished nightmares that came at night, the ones where my sister is burning—pleading for me to save her—asking why I abandoned her.

I closed my eyes, shut out the noise, and concentrated on my bar.

I concentrated on the few bloody tatters of me left and hoped it was enough to cobble together a life. To make amends with my daughter, Mary. Maybe even her mother.

I hoped it wasn't too late.

I was pretty sure it was.

Standing behind the bar at Bishop's Crossing on that day in mid-October, I had no idea what was coming, but then again, the one that gets you is always the one you don't hear. I was sitting at the back corner while my head bartender, Dave, took care of the few customers wandering in. New Orleans isn't a daytime sorta town. Mary was perched on a stool at one of the high back tables that allowed Bishop's Crossing to qualify as a restaurant instead of just a bar, chatting happily away while I drank Dave's latest attempt at a hangover cure-all.

"Ugh," I said, fighting hard against my gag reflex. "What's in this?"

Dave smiled. "Best not to ask, bossman. Family recipe."

I'd known Dave for a good six years now. We'd met when his family got involved with trying to open a doorway into our world using some old books, a virgin, and some very naughty words. Dave was the only one that saw the light and helped put a stop to it. He was a large dark-skinned man, topping six and a half feet tall and weighing well over three hundred pounds. His eyes were mismatched (one blue, the other brown), and his hair formed a large cloud around his head before merging into an equally impressive beard. He was a striking man and now the only survivor of his family. We hoped.

We were both sorta surprised that we had lived through the ordeal. Since he didn't have much in the way of non-occult skills (seems that being raised by evil cannibal cultists doesn't have as much portability as you might suspect), I gave him a place for a bit. He stayed around when I packed it in. Even when I'm "concentrating on my business," I'm still not the kinda guy that's good at showing up for a nine to five kinda shift. Dave, on the other hand, seems tireless and punctual. Some of the regulars ask him for his secret. He smiles at them, telling them they don't wanna know. He laughs. They laugh. I laugh.

But they really don't.

Still, he's good folks, and Mary took an immediate liking to him, which has never hurt.

"Uncle Dave, don't some of your family recipes have people parts in them?" she asked.

"Of course, Miss Mary," he replied with mock solemnity. "But those are only for holidays. This one's just because your daddy didn't pay attention to what and how much he was drinking last night."

Standing behind Mary, I raised my middle finger and smiled painfully as I fought down the remainder of the glass' contents.

"That's not nice, Daddy," Mary said without looking up from the book in front of her. Tolkien, by the look of it.

Dave smiled as I shook my head. The kid knew me too well.

"What are your plans with your drunken reprobate of a father, Miss Mary?" he asked.

"We're supposed to go shopping for a Halloween costume."

"Halloween costume? Him?" Dave asked.

"Yeah, Mom says Daddy's gonna take me this year."

"We were discussing it, yeah," I agreed. "But nothing's set in stone yet."

"It's in less than two weeks. I need my costume, and besides, Mom says you're way better with this 'Halloween Stuff' than she is."

Oh, for fuck's sake. Halloween stuff.

That's one way of putting it.

Jackie was my ex. We'd lived with each other and had a child together, but she didn't know what I had done or what I had been doing all of those times I wasn't around. She just knew me as a guy that was part of the sorta fringe scene the Quarter is famous for. Street artists, fake vodun priestesses, palm readers, psychics doing ghost tours, you know—general assorted charlatans. I was happy to keep her in the dark, at first, because I wasn't interested in yet another occult groupie and later because I realized I loved the hell out of her. I didn't want to expose her to the little corner of hell that I walked through some nights (literally in more cases than I care to count).

I was her quirky, moderately dangerous bad boy, and I played the part too well.

I wasn't the full-on douchebag. I never cheated on her, no matter how many offers came my way. I never hit her or did anything to make her feel unsafe. Instead, I treated her like some sort of manic pixie dream girl, ignoring everything that she wanted in a haze of sex, drinking, and drugs when we were together, chasing my obsession with finding the key to Hell when we weren't.

Most people say that for a relationship to fail, it takes two people. I sure as shit showed them, it wasn't true. I managed to tank what we had completely solo.

We had eight great years together.

No, that's a lie. We had *six* great years together. Then a mediocre year. Then a year where I was an asshole and drove her and my daughter away. I was convinced it wasn't my fault that she was being an unreasonable bitch. It's amazing, really. I'd spent all my time packing and storing my emotional baggage, but I was still shocked when Jackie packed their bags and left. The irony would be funny if it weren't so painful.

"What do you want to go as this year, Mare-bear?"

The offspring leveled a long-suffering look at me, rolling her eyes and sighing.

"I wanna be a voodoo witch," she replied with a nod.

"Witch and voodoo are two different things, kiddo."

"So?"

"So, you can't be a voodoo witch."

"Yes, I can. That's what I want to be. Last year Jessica went as a zombie cheerleader. And this year, Kayla says she's gonna be a vampire fairy."

Closing my eyes, I sighed. "Okay. Voodoo witch. Perfect. What's a voodoo witch look like? Do we pick this up at Toys R Us or something?"

"Daaaaad," she whined, sliding off of the stool so she could properly express her outrage. "I don't want to get a store-bought costume. I was hoping you'd take me to that supply store you and Uncle Dave are always talking about."

I sensed the danger in her request before my mouth ever opened.

"What supply store?"

"Papa Ivé's."

And the hits just keep on coming.

"Out of the question," I said immediately.

"Bad idea, princess," Dave added, looking at me with his most eloquent 'I told you so.'

"Why?" she asked, sliding out of her chair.

"He's in a bad neighborhood, sweetie. I don't want—I can't have you on their radar. It's not safe."

"Gangs," Dave added with a nod. "Big ones."

"Uncle Dave, you were supposed to be on *my* side," she said, stomping her foot in frustration.

"I am, princess. That's why I agree with your father. Ivé's isn't a good place."

Frustrated and confused, Mary looked between Dave and me, then sighed loudly and slumped back onto her stool. "Fine," she muttered, kicking the counter. "We can go to stupid baby Halloween Adventure."

Papa Ivé was a man of reputation in The Gloaming. The Voodoo King of New Orleans and, rumor had it, a direct descendant of Marie Laveau herself. He was a witch doctor of incredible power, considerable influence, and a legendary temper. Throw in the fact that I may have liberated some of his property in the past and not returned it, and you have the beginnings of a contentious relationship that probably doesn't end with an acceptable Halloween costume.

"I know some other places," I offered. "Some that aren't in the middle of gang territory. How about we avoid the pre-packaged costumes and hit up some other stores instead?"

Mary smiled, hopped over, and threw her arms around me.

"Thanks, Daddy."

And all was right with the world.

Spending the day shopping with Mary was one of those perfect days. The sun sat high in the sky, what clouds there were floated by, unthreatening, and my daughter spent most of the day smiling at me. You don't get enough days like that, and you rarely understand how precious they are until well after the day has passed. It took me too long to understand that time like this with Mary is limited. That after a very short time, she'll stop being interested in spending time with me, and I'll be the one chasing after her.

It's a limited window. A brief flicker.

God, I wish I'd realized it sooner.

But that wasn't the story for today. Mary and I rode the streetcar up and down the streets of New Orleans with an ever-increasing bag of purchases. I visited a few tourist stores and more than a few legitimate occult operations places that my shadow hadn't darkened in a year. We stuck strictly to the folks on the side of the angels, though some of them seemed downright nervous when I showed up at their shop.

The sun sat low in the sky by the time we finished. Mary was satisfied with her costuming choices. We'd stopped and eaten at one of the many small corner restaurants that dotted the city and were pleasantly full.

Jackie didn't live too far from me. While I was well off (you don't get to own a whole building in the French Quarter if you're a pauper), Jackie's fiancé, Victor, was wealthy. He was some sort of important oil executive and had purchased a home in the Garden District several years before. The Garden District is the best representation I've ever seen of the antebellum South brought forward into modern times. The homes are large, often have marble columns, and generally make me feel like I'm underdressed.

Walking her up through the intricate wrought-iron gate and knocking on the front door (framed by planters, of course), I gave Mary one last squeeze.

"Be good, kiddo. I'll see you soon."

"You promise?" she asked.

I nodded. "Scout's honor."

"Daddy, you told me you got kicked out of the Cub Scouts."

"And let that be a lesson to you. Those fascists don't have the market cornered on honesty, truth, or soapbox derby cars. Forge your own path."

"But is it really a derby if there's only one car?"

"Touché, daughter mine. Touché."

She giggled a bit as the door opened to reveal her mother, Jackie.

"Hey sweetie, did you have a good time?"

"I did," I said quickly before Mary had a chance to answer. Mary tried to suppress a smile while Jackie sighed and rolled her eyes to hide hers.

"Inside, sweetie. You need to put away your stuff and brush your teeth."

"Okay. Thanks, Daddy," Mary said, reaching up on tiptoes to wrap her arms around my neck and kiss me on the cheek. I watched her go inside, then offered a forlorn smile to my lady faire before turning to walk home.

"Jason?"

I paused. Not many people call me by my first name, and it always takes me a second to register; they mean me. I turned and looked over my shoulder.

Jackie stood about five foot nine, around three inches shorter than me. Her brown hair fell around her shoulders in waves, but her forehead was wrinkly with raised eyebrows. She was chewing on the right corner of her bottom lip, her hazel eyes looking around, for what I have no idea.

"Yes?" I turned and walked toward her as she closed the door behind her and took two hesitant steps toward me. "If this is one of those times you need someone to show your womanhood the ways of love, I'd be more than happy to oblige. I figure with all of the shrubbery you've got going on around here, it might not even be all that scandalous."

A laugh escaped before she could help herself, which drew a frown. I've always been able to make her laugh, which I've been told is frustrating as hell.

"Dammit, Jason. No, my womanhood is fine, thank you. This is serious. It's about Mary."

"What about her? We spent the day together, and everything seemed okay."

"Not according to her teacher and principal."

Uh oh.

"Is she not doing well in school? That doesn't seem like her. She's always gotten good grades before."

"I wish it were grades. The principal called yesterday and said it's behavior related. We need to go in to talk in person, first thing tomorrow. Eight AM."

"Mary's never had behavior issues before," I objected. "Are you sure he has the right kid?"

Jackie pursed her lips and nodded. "She. You know her principal is a woman, and yes, I'm sure. I need you to be there. On-time, Jason. I'm serious."

"I will be the soul of punctuality, my love."

"And stop saying that," she said.

I reached out and took her right hand in between both of mine, holding it tenderly.

"You're right. We both know the score. I don't need to repeat it like some sort of echo from the past. I know the way I was three years ago wasn't how someone can be if they're going to be in a relationship. I just need you to know that I get that, and I'm not that guy anymore, Jackie. I'm just a guy looking for another chance."

"You had lots of chances, Jason," she said quietly. "You left way before I did. If you were ever really there."

"I'm here now," I replied, trying to hide a wince.

She took her hand back from between mine, hugging her arms close around her middle.

"It's too late, Jason. Victor asked me to marry him. I said, yes."

I swallowed and nodded.

"Mary told me."

Jackie sighed, shaking her head. "We tried to keep it from her. To tell you first. I didn't want you to find out this way."

I smiled, nodding in reply.

"No, I get it. I'm happy for you. Victor's marrying way out of his league. Do I get an invite?"

"Is that a good idea?"

"Oh, *God,* no. But I do like to be invited to social events. I'm sure it'll be the place to be. When?"

"A year from now. Early October of next year."

I nodded once again.

"Make sure you guys tell me where you're registered. I'd hate to get the wrong china pattern."

Jackie laughed again, then stepped up and wrapped her arms around me.

"Are you gonna be okay?"

I returned the hug, putting my nose up against her hair and breathing in deeply, losing myself in the smell of her. After an eternity that was far too brief, I let go, stepped slightly back, and shook my head.

"Nope, but if you change your mind, you know where to find me. I know you've said yes, but hey, stranger things have happened, right?"

"You're delusional, Jason. We had our shot, and we blew it. Maybe some people just aren't supposed to end up together, y'know?"

"Some people, maybe. But what you just described sounds like the center of every great love story: overcoming the odds. Betting on the underdog, that sorta thing."

Stepping back further, I winked, shot her my best rakish smile, then turned, put my hands into my pockets, and walked into the deepening twilight.

As I walked through the Garden District's flower-scented streets on my way back to the Quarter, I mulled over my day. Out of all the names, Mary had heard Dave and I discuss, how had she locked onto Papa Ivé as the most significant? What did her principal want to speak with us about?

In the past, I would have immediately decided they were questions that needed answering. Probably kicked over a hornet's nest in the process. I've gathered that normal people just sort of worry about this sort of thing until the actual meeting, then deal with the issues from it after the fact.

It's always struck me as terribly reactionary. I prefer to be a bit more proactive.

But I walked away from that life. Now I'm just Jason Bishop, bar owner; not Jason Bishop, Occultist, Exorcist, and Demonologist, Miserable S.O .B...well, maybe I'm still a bit of the last, and while the latter title is more impressive, the former definitely has a much easier shot at a long and happy life.

Resigned to doing nothing but wait, I strolled through the door to Bishop's Crossing and waved to Dave behind the bar. "Why are you still here? I thought we hired a couple of kids."

"We did. Kid One is in the back workin' the grill. Kid Two is over there servin' drinks. I'm here waitin' on you, boss."

"Time's long past that I need a babysitter, Dave."

"I thought so too, but then someone came in askin' after ya."

Alarm bells immediately went off in my head.

"Tax guy?" I asked.

"You wish. Says he was in seminary with you. Looks like a spook to me. Ordinis Templi Erinnys. Seen enough of that type that I know when they look at me."

I didn't look.

"He's looking at me, isn't he?"

"Yup."

Fuuuuuck.

Way back in 1545, The Shadow Council of Trent was convened. The attendees included the hidden remnants of the Knights Templar (now called Ordinis Templi Erinnys) as well as representatives from the Vatican. They met with vampire bloodlines, the werewolf nations, the Seelie and Unseelie Courts, several Dragons, various and sundry other things that go bump in the night, and the Order of the Enlightened (we just call them wizards).

The Catholic Church agreed to knock off their surprisingly effective Inquisition against the supernatural in exchange for the monsters agreeing to something called The Liturgy of the Forgotten: the monsters were to stay hidden from the sight of humanity, never to reveal themselves. No supernatural creature was to be known to mundane humanity in any way, shape, or form, punishable by immediate and gruesome death. The supernaturals were supposed to mostly police themselves, but Pope Paul III wanted a safeguard to ensure that Mother Church's interests were protected, just in case the monsters weren't so keen on the spirit of their agreement. The Erinnys were the final arbiters of justice, working from the shadows and against the Forgotten to safeguard humanity. They were the judge, jury, and executioners of The Gloaming, often even more proactive than I used to be, heading off issues before they become a problem.

"Bishop. Been a long time, mon ami."

The voice came at my shoulder without warning, which put me immediately into a foul mood.

"Dave, I think I'm gonna need a whiskey for this one," I said as I turned to see who had disrupted my close-to-idyllic-as-I-can-get sorta day.

The face I saw was a familiar one. A black man standing a shade over six feet tall and powerfully built, he wore the ten years since we'd last seen each other heavily, especially in his eyes. The fact that he wore a priest's collar was amusing, mostly because most priests don't carry the sort of body count the Order racks up. Father Raimond Fortier had that; one look in his eyes was enough to make me certain.

"Raimond, to what do I owe this visit? Here to check on Dave, make sure he hasn't developed a taste for long pig in the last half-decade?"

"Leave me outta this, boss," Dave said, sliding the whiskey over and moving off toward the other end of the bar.

"Nothing like that, Bishop. I was in town and thought I might pass by. See my old seminary mate."

"Last time you passed by, you threatened to burn me at the stake if I recall correctly, so forgive me if I'm a bit skeptical of your noble intent. I'm out of the game, Raimond. Been that way for over a year now. I've got nothing to offer the Order except a hearty 'good luck' and the standing offer that you guys can drink for half price on Wednesdays."

"We don't drink alcohol, Bishop."

"For free, then. No danger to the bottom line!"

Raimond shook his head, then looked over his shoulder, taking in the bar with its scattering of patrons. The smell of alcohol and fruit chasers mixed with the heady roux from the back, the low murmur of conversation, and the ever-present music from somewhere out in the streets. New Orleans at its finest.

"You've got a good thing going here, Bishop. Nice place, busy enough to pay the bills, and never have to worry about money. The gaslights are a nice touch. Gives it that authentic feel the tourists love. You're close enough to Bourbon Street that you'll get random folks, but not directly on it, so you don't have to hose the place down to get rid of the vomit every night."

"Just when I try to help out in the kitchen," I replied. "Look, I appreciate that you like the place, but what's this about?"

"You're sure you're out? I got word earlier today that you and a kid were seen entering several different stores operated by legitimate practitioners of the Arts, plus one place run by a member of the Seelie Court."

I laughed, shaking my head. "Halloween shopping."

"Beg pardon?"

"I was Halloween shopping. For a costume. For the kid."

Raimond stared at me for longer than made me comfortable, then gave an almost imperceptible nod.

"That adds up," he admitted. "But isn't what I wanted to hear. Your city—*our* city—is a powder keg, Bishop. The fuse isn't long, and I'm afraid it's been lit."

"How do you mean?"

"Do you know Evangeline Grey?"

"I know *of* her. She is Ivé's kid. Probably somewhere around eighteen or so, right?"

"Seventeen. And yes, she's Papa Ivé's daughter. It's unclear if she inherited her father's gifts, but one thing is certain: she disappeared two days ago."

"What do you mean, disappeared? Are we talking like Bilbo Baggins disappeared? Poof?" I said, making an exploding motion with my hands.

"No, nothing like that. She's just—gone. She went to sleep in her room, same as always. When she didn't come down for breakfast, they checked, and she was gone. Missing. Her bed had been slept in, but there was no sign of her. Ivé has called on his resources to find his child but hasn't been able to find any trace of her."

"That sucks for Ivé, but I don't see what it has to do with me."

"Ivé suspects that the vampires have her. I'm not sure where he got the idea from, but if he doesn't get her back soon, or if he receives confirmation the vampires have her? It will be open war between supernatural factions."

"Shit."

"I agree. Do you remember what happened the last time there was this sort of disagreement? It ended up nearly going public. The Circle of the Golden Dawn and the Thule Society each used their arts to influence members of the government of their respective countries."

"England and Germany back in the '30s."

"Imagine both sides doing the same now, except the vampires and the vodun are both here in the United States. Both have influence in mortal society that we cannot allow to be brought to bear. The only option the Order would have would be Exterminii. We would need to wipe out everyone involved *before* it gets to that point."

"And while that makes me very sad, I've got no love for either Ivé or the vampires, so again, I ask you: what does that have to do with me?"

Raimond sat for a moment, quietly looking at his hands, then sighed.

"I love the Lord, Bishop. I love Him with all my heart, but I question some of the work I do in His name. The bodies we leave behind. So much blood. It's necessary. I understand that. I accept it. But what if there's a different way? What if I can praise His name and do so without being covered in blood? What if we can approach it without the deaths? I don't want this gir—this child's death on my head, Bishop. From all I can gather, she's done nothing wrong."

"Then don't. Call in your favors and find her."

Raimond shook his head. "The Order does not operate that way. We cannot be thought to show weakness, regardless of how distasteful I find the alternative. There can be no mercy. Only divine retribution. Without the shadow of the Order wielding the headman's axe and keeping the bonfires warm, what would keep the signatories to the Liturgy in line? What would prevent them from moving to outright predation on the Children of Adam? No. If the requirement for humanity as a whole remaining safe be that I spend some sleepless nights, then I am willing to make that sacrifice for the greater good."

"Damned zealot."

"If you like," Raimond replied with a soft smile. "But were *you* to search out the girl. Were *you* to find her. . . then the Order would not be involved. The Order would not have shown mercy and would remain feared, even if the Order would then be in your debt."

In my debt. That ain't nothing.

It's a get out of jail free card. A 'come in with guns blazing, no questions asked' card. Ideas like hospitality and debt are incredibly important in the circles that Raimond moves in. For him to offer a marker to me, not just from him but from the entire Order?

That's worth more than cash any day.

But it was also not something I had any use for.

"That's a great story and all, Raimond, but like I said: I'm out of the game. A marker from the Order doesn't do me a whole lotta good. As much as it'll make me sad if anything happens to the kid, I've gotta look out for me and mine. I've got enough trouble on that front without adding more to it."

Raimond shook his head. "What of the lives that could be saved, Bishop? What of the good you could do? Please, reconsider."

I shook my head.

"I know it makes me a special kinda bastard, but to be blunt, I don't know most of those people, and those that I do, I don't much like. The back room's locked up. The books are nice and dusty. The relics and items of power lie inert and under ward. I'm sorry, Raimond, the answer is not just no, but hell no."

Raimond fell silent, meeting my gaze and shaking his head, his disappointment obvious.

"Thy will be done, Father," he whispered, then looked me in the eye. "I understand. Should you have a change of heart, there is still time. I have other matters to address in this city prior to turning my full attention toward the disappearance of Evangeline Grey. If you do think better of your —" he trailed off, shaking his head, "—decision, come see me at St. Louis Cathedral. The staff there will know where to find me."

"Don't wait up."

Raimond stared me in the eye for a heartbeat before rising smoothly to his feet.

"Thank you for taking the time to speak with me, Bishop. I still think you would have been a great member of the Order had tragedy not struck."

"Don't think I was cut out for marching in lockstep, Raimond. Plus singin' kumbayas ain't really my style."

"Indeed not. The Lord has likely placed you precisely where you need to be. God Bless. And Blessings to you as well, David LeBlanc."

Dave looked up from the bar, where he was busily creating a drink for a customer.

"I appreciate 'em, but leave me out of this stuff," he said with a wink.

Without another word, Father Raimond left, leaving me to consider the things he'd said for the rest of the night.

I'm not a total asshole, at least I like to think I'm not, but as much as I wanted to make myself care about what Raimond said, my thoughts kept going back to Jackie marrying Victor. How could I even begin to entertain the thought of getting back into the same life that ended up costing me my relationship with her? It wasn't fair for him to even ask.

People would die, but not *my* people.

Lives would be ruined, but not the lives that were important to *me*.

You know, when I put it that way, I do sorta seem like a total asshole, don't I?

I leaned over my whiskey and rubbed the bridge of my nose.

"Should I have said yes?" I asked, not looking up.

"If you're serious about being out, then no way in hell, boss," Dave replied. "But I'm still not sold that you can ever really leave the life behind. Not really. Look around. You know this place is touched by The Gloaming. You know who some of the regulars are. What they are."

"That doesn't concern me. If they behave themselves and pay their tabs at the end of the night, we're all good. Their money spends, just like everyone else's." I said.

Dave shrugged. "I know you're doing this for Mary and Jackie, but is this the sort of thing they'd *want* you to pass up for them?"

I nodded. "Yeah, I think Jackie made that pretty fuckin' clear when she left me for doing this sort of shit, don't you?"

Dave snorted. "Boss, if you think that's why she left you, you're brain dead. Don't matter a whit what I've gotta say on the subject, anyway. You've already made your call."

"Damn right," I muttered.

So why did I have an uneasy feeling in the pit of my stomach that I would end up hip-deep in the mess?

Seven o'clock comes painfully early when you run a bar. By the time everything was closed up and cleaned up, it was nearly three a.m. Even my commute of "walk up the stairs" feels like it takes forever at that hour, and certainly much longer than it took when I first bought the place a dozen years ago.

Seven forty-five found me showered, dressed, and sitting with a coffee cup in hand and sitting next to Jackie outside of the principal's office.

"Do you think it's drugs?" She asked.

"Mary's eight."

"They say it starts early."

I frowned.

"But generally, not in fourth grade. That would be impressively precocious. Definitely one for the scrapbook."

"It's not funny, Jason."

Sadly, I never got to find out why it wasn't funny. The door to the office opened, revealing a rail-thin black woman with a face that had likely last cracked a smile during the Reagan years and whose hair was pulled back in a severe bun that highlighted her pronounced cheekbones. She was a striking woman, but there was nothing warm or remotely inviting about her. The fact that she'd chosen a career in education made me feel bad for the kids in her classes when she first started out.

"No, it's not. Mr. Bishop. Ms. Beaumont. Please come in." The principal's voice was harsh, sounding like her throat was clenched, or her teeth gritted. It was hate at first sight. I began to strain, pushing my senses forward to see what there was to see.

As we joined the administrator in her office, Jackie wore her worry on her face. I treated this like any other meeting I've had with a blood-sucking predator: Don't show fear, keep things calm, and avoid eye contact.

In retrospect, avoiding eye contact with the principal was probably unnecessary, but old habits die hard. Her office was severe. Clinical. Everything on her desk was arranged just so, all hard angles and straight lines. A plain white coffee mug held a handful of pencils, each sharpened and precisely the same length, and everything smelled of hand sanitizer. She was clearly a laugh a minute.

"Hello, I'm Dr. Simmons; please, sit down."

After we were all settled, she dove right in.

"I've asked you here because there have been numerous troubling incidents over the past month with Mary."

"Incidents?" Jackie asked, leaning forward. "I don't understand. I wasn't notified about any—"

"We prefer to address such things internally if at all possible," Dr. Simmons said, cutting Jackie off. "Until such time as it becomes clear that an internal approach is ineffective. In Mary's case, we suspect she's been cyberstalking several of her classmates and using the information that she's gathered to psychologically torment them, often hidden behind false sympathy."

"I don't understand," Jackie replied, her brow furrowing in frustration.

"She's saying Mary hacked some kids and is using what she got out of their computers to mess with 'em," I growled, looking at the spot-on Dr.

Simmons's face in between her well-manicured eyebrows. "She's saying that Mary is a bully."

"We don't like to use that terminology here, but yes. That is the gist of it. The things that have been reported are deeply troubling. Things your daughter has said to other children here at the school."

"What things?" Jackie asked, her voice taking a harder tone as Dr. Simmons accused Mary of something entirely out of character.

"Things about dead family members not approving of the way they dress and talk. She told one child that her therapy wasn't helping. She told another child who was depressed that her parents' divorce wasn't her fault, no matter what her father said. There are other examples, troubling ones. Everything she has confronted other children with that we can verify has been highly accurate and incredibly sensitive information. Information that she could not have been privy to without her taking some sort of extraordinary steps."

Shit. That sounded distressingly familiar. I held onto my poker face as the ladies discussed it.

"Ms. Simmons—"

"Doctor Simmons, if you please, Ms. Beaumont."

Jackie blinked, replied through a clenched jaw. "*Doctor* Simmons, our daughter isn't a hacker."

She wasn't. But she might have some gifts. Like the people, I used to work with. Like me.

"Parents are often the last to know about this sort of behavior."

Talking about magic stuff wasn't an option. I needed to spin things.

"No, *you* don't understand, lady," I replied as Jackie blinked in surprise at the woman's gall. "Jackie doesn't let Mary go online. She doesn't even have a smartphone. I don't have a computer in my place at all. Just good ol' fashion analog books."

"Then how do you explain her insight into the private home lives of these other children?"

I had some ideas, but there were none I was willing to share at the moment.

Jackie jumped in before I could respond. "Mary's always been a precocious kid. Very observant. Maybe she overheard something. Maybe she could tell by the way kids were acting. Lucky guesses. Maybe she overheard gossip. I don't know, but I think it's in horrible taste for you to call us both down here, worry us to death and then act like our daughter is some sort of supervillain who is terrorizing the other children!" Jackie leaned forward as she spoke, her voice getting louder as she began to wrap herself in her righteous indignation. "Mary's a good kid. Smart, friendly, and respectful. I just can't imagine her being as devious as you're trying to make her out to be."

"Children often act differently at home than they do at school, Ms. Beaumont. Especially in cases like Mary's with, quite frankly, less than ideal home situations and...questionable role models."

Jackie sat back in her seat, her eyes going wide at the gall of the woman, sputtering over her words as she looked for the proper response.

I, on the other hand, had a pretty good idea about where I wanted to go with this.

I'd seen enough. "What did you just say to us, you dried up old battle-ax? Where the fuck do you get off insulting us and our daughter? I don't give a rat's ass who you think you are or how many letters you've got after your name. I won't sit here and listen to you run down the two people I love the most in the world." I spat, leaning forward in my chair.

"Mr. Bishop, I assure you—" she began. "*I'm not done yet,*" I re-interrupted, my eyes going hard. "Me? You can say what you want about me. Most of it's probably deserved, even a bunch of stuff that probably wouldn't occur to you. But Jackie? If you're stepping up to the plate against her, you're out of your league, sister. All she's ever done is take care of other people, donate her time to charities, and make the world a more beautiful place. Where do you stack up? Before you answer, let me help you out with a few things about you that you didn't know before: You're pissed at Jackie because she's pretty, but you look down on me because you think I'm a drunk that threw away my family and my education. That's all accurate, aside from the drunk part. You can't let shit go when someone pisses you off, and God help anyone that shows you up in public. You don't have many friends, and you're in a loveless, sexless marriage to a man who cheats on you just about every time you're out of the house for more than two hours. Sound about right?"

Both Dr. Simmons and Jackie gasped at me in horror, Dr. Simmons's face going ashen while Jackie's went crimson. She took a deep breath, then opened her mouth, but was interrupted by Dr. Simmons.

"What...how...?" The woman across the desk sputtered.

"Student of humanity," I lied. Dr. Simmons wore slights against her like badges on a sleeve, and reading it reflected in her aura was child's play. Though I have to admit I made the husband part up based on the pictures she had in her office. Because fuck her, that's why. I also figured if I pulled the same trick as Mary, it might confuse her enough to muddy the waters.

"I think we're done here," I said. "Or at least I am. Jackie, did you have anything else to say to Dr. Simmons?"

Jackie looked up at me, then back to the woman across the desk, sitting with her back straight, and jaw locked, then shook her head.

"No, I think you covered it, Jason. Thank you for expressing your concern, Doctor. We'll talk to Mary about being a bit more—ah, the hell with it. You pull a stunt like this with her again, and we'll see you in front of the Board of Directors, lady."

She even slammed the door on her way out.

We walked together in silence until we got outside of the building, at which point Jackie turned, looked me in the eye, and punched me hard in the shoulder.

"What the hell was that?"

"What?" I asked, rubbing the impact point. The girl could throw a punch.

"In there. Mary could already be in trouble, and you antagonize her principal? How was that smart, Jason? How did that help her? All it did was soothe your ego since she was saying mean things about your little girl."

"And you."

"Don't you get it? This is the grownup world, Jason, not your bar. You don't get to try to solve every situation by throwing a punch, literal *or* verbal!"

"To be fair, *you're* the one who punched *me*."

Which she did again.

"Ouch! Quit it, dammit!"

"You need to listen to me. Mary needs our help. Your help. Based on your performance in there, she's clearly pulling the same sort of bullshit at school. You're going to talk to her. You're going to explain to her why it's not a good way to live your life. This whole 'I'm better now' schtick doesn't track...not after what I saw. You were just as mean in there as you ever were before. Just as spiteful," she stopped and took a deep breath. "Look, you both clearly have a ton of insight into people. Maybe show her how to use that as a positive thing." Eyes downcast, she shook her head. "I've gotta go. I'll call you later."

I stood there in silence as she set her shoulders and stalked down the street, spine rigid.

Mary was pulling the same bullshit as me. Not really what I wanted to hear, and if she was able to read an aura for surface information at eight, that meant one thing: she had the potential to be a willworker. She had

Talent. She'd shown some flashes in the past, but nothing concrete. This was the first "smoking gun" I could point too.

She might just be able to see auras like me, but given the signs showing up this early, chances are that Mary was someone who would be able to alter reality with her will. She'd be the type of person that was chin deep in The Gloaming. The type of person the Order would keep a close eye on. Kill if she stepped out of line.

I grumbled and shook my head.

"Son of a bitch. I'm gonna have to take this fucking job."

Stuffing my hands into my pockets, I started off into the October morning to meet with Father Raimond again.

October mornings in New Orleans can be hit or miss. This one was more miss than hit. There was no actual rain, but the clouds hung low overhead, and a fine mist had settled in over the city, coating everything. It was days like this that I was glad for my navy surplus peacoat.

Before you start in, I know. The cliché is that guys who work in the field I do wear a trench coat. Used to do? Am about to do? Shit, I don't know. In any case, the trench coat seems like it's part of some sort of uniform, along with disrespect for authority and potentially self-destructive tendencies, but the things are a nuisance, and I don't care. Get over it.

Even with my foul mood, I managed not to draw any sidelong looks as I walked through the quaint streets of the Quarter through Jackson Square Park and up to the front door of the Cathedral.

Now, I've had my issues with the Mother Church. Clearly. You don't end up with my checkered past if all is right with your ideas of faith and divinity. That being said, no one does pomp and circumstance like the Catholics, and the Cathedral of St. Louis in New Orleans is a prime example. The place is breathtaking, with marbled white stone on the exterior, a trio of towering steeples, and a big clock in the middle.

The inside, though? That's where it makes a play for making you believe in the divine.

Sweeping arches supported by marble columns, a marble floor with white and black diamond patterns polished to a high sheen, illuminated manuscripts, and enough gold to make a Vegas casino blush. There was a pleasant smell of incense and a feeling of peace and acceptance that embraced you as you entered. I'm surprised they don't get more spontaneous conversions from the tourists.

I paused at the back, taking in the atmosphere for a moment, and allowing a pang to hit the empty spot in my middle, the place where my faith used to live. I followed the left path, walking along the outside aisle of the pews and toward the door past the altar.

Pushing my way through, I almost collided with a nun, busily typing away on an iPad as she went.

"Oh, excuse me, but you're not supposed to be—oh. It's you."

Sister Mary Elizabeth still hadn't forgiven me for—actually, I'm not sure why she hates me. But what I lack in certainty, I more than make up for in the intensity department. She *really* hates me.

"Sister. I'm here to see Father Raimond."

"Of course you are, Mr. Bishop," she said. "I'm fully aware that your...deficiencies wouldn't allow you to be here otherwise."

Dammit. I hate it when they get the better of me. Lacking any sort of witty response, I just forced a smile, nodded, and continued down to Raimond's office, finding the door standing open and the large priest seated behind his plain wooden desk, making notes in a large book.

"Raimond," I began.

"You'll do it?" he interrupted.

I locked eyes with him, then shrugged.

"Same deal as you offered at my place. Let me deal with it, and you owe me. No questions asked?"

He frowned, then leaned forward.

"Why the change of heart?"

"I want to make sure I don't end up with skin in the game, that's all," I replied, partially dodging his question.

"I know not to look a gift horse in the mouth, so I won't press. You have three days, Bishop. In three days, I'll need to start investigating, and only then if neither Ivé nor the vampires do anything untoward. The Order's mission must remain paramount in this, as in all things."

I sighed. "You know this could get bloody, right?"

Raimond nodded in reply.

"But it will be buckets of blood, as opposed to the rivers that will run if the Order takes the necessary steps. Lives will be saved."

I nodded, thoughts of Mary running through my head as I left the Cathedral.

Evangeline Grey was missing. Vampires were suspected. Her father would have his people out looking, which could be unhealthy for me if they ran across me. That meant going to see Papa Ivé myself.

I paused at the doorway leading out of the Cathedral and looked at the crucifix hanging above the altar, then shook my head.

Pomp, circumstance, and a damned twisted sense of humor.

Just my luck.

You don't need street signs to tell you when you've entered the Ninth Ward in New Orleans. A little bit to the north and quite a bit east of the French Quarter, it may as well be in another country. Another world. While the devastation from Katrina had been erased elsewhere, there were still signs of its aftermath here in the Ninth. Even after all this time, there were abandoned homes whose owners never came back and flooded-out cars abandoned beneath overpasses. Worst of all was the wary, haunted look the Ward's residents gave to any outsider who strayed into their world.

Papa Ivé was the undisputed ruler of the Ninth Ward and one of the more influential figures in all of New Orleans, even if the average Joe had never heard of him. A powerful willworker and the self-styled voodoo king of the city, Ivé's home had served as a rallying point for the people of his neighborhood during the catastrophe. He acted as the sole source of order, stability, and authority during the chaos and looting that followed the levees' breach. Partially by ignoring the standard rules of the Liturgy of the Forgotten, Ivé was able to save hundreds, if not thousands, of lives. He kept his people safe and fed, gaining their admiration and unquestioning loyalty ever since.

His home stood out amongst the rows of single-story cookie-cutter homes: different colors, but each with the perfect "V" roof and an ample porch. It was a large, two-story building with a basement, which in itself was a testament to his power. New Orleans' status as 'below sea level' is infamous, but the side effects aren't immediately obvious, and the immediate flooding of anything below the street is a big one. Ivé managed to keep his through the judicious use of spells and bound spirits. His home was fronted by a 'Practical Voodoo Shoppe' storefront that served as his source of taxable income. It seems that even massively powerful Voodoo Kings need to step lightly around the IRS and their particular brand of bloodsuckers.

My cab (a rarity itself in the Ward) dropped me off around the corner and drove off before I'd even managed to get both feet onto the sidewalk.

"It's almost like you're trying to tell me something," I commented to no one in particular.

Much to my chagrin, I received an answer.

"It's telling you that it was damned stupid for a motherfucker like you to step foot in the Ninth with everything that's going on right now, you piece of shit con man."

I raised my hands, assuming the worst, then turned around to see who was behind me.

I breathed a sigh of relief when I saw Scrabble.

Scrabble was a thin black guy in his late twenties or early thirties who got his name on account of his inventive spelling. Anyone who has ever had the misfortune of trying to translate a written message from Scrabble expressed shock and awe at the damage he'd done to the English language. More importantly, for me, he was a professional snitch. One that I'd done business with previously.

"Scrabble! I haven't seen you in—"

"Cut the shit, Bishop. You almost got me skinned alive, motherfucker."

"Skinned alive? What are you talking about, Scrabble, I didn't—"

"The Holy Oil."

"—Oh."

"You tole me it was legit, fucker. I took that shit and went into a nest of bloodsuckers. Was gonna impress Ivé an' get moved up into the Inner Circle, dawg. Make me a player in this town. What was that shit you sold me?"

"It was a long time ago, Scrabble, I don't really—"

Scrabble reached behind his back, producing a large handgun and leveling it at me.

"What. Was. The. Oil?"

Shit. So much for old times.

"Now, it's been years, so I'm a bit hazy on this," I said, trying to stall.

"See if you can remember, bitch. I'm layin' bank you don't forget it when you fuck someone as hard as you did me."

"Lamp oil. From Home Depot. With some ginger powder added in to give in the right smell," I finally admitted.

Scrabble clenched his jaw and made odd gestures with the gun in my general direction.

"You nearly got me *killed*, motherfucker! I went in there with that stuff on me thinkin' I'd be protected. That those bitches couldn't touch me."

"A lot of times faith by itself can be enough—"

"Stop bullshittin' me, Bishop! One of those fanged fucks grabbed me by the throat with that oil all over me and tossed me through a wall! Broke three of my muthafuckin' ribs! Papa an' his boys laughed at me. Why would you do that to me, man? We were tight! I trusted you!"

I swallowed. When people think you screwed them, they can get dangerous. Unpredictable. And Scrabble more than thought I'd screwed him; he *knew* I'd screwed him.

"Look, Scrabble, it wasn't anything personal. I needed a distraction. Something to grab the nightwalkers' attention at the front of their crypt while I dealt with something in the back."

Scrabble glared at me hard. "What was so important you were willing to risk my life for it, asshole?" he shouted.

"I needed the ashes from an old vampire for a spell I was working on. Three hundred years plus. There was a rumor that one was in residence there."

"You fuckin' set me up for a goddamned grocery list? *Asshole!*" He jabbed the gun into my right shoulder, knocking me off balance. I had begun wishing we were *anywhere* else in New Orleans. If we were, a cop might happen by. Here that chance was right around zero. Ivé was the law here, and everyone knew it, cops included.

"It wasn't personal, Scrabble. The vamps weren't going to do anything permanent to you. They know you're under Ivé's protection. I was banking on that."

"You think that shit makes it better? That it wasn't personal? You gambled with my life, asshole," he said, looking more hurt than angry. It was justified. Scrabble had counted on me as a friend, and I'd let him down because I was working a job that I considered more important than either him or our friendship, such as it was. There was a ghost on the loose at the time. A nasty one. It had been possessing teenagers and driving them to suicide. I'd managed to put a stop to it, but the trail of young bodies it had left behind was appalling. The fact it happened around the same time Jackie and Mary had left contributed to the fact that I hadn't been in the best of headspaces. I'd been reckless with his life; there was no denying it.

Sadly, I didn't think that admission would get me any points at the moment.

"I been on the outside lookin' in, dawg. Ivé called me a worthless child. A moron. Called me out in front of the whole crew. *You* did that to me, Bishop. You."

"I didn't mean—"

"Don't matter what you *meant*, bitch. It's what you *did*. You ruined my life. Your fuckin' game kept me out. But now you're gonna be my ticket in."

"Look, Scrabble. I—"

"This ain't a negotiation, Bishop. Ivé put the word out that anybody sees anything strange in the Ninth, they bring it to him. A fuckin' blade of grass out of place an' he wants to know. Ain't nothing stranger than seein' your white ass walkin' the streets around his house right after his little girl gone missing. Ain't nobody seen you in a year an' all of a sudden you're here? You sure as shit ain't above gettin' involved in snatchin' someone's kid, an' if you didn't do it—" he trailed off, looking me up and down, then shook his head. "Naw. You're up to something."

I raised my hands in a shrug. "Look, Scrabble, I heard about Evangeline. I'm here to help."

"Like you helped me? I don't think Papa's interested in your kinda help, Bishop. But maybe you're on his grocery list."

In retrospect, I think that sigh of relief when I saw Scrabble might have been a tad premature.

Scrabble led me at gunpoint around the block to the front of Papa Ivé's home. Bustling with activity, there were armed men stationed on the porch and the small patch of lawn. Ivé had shed the "nondescript" façade and gone straight to "armed encampment." It appeared he was taking his daughter's disappearance about as well as you'd expect.

The guards stepped forward as we approached, then saw my face. The one on the right raised his assault rifle while the one on the left took an inadvertent step back. It always feels good to be remembered.

"Scrabble, what the fuck you bring this asshole here for? Ivé don't got time for seein' tourists," the guy on the right spat. He was young, not quite eighteen. He almost certainly didn't know my face.

"Floyd. Can it. That there's Jason fuckin' Bishop."

Floyd snorted, looking me up and down. "Bishop? That guy everyone tells the boogeyman stories about? This cracker don't look like a warm pile of shit. What about it, tough guy? You here to bust up some heads? Set us on fire?"

"I caught him on the street," Scrabble said, stepping in. "Thought Papa would want to talk to him."

"Where the fuck do you get off *thinking*, Scrabble?" Floyd spat before starting in on my captor.

Floyd was a typical product of the worst parts of what the Ninth had become. He'd grown up hard and fast. Drugs had ripped his family apart, forcing him to be a man far earlier than he was ready for. He'd killed before and would do so again without hesitation. The back and forth that he and Scrabble were engaged in was likely to get bloody quickly.

Floyd started forward, murder in his eyes. Scrabble stood his ground.

I stepped directly in Floyd's path.

"Floyd, don't you want to tell your boss that I got brought in, just in case he *does* think I have something to do with Evangeline's disappearance? If even half the stories you heard about me are true, it's something I'm capable of, right?"

Floyd's angry gaze shifted from Scrabble to me and was quickly followed by a punch to the gut that doubled me over and left me gasping for breath.

"You don't look like a damned thing to me, asshole. Just a motherfucker 'bout to die."

Still gasping for breath and doubled over, I could see Floyd's gun coming up to his shoulder and cursed, then held my right palm up between us and called on my compact, whispering "Ignem."

Silvery white flame erupted from my hand, engulfing the barrel of his gun and heating the rest red hot. The smell of burnt flesh surrounded us as Floyd fell backward, howling in surprise and pain.

Years ago, I had been approached by an angel. Which one? My client list is confidential, so you'll just have to guess. They needed something retrieved from a library that they couldn't enter. In exchange, they granted me a boon. Angel Fire. Stuff allows me to channel a bit of the fire of Creation itself. It's spectacularly destructive and exhausting to use but comes in *very* handy in a pinch.

My vision swam as the fatigue washed over me. Realizing I was a dead man if I passed out, I fought it back and struggled to my feet, then looked over my shoulder at Scrabble.

"I'm guessing Papa will see us now."

A moment later, the door to the home burst open to reveal Papa Ivé in all his glory. Standing six and a half feet tall, Ivé was an impossibly thin, dark-skinned black man with a shaved head and a jet black, neatly trimmed beard. I didn't say African American because I have no actual information that says he was, is, or ever will be American. Or African, for that matter. His voice was accented with a soft patois that suggested either creole or Haitian as his origin, but at times his accent drifted into something else entirely. Something older. He was one of the most dangerous men in New Orleans, if not the world.

He looked pissed, which was probably my fault.

"Who dares? Who dares channel magic on my very doorstep?" he demanded, his voice booming out from the front porch. His dark eyes scanned the crowd and quickly locked on the one person who didn't belong. "Bishop."

He spat my name out like a curse.

"Ivé, before you start, I heard what happened and came to offer my help."

As soon as the words were out of my mouth, I realized my mistake: implying that the great Papa Ivé needed help from someone like me in front of his people. Questioning his strength. His eyes went wide, and his nostrils flared slightly.

Not good.

Ivé stalked down his stairs, his dark eyes locked on mine. I'd read his aura once when I'd first met him over a decade ago. It took days for the images to fade from my mind. Ivé had seen and done things that few mortals can claim to have witnessed and survived, and the man's aura still carried the scars.

Then again, I have no more evidence that Ivé is actually mortal than I do that he's American.

"You filth! You dare come to *my* home in a time of crisis and feign to offer *me* help? *Me*? An ant has as much to offer a lion as you can offer me, charlatan. You," he barked to Scrabble, "take him inside. The rest of you find somewhere else to be."

He paused, looking down at Floyd and sneering. "And teach this one not to fall for parlor tricks."

Scrabble puffed up with pride at receiving a direct order from Papa and pushed my right shoulder, sending me stumbling forward toward the front stairs.

"It doesn't need to be this way, Ivé. I can help you. People will talk to me who are afraid to say anything to you."

"If they think they're afraid now, let me find out that someone has information about my Evangeline. I'll teach them what it means to be afraid."

Scrabble shoved me again, and I tripped up the front steps of Ivé's home.

I was roughly guided through the Practical Voodoo Shoppe, through the beaded curtain, and into the living quarters beyond. Decorated with dark, rich burgundy furniture with shadows dancing maddeningly in the corners, it wasn't the sort of room to put a body at ease. Or maybe it was the feeling of overwhelming dread I was experiencing. To your average soul-devouring voodoo practitioner, I'm sure it could be quite lovely.

Scrabble pushed one last time, sending me crashing into the large couch. I turned to reason with him. Plead with him. Anything, but Ivé was in the room before the first sound escaped my throat.

The eerie lighting in the parlor did nothing to soften the Voodoo King's nightmarish appearance. The unnatural shadows clung to the willworker and highlighted the skull-like appearance of his face, giving him the visage of an angry god of old. Glancing briefly at Scrabble, he waved, dismissing him.

Scrabble showed that he was smarter than I gave him credit for and left without a peep.

"Your life hangs in the balance, charlatan," he growled at me, "I will ask you one time and one time only: Where is my daughter?"

I swallowed, trying to figure out what combination of words allowed me to continue drawing breath. "Ivé," I began. He didn't let me get any farther.

"Don't bother. The loa already tell me you know nothing."

The words hung in the air between us for a heartbeat that seemed to stretch into eternity, Ivé's eyes drilling holes into mine. Finally, he shook his head and slumped down into the overstuffed armchair behind him, his furious demeanor gone. The Papa Ivé of legend vanished in an instant.

The towering presence from outside deflated and was replaced instead by a father concerned about his daughter.

"Why would you come back, Jason? My people, the spirits, even the other signatories of the Liturgy of the Forgotten all agreed. You had moved on, attempted to settle with your wife and child. Why risk it now? The timing of your appearance so close to Evangeline's disappearance raises questions."

I breathed a massive sigh of relief. I'd worked with Ivé in the past. While we were never friends, we each knew the other and (I hoped) had some respect for each other's character. The fact that he was talking right now was a good sign.

"Mary," I responded simply. "She's showing...signs."

Ivé leaned forward.

"Mary is your daughter?"

"She is," I replied.

"And this concerns you because?" he trailed off, then shook his head. "The Church. They are threatening your daughter. Forcing you to help put a stop to my retribution against whoever has taken my Evangeline."

"Close," I replied. "Mary is showing signs, but she's not on their radar yet. Raimond is offering me a blank check favor if I can stop whatever is about to go down between you and...whoever ends up in your crosshairs."

"It amounts to the same," Ivé said flatly. "If you think the offer was made without knowing about the situation with your daughter, you *have* been away from the game too long. Your bar has dulled your wits, Bishop."

I opened my mouth to disagree, then closed it with a snap. Ivé was right.

Raimond didn't make offers without knowing *exactly* what was on the table. He certainly didn't give a blank check to someone he considered to be a wild card. But a desperate father looking to protect his daughter? Someone he knew would go to any length to keep his family safe?

That's the exact sort of person Raimond would make an offer to.

The asshole.

"Now you're thinking again." the Voodoo King intoned, his voice echoing in the parlor. "You'll need that. As much as I'd like to help you with your situation, my daughter is missing, Bishop. Taken. This assault on my family cannot be allowed to stand. I will find those responsible, and I will see everything they hold dear burned to ash around them. Their suffering will become the stuff of stories told in hushed voices in back rooms and parlors. They have crossed a line, Bishop. A line that I cannot allow any to contemplate approaching again."

My heart sank. So Ivé wasn't actually going to be helpful. Figures.

"Look, Ivé, why not just stand your people down? Bring back the loa you've tasked to this, tell your contacts and followers all the attention is scaring your daughter and sending her to the ground. Clear them out, and let me see what I can do."

Ivé sneered, shaking his head.

"You? Who a moment ago couldn't see he'd been set up by his formerly beloved Mother Church? Don't be foolish, Bishop. I will do as I have always done—protect me and mine. It seems that some here in New Orleans have forgotten what it means to court my wrath. I will remind them."

Ivé paused. Taking out and lighting a cigarette, he took a long drag, closed his eyes, and savored the flavor before continuing. "I truly am sorry that this bodes ill for your daughter, but neither she nor you are one of mine."

He opened his eyes as he exhaled, surrounding himself with an ominous haze of smoke.

"I sorta figured," I replied through gritted teeth.

Ivé's lips split into a wide, mirthless grin, revealing too-white teeth. "I would expect nothing less, priest. May the best man win."

*Chapter
Four*

As I left Ivé's, I felt deflated, but I was still drawing breath, so I decided to chalk that visit up as a split decision, all things considered. Even the shocked expressions on the guards' faces outside as I walked across the lawn did nothing to soften the blow of not managing to pull off not-a-loss. In addition to not getting Ivé to back off, I'd been grabbed so quickly after my arrival that I hadn't had a chance to put my ear to the ground and find out anything useful. I needed information, and I needed it badly.

There were few options available to me on that front, and the ones that I had each presented its own inherent risks. My back room at Bishop's Crossing had enough ritual books and supplies that I was certain I could find *something* if I dug through them. The problem was that sort of re-search is slow and tedious, and Ivé didn't give me the impression he would be waiting. Hell, I wouldn't have been if the shoe was on the other foot and Mary was the one in the wind. Difference is that I'm not capable of starting a supernatural blood feud if I lose my cool. Ivé is. All it would take was the hint of a whisper that Evangeline was somewhere he didn't approve of, and there'd be bodies on the ground.

That meant slow and tedious was out. I needed to start reaching out to the other things in the city that go bump in the night.

The vampires were never a great place to start. When someone looks at you like you're food, it's tough to reach the kind of understanding required to do business together. Last I'd heard a guy named Conrad was in charge of the bloodsuckers. Considered himself to be some sort of businessman. A thoroughly modern bloodsucker. I might be able to cut a deal with him for information if push came to shove, but it was also entirely possible that his price would be something I didn't want to pay.

The werewolves were around in small numbers, but they tended to be a bit kill-crazy for my taste. Like the beasties they turn into, they run around in packs, so a one on one chat would be tough to arrange. They can be useful in a pinch, but only in very small doses. Plus, I'm pretty sure their current leader was someone who's not a member of my fan club. Big part-time fuzzball named Donovan. Like a lot of the other names in the city, we had a history.

There were other assorted willworkers, witches, ghosts, and fae, but none of them had the kind of reach or organization to cast the broad net I needed. The more I thought about it, the more I realized that I already knew where I needed to go and who I needed to see: Ava Dufrense at the Bayou Review over on Canal Street. Ava's a torch singer. One of those ladies who wears a slinky dress and sings while writhing around on top of a piano. The tourists eat it up, but Ava's something special. When she performs, *everyone* eats it up. You see, Ava's a succubus, so all of that squirming has a purpose. It helps keep her fed. Born to a human mother and a demon father, she's got some abilities that make this line of work come naturally to her. In addition to a supernatural ability to play with people's emotions, she's a shapeshifter. To a point. Succubi and incubi (the male version) can assume the form of anyone of their own gender. They're stronger, quicker, and tougher than normal folks and heal a whole lot faster. I'm sure you can figure out why all of this could be useful in their standard line of work.

In Ava's case, she has some other really useful skills, namely that she sucked up information like a sponge. If something was happening in New Orleans, Ava knew about it. She's not someone who has a burning desire to see me dead most days, so I count that as a bonus.

Unfortunately for me, Canal Street is nowhere near Papa Ivé's (remember how I said earlier it was like going to a different world?). Since I was more likely to find buried treasure here than I was to find a cab, I decided that walking in a straight line toward the Quarter was my best bet. I started heading west at a brisk pace, muttering an ancient incantation as I walked. The words spilled out of my mouth in time with my steps, setting a steady rhythm.

Before I knew it, I was in the Quarter.

There are a lot of old terms for what I'd done. Some would call it magic. Some try to cover it with teleportation or time-shifting. Other people say that you walk in shadows or through broken moments. I don't really understand the metaphysics behind how most hedge magic works, only that it does. It's less flashy and less effective than the sort of will working that Papa Ivé can do, but it's also a much, much quieter trick. Where willworkers take reality, then bend it to their purposes, hedge magic is more like a bug in reality's base code. Quieter, simpler, and anyone could learn how to do it.

I stopped by my place for a layover since the Review wouldn't be open for another few hours and laid myself out on the couch.

Considering how the day had gone so far, I figured a reset wasn't the worst idea in the world.

Nine o'clock found me standing outside of the Bayou Review. Like most of the businesses in the Quarter (including mine), it wasn't exactly spacious but made up for it with its unique New Orleans vibe. Outside, Spanish moss ran down the side of the red brick building, surrounding the gaslights flickering from their sconces as they sent out their small globes of light into the hazy, diffuse darkness around them. Palm trees jutted out from the center lane of Canal, standing vigil around the streetcar tracks that ran down the middle of the thoroughfare. A small wooden sign declaring the establishment's name hung over the door, and on the right side, a menu warned patrons of the highway robbery that was about to be enacted on them. Given the size of the crowd outside, I guessed word had spread that Ava would be performing.

She definitely knew how to draw a crowd.

I skipped the line and approached the door of the Review. A glance above the heads of the throng outside told me that Zeke was working the door tonight, which at least didn't work against me. Zeke was a mountain of a man, standing damned near seven feet tall, with muscles on top of his muscles. He was a massive, bald, racially ambiguous man who wore menace like a second skin. For years, I was convinced he was some sort of supernatural something or other. I dug into every iota of his life and came up blank. I scanned his aura twelve ways to Sunday and saw nothing.

I'm still half-convinced, but I could never make it stick. Zeke is a mystery wrapped in an enigma.

"Bishop," he rumbled with a voice that harkened to Barry White. "Thought you were dead."

"No such luck. Just retired."

"Then you can get in the back of the line and wait your turn."

"That was yesterday. Now I'm only semi-retired," I tried what I hoped was a winning grin. He didn't seem impressed.

"Semi-retired. I don't even know what that shit's supposed to mean. This ain't Wall Street, Bishop. You're either in, or you're out, my man. If you're out, you pay, just like everyone else. If you're in, Ava says to let you through. I don't think she'd be happy if I only let half of you in: she always had a soft spot for you for some reason."

I looked down at Zeke's knuckles, scarred with the memories of count-less street fights, and swallowed.

"That's something I'm incredibly grateful for right now."

He grunted and gave a brief shrug.

"Go on in, Bishop. Keep your nose clean and stay outta trouble. Her set's on in fifteen. Should be done in about an hour. Same rules as always."

I slipped a twenty into his hand on my way by just to forestall any murderous impulses he might be feeling. "Appreciate it, Zeke."

He didn't bother to respond as I walked into the warm, dark room he was guarding. Festooned with red curtains hiding the walls and lit by flickering gaslight sconces similar to the ones on the exterior, the shadows played tricks on your eyes if you weren't prepared. They danced around the edges of your vision and calling out to the unprepared, offering forbidden mysteries and taboo delights. Offering to help you lose your worries and possibly your sanity.

I breathed in the perfume of the Bayou Review as I walked: a mixture of vanilla, cinnamon, and sweat. It added to the ambiance of the room and drew you in, worming its way into the parts of your brain where you made your decisions and encouraging you to make the best kind of bad ones.

I moved to the left side of the room, taking a table near the entrance to the backstage area. Not the best sightlines, but I wasn't here for the show.

And yet.

When the gas lights dimmed, and the soft wail of a saxophone droned out across the room, mingling with the melancholy tune of the piano, my breath caught in my throat. Ava's voice made an appearance, deep and throaty, singing about love lost and a woman wronged. She emerged from behind the red velvet curtain wearing a shimmery dress of black satin that seemed to be half a breath from sliding off of her lithe form at any given minute. The spotlight hit, kissing her pale skin and setting her fiery red hair ablaze in its embrace.

I found myself lost in the sound of the song more than the lyrics. The feel of it. The way her lips formed the words. The rise and fall of her chest. The swish of her hips as she moved around the stage. Our eyes met for a brief slice of eternity, and my breath caught in my chest. She gave the slightest hint of a smile and then moved on to the next mark.

My God, she was mesmerizing.

As she sang song after song, I became lost in her voice, wondering what might have been had I made different choices, longing for the chance to make up for past mistakes. Wondering if—

"Madame Dufrense will see you now."

I startled, my head whipping up and around to face the man standing next to my table. It took me far too long to register that someone was speaking to me. I blinked owlishly up at the waiter staring down at me and nodded, my voice failing me.

He waited a moment, then shook his head and vanished back into the haze of the dimly lit room.

I rubbed my eyes, then slapped my cheek, trying to clear the effects of her song and to break the reverie. Failing, I shoved my right hand into the pocket of my coat and gripped the silver crucifix inside hard enough that the edges dug into the palm of my hand. The pain gave me something to focus on, a metaphysical splash of cold water to my face. I felt my brain moving, grinding back into its natural setting, and took a shuddering breath.

"Too close," I muttered as I came to my feet.

I moved to the stage door on rubbery legs and slid past the security guard with a brief nod. The backstage area was entirely distinct from the lounge: harshly lit by incandescent lights, its bare brick walls and stark wooden steps showed a no-nonsense approach to the business that might have shocked the crowd that had just been so cunningly wrapped around Ava's little finger with her mixture of music, talent, ambiance, and booze.

As I mentioned, the Review wasn't spacious, so I was in front of Ava's dressing room door within ten steps of hitting backstage. I was pretty certain it had started life as a closet of some sort. Ava's name was on the outside, and it stood slightly ajar. Swallowing, I knocked firmly on the frame.

"Come in, Jason. Close it behind you."

I did. The dressing room was utilitarian, like the rest of the backstage area. There was a rack for dresses. A small dresser/chair/mirror for makeup and a screen to allow for changing, which currently concealed Ava, who tossed the slinky black number onto it from behind.

"Didn't expect to see you. You made a huge deal about going legit. Stuck to your little bar and didn't come around and socialize with us spooky folks that go bump in the night anymore. Decided to trade in the life for some domestic bliss with your normie...you were trying to make her into an honest woman, right?"

"Something like that, except more like trying to let me show her that I can be—ahhhh, doesn't matter. How've things been, Ava?"

"Kind of boring, honestly," she called out from the other side of the screen, her voice randomly tensing as she took off and put on clothing. "Things have always been a lot more fun when you're around. What brings you back? Don't tell me you're just here for old time's sake. You said that Julie..."

"Jackie"

"Right—Jackie—you said she didn't really approve of you hanging around with your exes."

"Not just my exes. People from the old life. Plus, she felt a bit threatened by you. Do you blame her?"

"Hey, once you said we were platonic, I respected that. I don't make a play where I'm not wanted."

Stepping out from behind the screen and ruffling her shoulder-length hair, she offered a shrug.

"You picking someone else over me is just a statement about your lack of taste, Bishop. It has no bearing on me."

I laughed and shook my head. Ava had changed into a cropped, over-sized white t-shirt with "Frankie Says Relax" emblazoned across the front in black letters and a pair of low-rise blue jeans. So far, she hadn't located her shoes. She was five foot eight with killer cheekbones and a lopsided smile that I couldn't help but find charming. I was relatively certain that this was the 'real' Ava, but since she was a shapeshifter, it was hard to tell. I know that when she falls asleep, this is the form she reverts to, in any case.

Okay, when she's sleeping, there are also little horns on her head, which she wasn't sporting at the moment, but that hardly counts.

"So—?" she asked, her hands on her hips as she waited. "What brought you in here? I'd love to hang out and catch up on old times, but I'm guessing you've got an agenda. You've *always* got an agenda."

I looked down at the floor and nodded before looking back up.

"Yeah, 'fraid so. I need to find Evangeline Grey."

"Ivé's daughter?"

"The same."

Ava whistled and shook her head.

"You don't believe in swimming in the shallow end, huh?" she mused. "I heard you were skulking around Ivé's place earlier today. That would explain that."

"How the hell did you hear that already?"

"You leave an impression," she shrugged with a smile. "And people like to tell me things."

Remembering back to how I felt during her song, I shook my head. "Yeah, I'll bet."

She ignored me and pressed on. "I might have heard something, but first I have to ask why."

"'Why'?"

"Yeah. You were out. And you were out because it was the only way for you to be with someone you clearly cared about a ton. I told you, I'm not gonna jeopardize that for you, even if you've decided you want to."

I frowned a bit, then looked up and met her eyes. She was Ava, a force of nature and always in control of every situation. Ava knew everything. Always. There was no way she hadn't known Jackie's name earlier. She was Ava, same as always, but this time there was something else. Some subtext I hadn't seen before.

She was hurt.

"I did. I do," I replied, feeling nervous about where this was going.

"Obviously. So why risk it? From what you just told me—hell, from everything that *everyone* has ever told me, if she finds out you're out and running with your old crowd again, any chance you have of prying her away from that oil exec is through. So why? What the hell do they have over you that you'd risk losing your Jackie over?"

"Mary."

Ava stared at me for a heartbeat, her eyes widening slightly.

"Mary? Your daughter Mary?"

"Yeah," I replied.

"Shit, Jason. She's what, like ten?"

"Almost nine."

She shook her head, angrily. "Who has what on her? I'll help you feed 'em their livers," she growled, her irises flashing red for a split second.

I shook my head, holding up my right hand. "It's not like that. Mary's—she's great. But she's showing some signs."

"Signs?"

"Yeah. Signs that she might be a willworker."

Ava stood quietly, weighing what I'd just said, then shook her head.

"Who knows?"

"The Church. Raimond approached me about Evangeline. If I can find her and put a pause to this crusade that Ivé's about to embark on, he'll owe me a favor. Carte blanche on anything I ask."

"Like not putting Mary down, long enough for you to find her a teacher?"

"Exactly like that."

My words hung in the air between us while Ava and I looked into each other's eyes. The sounds from outside faded from background noise into a half-remembered mist.

"Fuckers set you up, Jason. You know that, right? You haven't been retired that long, have you?"

I shrugged, anger bubbling up from my gut. "Blatantly and obviously. It wasn't even particularly subtle. Raimond knew the score on Mary before I did. I don't know how, but—" I shook my head. "Otherwise, he never would have come into my joint and talked to me. That bastard never asks a question he doesn't know the answer to if he can help it. He's using my daughter as leverage on me, which is part of why I tried to get out. To head this shit off."

Ava took a deep breath, then nodded.

"And that's why you need help this time."

"Come again?"

"You've been out of the game for nearly two years. People change, and things move. If Raimond set you up on this, there's a chance he's not interested in seeing you come out the other side. That means you need someone you trust to watch your back."

"And you're volunteering?"

"I—yeah. Yeah, I am," she replied, turning her face away and looking toward the wall, "No girl should ever have to grow up without her dad. Even if her dad is a special kind of bastard sometimes."

I opened my mouth to reply but thought better of it at the last moment, instead deciding to say the right thing for once. "Thank you."

Ava looked back at me, forcing a slight smile.

"So," she said, a bit too loudly, "what's your plan for finding Evangeline in the event I didn't have her locked in my dressing room?"

I frowned, thinking. "If you don't know where she is, that means she's probably not in circulation right now, which is either a very good sign or a very, *very* bad one. Ivé's people would have seen her if she were on the streets. Word would have reached you if she were in any of the private clubs. The loa would have told her father if she were dead."

"I'm with you so far, so what's the other option?" she asked.

"I'm starting to entertain the idea that Ms. Grey isn't someplace she wants to be, and the someplace is protected enough to hide her from daddy dearest. Anything with the juice to pull that off falls into the realm of organized crime with connections to the supernatural. If it was just regular human traffickers, Ivé's loa would have found her in half a second. This has to be somebody connected."

"The vampires have gotten into that business over the last few years," Ava offered. "They move people in and out of the city regularly. New Orleans's port is lousy with them."

Vampires. Awesome. Just like I called.

Ava saw how concerned I was at the thought and smiled.

"Oh, come on. Everybody knows that you stuff your pockets and that backpack of yours with an arsenal every time you go out on a job. Holy water, crucifixes, stakes, silver, iron, gold, salt, and mirrors. You become a walking billboard for what happens when someone violates the Liturgy of the Forgotten. A few vampires have you worried?"

"Yeah. The vampires had started to really organize around the time I left. One of the Corrupter vamps got it into his head to eliminate the family issues they have and see if he could bring all of the bloodsuckers in town under the same leadership. The heads of the other families didn't like it too much, but it looked like he was gonna pull it off."

Ava crossed her arms across her chest, cocked her hip out to the left, clenched her jaw, and gave me a look that made me feel like I was a bug she'd just scraped off the bottom of her boot.

Uh oh.

"I love it when you tell me things I clearly already know, Jason. It's every girl's dream to be mansplained to. Oooh, I know! Can you teach me about lounge singing next, you jackass? Hello? I've been *living* in this world while you've been slinging drinks to tourists. You came to me because I know the lay of the land, didn't you?"

"I—"

"Shut it. If you were gonna trust my information before when I was a contact, why not now when I'm offering to partner up? Men and their fucking egos." She paused and shook her head. "The guy you're looking for is called Conrad and most assuredly *did* get all of the other vampire families to toe the line. Mostly by sending his thralls in after the sleeping family heads during the day and bathing them in sunlight. It was brutal."

My heart sank. "I'd heard the name, but the tactics lesson is new. So you're telling me that we have a vampire lord who's smart, ruthless, and isn't afraid to work outside of the box?"

"Yeah. He's mostly kept his kind under control since he took over, but I think the way he did it is by kidnapping a lot of the types who don't get missed. If they grabbed Ivé's little girl on Conrad's say so, it wouldn't be an accident."

I cursed long and loud in my head before sighing and nodding.

"Awesome. Any idea where I—where *we* can find the bloodsucker?"

"Better. He doesn't hold court like the old family heads used to. Treats the whole thing more like a business. He's set up in a shipping company called Consolidated International Holdings. They own a bunch of warehouses and boats outright, plus a fuck ton of other shit through a maze of holding companies. I've never met the man himself, but everyone I've talked to says the same thing: The guy's smart. He's married old school supernatural powers with modern organized crime."

"So what you're saying is—"

"If Conrad grabbed her, you're fucked."

"What happened to 'we?'" I asked with a sigh.

*Chapter
Five*

Okay, there's a bit of background you need going into this.

First: Clear your brainpan of anything you learned about vampires who sparkle in the sunlight—that shit's bonkers. Ignore anything you've heard about vampirism being a virus or disease. It's a cute idea, but it's also complete bullshit. In all my research, I've managed to piece together a few things on the night-stalking bloodsuckers, and it's kept me alive through my less than congenial encounters with the bastards.

Second: Vampires aren't misunderstood anti-heroes pining for their lost humanity. They're not romantic figures or a stand-in for repressed Victorian feelings about sex and fluid exchange. Vampires are predators who have a transmittable curse that was placed on their forebears by God Himself.

No, I'm really not joking.

Near as I can tell, there are four main "families" of the bloodsuckers, each descended from a different cursed individual or individuals. Each of the families has a different set of abilities and weaknesses, some of which have even shown up accurately in pop culture over the years. Every one of them is stronger, faster, and tougher than regular humans. They all drink blood, and if they feed their blood to a human, they can turn that person into a thrall. That's basically a slave under the vampire's control. Like Renfield. Okay, fine: Bram Stoker didn't get *everything* wrong.

From there, things need to be a bit more nuanced.

The oldest of the family lines are the Descendants of Lilith. Y'know, Queen of the Monsters? Yeah, her. First wife of Adam, who fled the Garden of Eden after refusing to be subservient to her husband, which resulted in her being cursed by The Almighty.

Yeah, I know. Women's Rights weren't exactly advanced back in the day.

Anyway, Lilith ran to the banks of the Red Sea, where she mated with a bunch of demons, giving birth to monsters. One type of monster she squeezed out during her demonic orgy was the Lillin Vampires. These night stalkers can cover themselves in an illusion to pass as normal, but without that, they're absolutely grotesque to look at. They're incredibly strong, fast, and resilient (even for a vampire). Only way I've ever heard of killing them is exposure to sunlight or decapitation. Nasty fuckers.

Next oldest of the vampiric families are the Descendants of Cain. Yes, the Cain from Cain and Abel. After Cain offed his brother, God laid the whammy on him with the Curse and Mark of Cain (catchy, right?), basically making him a vampire of the kind that would eventually be described by the aforementioned Bram Stoker in his book. Descendants of Cain cast no reflection, can't enter a home without an invitation; they can control creatures like wolves, bats, and vermin. Older members of the family have the ability to take the forms of these animals, as well as mist. A stake through the heart, beheading, fire, and sunlight will all close the deal on these guys.

The third family of vampires are the Descendants of Judas Iscariot. After taking thirty pieces of silver to betray Christ, Judas attempted to hang himself in a fit of regret. The Heavenly Father wasn't quite through with him yet and bestowed the curse of vampirism upon him, forcing him to live with his actions until the End of Times. His descendants are corrupters. They whisper in the ears of humanity, driving people to engage in their vices and destructive impulses. They're really good at subtle mindfucks with control over emotions, minds, and stuff like that. They're the least physically imposing of the bunch and the most numerous. Fire, sunlight, beheading, and silver will all do the job on them.

The last family is the rarest, thank God. For a brief time, Lilith and Cain were an item and had some kids.

It takes all kinds, right?

The combination of their curses produced truly frightening vampires that became vampiric sorcerers of incredible power. They can manipulate the stuff of reality itself, but not quite on the same level as guys like Papa Ivé. In all my years dealing with the things that go bump in the night, I've only ever heard credible stories about two of these guys, and I've never so much as caught a glimpse of one.

I hope that never changes.

I'd called ahead to Consolidated International Holdings's offices, located in One Shell Square, a massive block of a skyscraper located a few blocks outside of the French Quarter proper. After asking for the boss by name and pointing out that I needed to meet with him outside of normal business hours (the code phrase helpfully provided by Ava), I was told that

Mr. Conrad could see us in half an hour if we could be at their offices by then.

Ava objected, pointing out that it was probably a trap. I disagreed.

It was *definitely* a trap.

Unfortunately, the trap was also literally our only lead, so I didn't see what other options we had. A quick call to a cab found us standing at the reception desk on the forty-third floor, facing a pleasantly smiling young light-skinned black woman. The reception area looked like it came out of central casting for reception areas. There was a long dark brown counter-desk staffed by the pretty receptionist, a set of four chairs and a couch arranged around a glass table, a scattering of plants, and some generic landscapes hung on the walls.

"I'm afraid that Mr. Conrad was quite specific. He's willing to speak face to face with Mr. Bishop and Mr. Bishop only." Her voice rang out with the slightest hint of a southern drawl, which only highlighted her over-produced, peroxide blonde exterior.

"Out of the question," Ava growled. "He knew two people were coming to see him when we made the appointment twenty minutes ago. He had both of our names."

The smile on the receptionist's face remained in place. "That may be the case, but his instructions are clear: Mr. Bishop is to be shown into his office while you are free to go, Ms. Dufrense."

Ava glared, then turned to me.

"I don't like it."

"Neither do I," I agreed, looking away from the receptionist, who offered me the same impervious smile she had, Ava. "I also don't see what other choices we have. Conrad's pulling a cheap power play, that's all. He wants to watch us squirm and prove to his people that he's the head man in charge. That means if we want him to talk to us—"

"You," Ava corrected. "I'm not invited, remember?"

"Right. Me. If we want him to talk to *either* of us, we need to play ball. As soon as I'm finished with him, I'll meet up with you back at my place, and we can figure out what's going on. Would you rather just cool our heels in his waiting room all night?"

Ava opened her mouth to object, then just shrugged and threw her hands up.

"Your place. One hour. I'm serious, Jason. Things have changed in the last couple of years. You don't know how dangerous he is, but *I* do," she replied before turning to look at the receptionist's nameplate. "Right. Amanda. If I don't meet up with this man in the next hour, I'm holding you personally responsible, do you understand me?"

Amanda's smile faded slightly, but only just. "Miss, I'm sure I don't know what you mean."

"Yes, you do, thrall," Ava spat back. "You. Responsible," she said, locking eyes with the girl for slightly longer than was comfortable for either of them. Amanda swallowed, then Ava stalked toward the elevators with a shake of her head. Entering the metallic box, she turned and glared back into the reception area, her brown eyes flashing as the doors slid shut.

Amanda took a deep breath and re-installed that same smile from before.

"Mr. Conrad will see you now, Mr. Bishop. Straight through those doors. His office is at the end of the hall."

I locked my jaw and walked through like I didn't have a care in the world. I would be damned if I let the bastard see me sweat.

The hallway was nearly as generic as the name of the company. The interior sported a tiled floor with grey-toned walls, four doors placed at even intervals on either side leading away from the lobby, with a large set of dark double doors standing sentry at the end, their silvered knobs standing out in stark contrast to the grain of the wood.

I wrapped my hand around the doorknob, taking a moment to brace myself before turning it and striding in as if I didn't feel like this was the march to the gallows.

Conrad's office was a spacious corner deal on one of the highest floors of any building in the entirety of New Orleans. It had floor to ceiling windows that offered a stunning view of the city and the Mississippi. There were a couple of plants, a bar over to my left, a table with four chairs on my right, and a massive glass and steel desk straight ahead with the object of my inquiry sitting behind it.

Conrad looked to be in his late twenties or early thirties. He was a bit under six feet tall and on the slender side, with neatly trimmed dark hair that he wore slicked straight back from his pale face and was wearing a suit I'm almost certain was more expensive than most of the cars currently occupying the city streets below. I'm sure he had eyes, but I couldn't tell you what color they were.

Never look a vampire in the eye. Too many of their dirty tricks start with eye contact. Anyone who doesn't learn that early on in dealings with the bloodsuckers doesn't get a chance to have *more* dealings with them. My preferred trick was to look at their hairline. The Gordon Gekko wannabe in front of me offered plenty of forehead to gaze into with his choice of hairstyles.

He noticed my lack of eye contact almost immediately. I could see his smile widen in my peripheral vision.

"Mr. Bishop, so nice to hear the rumors about you coming back into the fold are true! Welcome!" He started around the desk, offering me a hand. I held mine up to stop him.

"Please," I said. "I know better than to get touchy-feely with someone who can pull my arm out of its socket."

His smile almost skipped a beat, and his eyes narrowed ever so slightly.

"You're not stupid; I'll give you that. But you're not as smart as you think you are either, Mr. Bishop. If you're truly concerned about what I might do to you, you should have brought your succubus friend."

"I don't need Ava as a bodyguard, Conrad. I'm not here for anything that touches on you or yours. All I want—"

"You have no *idea* what touches on me or mine, Mr. Bishop. Please, take a seat."

He moved away from me, back around his desk and into his large, executive chair. I thought about standing, just to be difficult, but decided against it.

Diplomatic as hell, that's me.

"You're looking for Ivé's girl, yes? We don't have her," he said simply.

"What makes you think I'm looking for Evangeline?"

"Because I am also not stupid," he replied.

Touché.

"You, who have been out of contact with everyone in the occult world for the better part of two years, all of a sudden become active within days of the girl's disappearance. Within twenty-four hours, you manage to speak with Papa Ivé, a man who reportedly hates you, and live to tell the tale. You manage to convince the succubus Ava Dufrense to help you, and then you arrange to place both of you in my office. What else could you possibly be looking for?"

Butterflies began to gather in my stomach.

"Almost. I didn't quite *manage* to get Ava into your office," I said. "So, you're having me watched?"

"Of course, Mr. Bishop. I have every one of note in this city watched, both in the occult community and the mundane," Conrad replied, that same smile etched into his features.

What was it with this place and smiles carved out of marble? It was starting to piss me the hell off.

"I'm not anyone of note. Not anymore. I own a restaurant and bar."

"And yet, here you are. I can assure you, Mr. Bishop, if you were indeed a simple restaurateur, you would not have found your way into my office. People like you never leave the life behind, Mr. Bishop. They don't buy houses in the suburbs. They don't have white picket fences, they don't have dogs, and they don't get to have a wife and kids."

"You keep any mention of my family out of your mouth," I flatly reply. "I'm doing a favor for a friend. That's it."

"You're doing this, but it's not for a friend," he said, waving his hand. "You're doing this because you can't let it go. The life. The excitement. The chase. You're an addict, Mr. Bishop."

Conrad leaned back in his chair, shaking his head.

"I recognize a junkie when I see one, and being 'in the know' is your drug of choice." He paused, shaking his head. "Where are my manners? Would you like a drink?"

Distracted, I shook my head.

His lips twitched slightly before he nodded.

This conversation hadn't gone where I'd wanted it to at all. The vampire had too much information on me and had been prepared for me to show up. He'd planned for this. Done his homework.

But why?

"All of this is immaterial, Conrad. We're not here to psychoanalyze me. We're here for me to find a way to convince Ivé that you don't have anything to do with his daughter's disappearance. To avoid Ivé and his people declaring open season on every vampire in the city of New Orleans."

Conrad threw his head back and laughed long and hard from deep in his gut.

"Oh, Mr. Bishop. I'd been told that you were a hard man, not that you were a comedian."

My head was spinning. Conrad was too smart by a half. Ava was right: I might be out of my league.

"Come again?"

"Do you have any idea how many vampires are in New Orleans?"

"In the metro area? A couple hundred, I'd guess."

Conrad's laughter trailed off.

"Vampires are a renewable resource, Mr. Bishop. All we need is a bit of time and one of the thousands of people that stream through this city like water in the Mississippi. Anonymous and useless to the world they live in, they swell our ranks.

"There are thousands of us, Mr. Bishop. Members in every walk of life, from the mayor's office to the street sweepers. We flow like water, getting into every crack, and crevasse.

"You think I'm afraid that a relic of a bygone age and his dolls are going to put a stop to us? To what I've built here? We're the future, Mr. Bishop."

His news left my mouth dry. I swallowed to fight the nerves back down.

"That's nice and all, but his daughter?"

"I couldn't give a shit about him misplacing his brat," Conrad spat. "But I welcome the conflict. I've been preparing for this since I first seized control. It will serve as an announcement to all the members of the Liturgy of Shadows, from the Ordinis Templi Erinnys to the Werewolf Nations that the Vampire Bloodlines are *the* force to be reckoned with here in New Orleans."

"And will it send the same sort of message to the vampire lords across the United States? Announce you as a big player on the scene?"

Conrad leaned forward, resting his elbows on the desk and steepling his fingers.

"One step at a time, Mr. Bishop. No need to get ahead of myself."

The feeling in the pit of my stomach had spread to a full-blown sense of dread. I was feeling light-headed and dull. Slow witted.

"You're a monocle and a Persian cat away from Bond-villain territory, man. You're offering the full villain monologue: why?" I asked.

"Clearly because I don't intend to let you live, Mr. Bishop."

I was on my feet and backing away from him before the sentence was past his lips. I held out my left hand, trying to steady myself as the room spun.

"What—what have you done?" I slurred.

"One of the great advantages a vampire has in dealing with the living is your dependence on breathing. It provides substantial opportunities to deliver incapacitating agents that have utterly no effect on my people. The one you've been breathing in was liberated from the Russian government at great expense. A chemical compound known as Kolkol-1. They used it in 2002 to neutralize a threat to some theater patrons after Chechnyan separatists took them hostage. It's a marvel, wouldn't you agree?"

He'd stood up from his desk and moved around it, his hands in his pockets. I tried to back away but lost my balance and fell to the floor on my back.

"You didn't meet my eyes, so you limited my ability to manipulate your emotions or to control your mind. You avoided physical contact and kept the desk between us, so you negated my physical advantage. You undoubtedly could have summoned the fire that you're so famous for well before I would have been able to reach you. You really are quite good."

He squatted down, his green eyes locking onto mine. I tried to call the Angelic Flame, but the word was slippery in my mind, sliding away more quickly the more desperately I tried to grasp it.

"Or, more accurately, you *were* quite good. Goodbye, Mr. Bishop. Please take solace in the fact that you never stood a chance. You were out of your league from the start and would have been even had you not been out of practice."

His mouth opened, revealing the classic pronounced canines.

I closed my eyes, then felt the unmistakable sharp pain in the side of my neck and the rush of warmth at the site.

The fucker was drinking my blood.

Chapter
Six

The bite's pain faded immediately, replaced by a crushing wave of euphoria that washed away all other thoughts and concerns. It was one of the most insidious aspects of dealing with vampires: their ability to make you *want* to be their food. The sensation is like no other—a heady shudder that dug into your soul and left you craving more. Deep down, a part of my mind was screaming, fighting the fact that I was dying by inches. The rest of me didn't care.

I was awash in a warm sea of contentment, even as Conrad pulled the life-giving blood from my body. How long had he been doing this? A minute? Five? Not long enough (too long, the buried part shouted). My eyes fluttered as I tried to open them, but it just wasn't worth the effort.

I was out of my league. He'd said so, and he was right.

No. You can't do this, Daddy. Wake up. Fight back.

What the hell?

The screaming part of me latched on to the small, female voice. The voice that sounded unmistakably like my daughter.

He's killing you, Daddy. He's taking you away from me. You have to fight him.

The screaming part of me fought back harder, pushing the contented, happy feelings aside, clawing its way past them. It was like being out of air as you clawed your way to the surface of a lake. Every moment was torture, but failing and giving up meant death. Sensations other than Conrad's bite began to trickle into my consciousness. The coarse feel of the carpet on my back. The pressure of the vampire's hands. I focused on Mary. On any sensation other than the delicious pain of the bite. My arms moved, pushing against Conrad.

The vampire paused for a moment, tensing. A thready heartbeat later, I felt him stand as someone else came to take his place.

I hadn't realized anyone else was in the room with us. I'd say I was slipping, but that seemed pretty obvious based on my current predicament.

I pushed harder, but the vampire didn't move. My hands slid ineffectually to either side of his head.

"Are you still fighting, Mr. Bishop? Do you somehow think you can *win*? No mortal can escape the Dark Kiss. All you're doing is turning a peaceful death into—"

You can win, Daddy. I believe in you. You have to.

Steeling myself, I mentally focused all that I had on the small voice, trying to ignore the light-headed, wispy feeling in my head. I gritted my teeth and breathed out.

And then I called the fire.

"Ignem," I whispered.

Silvery flame erupted from both of my palms, instantly incinerating the head of whatever poor slob Conrad had put in his place to finish draining me and covering me in a fine layer of ash. Opening my eyes, I rolled onto my side, then came to my hands and knees as Conrad backpedaled away, emitting a loud hiss. "That's not possible!" he shouted. "How— *What* are you?"

I took a deep breath, trying to focus my scattered thoughts. It was like trying to swim through molasses. "I'm...the guy...who's gonna fucking end you," I rasped in response. Not my best work, but with my head spinning, it was all I could manage.

Thankfully, it was enough to break Conrad's resolve. The head blood-sucker in charge blurred (or maybe that was my vision) and vanished behind a spinning panel behind his desk.

I was alone in the room on my hands and knees with an open, bleeding wound in my neck. My heart hammered away at my chest in a way that was telling me the blood-drinking had gone on for far longer than I realized. I was cold. So very cold.

It was then that I realized I was dying.

"Well, fuck me."

Grabbing onto the overturned chair, I pulled myself to my feet, but only just. I staggered off the chair and slammed into the wall like a drunk, feeling the impact run through me.

"How do you eat an elephant?" I asked myself. "One bite at a time. You got this."

I hoped that if I didn't try to think too far ahead, I could focus on one thing, then the next, until I was safe. The next obstacle was the door to the office. I slid along the wall until I reached it, then fumbled with the knob.

My hand fumbled for it three times before I finally managed to turn the damned thing, dispelling the fear that it was locked from the outside.

The door opened, allowing me to slide through, then lean back against it for a moment, praying my legs didn't give out.

Next: the secretary's desk. Leaning hard against one wall of the same generic hallway I'd traversed less than ten minutes before, I made my halting, stumbling way toward the lobby, pausing once I was perpendicular to the desk.

Conrad's flight must have triggered some sort of alarm. The outer office area was abandoned. I staggered forward, practically lunging toward the desk, then nearly collapsed as I came into contact with it.

"No. No falling. If you fall, you die," I said to myself. Or possibly just thought. It was hard to keep track. Everything was cloudy, and it was getting harder to think. How long did I have? How long can a person go after suffering severe blood loss before irreversible damage sets in? Even if I normally knew, my brain couldn't produce the answer. I suspected the answer was 'not too much longer,' so I locked onto my next goal: The elevator. Its shining doors seemed impossibly far away. A distance that was completely negligible on the way into the office now seemed insurmountable on the way out. The placement of the desk offered no walls to lean against. No support. It was just a straight walk across the open marble-tiled floor to the elevator.

I was shivering but covered in sweat as I panted against the desk. I leaned back against it, then forced myself upright. I picked up a foot that felt as if it were encased in cement and dragged it forward. Then the other. I repeated the process more times than I thought possible, getting closer with every herculean effort, but still too far away. The room was spinning; breath was coming in gulps.

And then I was on the tiled floor.

I didn't remember falling, but the smooth tile was hard against my sweaty cheek.

Not good.

I tried to return to my feet, but the effort was beyond me, so I took the only option left to me. I crawled.

Inch by excruciating inch, the cold tile sucked what little warmth was left out of my body as I dragged it across the lobby, clawing my way toward the salvation that was just a short elevator ride away. Every movement was torture. My heart hammered irregularly against my breastbone while my muscles became less and less responsive.

It might already be too late.

Regardless, I reached the elevator and flailed up at the pad until I managed to hit the down button.

The soft chime that announced its arrival was one of the most beautiful noises I'd ever heard, and as soon as the doors slid open, I tried to crawl inside.

Sadly, my legs didn't seem to want to cooperate.

I tried a second time. A third. Still nothing.

Fearing the elevator would descend without me and positive that would mean the end, I rolled, flopping myself into the elevator with as little care for dignity as a human being is capable of. Repeating the exercise that had summoned the elevator, I managed to key it to move to the lobby.

And then, the darkness swallowed me.

I had the vague impression of voices. First one, then many. I was irritated at my inability to make out what they were saying, but they all seemed incredibly insistent. I was moved around, covered in blankets, stabbed (I objected to this to the best of my ability), and pumped full of what felt like liquid fire.

I thrashed against the strong hands that held me down as the burning traced a path from my arm, up my shoulder, and into my chest. My mouth opened to scream, but no noise could escape, just a quiet hissing as breath left. The voices started again, and then I relaxed, falling once again into the hungry darkness.

It eventually seemed possible that I wasn't dead, which came as something of a surprise to me. My mouth tasted like someone had used it as a urinal, and everything hurt. I didn't think death was likely to hurt this much, so I was almost certainly alive.

I forced my eyes open and was immediately flooded with regret.

The light coming from the fluorescents was painfully bright, to say nothing of the light filtering in around the outline of the window shades from outside.

"How long?" I attempted to say. It came out sounding more like "Harong." Insightful.

A nurse started at my eloquence, then frowned.

"What was that, darlin'?" she asked.

I swallowed the little spit that was in my mouth. "How long? How long was I out?"

"You only got brought in last night," she replied. "Most miraculous recovery from that sorta blood loss we've ever seen."

"Brought in?" I asked, confused.

She nodded, picking up my chart from the end of the bed and checking it over. "Yeah. Your wife said she found you like this. Got jumped by some kids who wanted to play vampire or something. They managed to drain a lot of blood out of you. It was touch and go, what with you being O negative. Lucky for you, your wife is the same blood type. Those are some long odds working in your favor, Mr. Bishop."

Frowning, I shook my head.

My wife?

"That's not right," I said. "Jackie's blood type is A positive."

The nurse shook her head. "No. O negative, just like yours. She donated as much she could and stayed right next to you all night long. Poor angel, she fell asleep about an hour and a half ago. Careful not to wake her."

My gaze followed hers to the figure curled up in the chair in the corner.

The chair where Ava, dressed in hospital scrubs, quietly slept.

My brain finally started working properly.

My wife. Ava. Ava had found me in the elevator and brought me to the hospital. Ava had donated blood to save my life. Ava, who was a succubus. Ava, who was a shapechanger. Ava had donated blood to me.

I swallowed hard.

"Yeah. That's some luck." I agreed.

"We tried to send her home, but she wouldn't leave. Was too worried about you after saving your life. Little thing like her, dragging a guy like you all the way here. It must have been a sight to see. You make sure you treat her right."

"No worries on that front," I agreed, distracted by the thoughts racing through my head.

I stared over at Ava as she slept, her head resting on her folded arms, and her bare feet curled under her. Her arm twitched, bringing a soft snore out of her. Her white t-shirt had been replaced by a blue hospital scrubs top, which she still managed to make stylish. The slightest hint of a pair of tiny horns poked through her mussed hair, seemingly unnoticed by the nurse.

I shook my head, expecting it to set off a lance of pain where Conrad had made a snack out of me. It didn't. That was concerning in its own right. I refused to believe Ava had done something like that to me. I'd known her for too long. Been through too much with her.

Besides, she'd been pissed about being excluded from the meeting with Conrad and could have easily left me to die if she'd wanted to bring me to harm. She'd done the only thing she could to help and put herself into danger to do it.

I moved the adjustable bed into a sitting position. Then, when it was clear it had caused no issues, I lowered the rail on the left side of the bed and swung my feet over the edge, taking a blanket and laying it gently over the sleeping succubus.

"Jackass."

Correction: The allegedly sleeping succubus.

"You're back in the game for one day, and you let some second-rate Bela Lugosi knock-off get the drop on you? I'm starting to think your entire rep is just stories you made up to scare the tourists, Jason," Ava uncurled her legs and sat up, glaring.

"How was I supposed to know he was gonna gas me?"

"That's part of your rep: Jason Bishop: the man that can't be taken by surprise. Jason Bishop: the guy who prepares for every contingency."

"I think you have me confused with Batman."

"I had you confused with someone who knew what the hell he was doing. With someone who still belonged in this world."

"Had?" I asked.

"Had," she spat back. "Not anymore. You don't belong in this world anymore, Jason. If you ever did, you lost it in that year off. Go back to Jackie. Go back to Mary. I'll find Ivé's kid and tell you when and where. I only stuck around to make sure you were okay. And to make sure there were no—"

"Unexpected side-effects?" I asked.

She frowned, her eyes becoming downcast, then nodded.

"I didn't want to. I swear I didn't. But the doctor said the blood supply they had on hand wasn't enough because you've got some sort of stupid designer blood. And what kind of jackass has blood that's that picky? Seriously!"

"Thank you," I replied.

She didn't hear me.

"So they said there was nothing they could do. Then I asked them 'Well, what if I'm a match?" and they asked me if I was, so I said yes, then I concentrated and was."

"I said, thank you."

Still nothing.

"But I don't know what my blood will do to you. It was that or just let you die, and even though you were a dipshit, I couldn't just sit back and do nothing, but now I did this, and I have no idea what it means...what it's going to do to you."

"I said thank you, Ava," I repeated, louder.

"Well, you shouldn't," she snapped back. "You don't know what this is going to do to you either. It could make you my mindless slave like a vampire thrall. It could call to you and corrupt you. Make you want to do horrible things to people. Even the people you care about. It could—"

"I'm pretty sure I'm not your mindless thrall," I replied.

"No, just mindless."

"It certainly feels that way, but I was like that before the transfusion."

"I changed who you are," she replied miserably.

"No. You just saved who I am when you saved my life. Who I am isn't going to be changed by anything like this. I'm way too stubborn for that. But who I am is telling me that we need to get the hell out of this hospital and get to work unless we want Ivé and his people to do a lot worse to a lot more people than what Conrad did to me," I paused, looking around, then offered what I hoped was a disarming smile.

"Any chance you know where my clothes are?"

Fifteen minutes later, I was checked out over my doctor's objection and wearing a full set of hospital scrubs. My clothes had been destroyed. Seems that being covered in blood classified them as a biohazard.

If only they knew.

Their objections became even louder when I eschewed the need for a cab, heading toward the streetcars that ran down Canal instead. Braving the manageably chilly morning air, we sat in the streetcar as it clacked down the broad avenue, the scattered palm trees gliding steadily by while the other passengers stared at the two of us.

Catching our reflections in the window while I looked out at the street rolling by, I had to admit it was probably mostly me that was drawing their attention. The gauze bandage on my neck and full hospital scrubs was bad enough, but I was certain they hadn't quite cleaned off all of the blood that had crusted in my hair as I was lying in the elevator. Standing next to Ava, who had never wholly cleaned off her makeup from the performance the day before, we looked a hot mess. Or possibly escaped mental patients.

Our reflections were finally a point too far in all of this. It was utterly absurd, so I did the only thing I could think of: I burst out laughing.

Ava looked askance at me while I was in mid-guffaw, so all I could do was point at our reflection, then wave vaguely at the other passengers, which did nothing positive for their opinion of my sanity. Ava's eyes tracked my gestures, going wide at the sight of herself in the window, at which point she let out a loud snort and joined me.

The laughter was like a dam bursting, letting out the fear, frustration, and tension from the previous evening in a torrent. It obscured whatever fresh hells laid in wait. The red streetcar clacked its way down Canal, passing the stately palm trees and pushing through the aromas of fresh beignets cooking. In this moment, in the now, we were alive. We looked ridiculous. It was awesome.

People began clearing off of the streetcar at the next stop while our geyser of laughter finally subsided to a few chuckles as we were carried toward our destination.

*Chapter
Seven*

Bourbon Street is always a strange animal in the morning. A creature of the night just as surely as the vampires I'd just escaped, it offered a different face while the sun was shining. Most especially before noon, when the entire street felt like it was awakening from a coma and sporting a killer hangover. Which it probably was.

We passed a few tourists, who ogled us just as blatantly as the passengers on the streetcar had then made the right-hand turn onto Toulouse that would take us to Bishop's Crossing. Dave was there (as he always seemed to be), waiting behind the bar. One sight of me brought a shake of his head and a low whistle.

"Damn, Bishop. Looks like you shoulda stayed retire—"

He stopped abruptly and did a double-take as he recognized who was with me.

"Ava! I ain't see you in forever, girl! How'd this reprobate convince you to help his ugly ass?" he asked as he came around the bar to give her an enormous hug. Dave's massive form enveloped Ava, who chuckled and hugged the big man back.

"I have a rule about helping pathetic things. Wet kittens, sad puppies...Jason..." she replied. "Why are you still with this loser? Thought you'd have opened your own place ages ago."

Dave shook his head. "And miss out on the mess Bishop makes of his life? You can't get that kind of entertainment on cable."

I cleared my throat.

"I'm standing right here," I objected.

"We know," Ava informed me. "But don't let us hold you up: You stink. Go shower."

I opened my mouth to object, drawing a raised eyebrow from Ava and a shake of the head from Dave.

"You're gonna scare off the customers, boss. That look is a bit too 'Nawlins for the daytime."

Ava made a shooing motion toward the stairs up to my apartment. "I'll grab a shower after you're back down," she informed me. "Then, we can figure out what the next steps are."

"You guys came up blank?" Dave asked.

"Not quite. We definitely found something," Ava replied. "Conrad tried to kill him."

"Yeah," I groused. "It's really the best news we've had since I started on this."

"How's that good news?" Dave asked.

"Because it means we're on to something," Ava replied.

Within five minutes, I was standing under a steady stream of hot water in my shower, allowing it to wash the crusted blood out of my hair. I replaced the gauze bandage and discovered the wound wasn't nearly as bad as I feared it would be. Two small holes with highly developed scabs were all the evidence my brush with death had left behind.

"Wake up, daddy. Fight back," I muttered. "Dammit, Mary. What did you do?"

Sighing, I finished showering, then toweled off, got dressed, restocked my pockets with the usual paraphernalia, and headed back downstairs. As soon as my feet were on the ground floor, Ava uncoiled from the chair she had claimed at the corner table and padded up the stairs for her turn. I collapsed into her recently abandoned chair and frowned, staring down at the table and turning the puzzle pieces over in my head.

"That bad, boss?" Dave asked, breaking me out of my reverie.

I looked up to find the big man standing at the table across from me and offered up a sad smile.

"I'm not sure about bad, but it certainly falls into 'strange.' Last night, a vampire got the drop on me. Used some sort of paralytic gas that put me down like I was tased, then started to drain me dry."

"Ava, bail you out?"

I shook my head.

"You broke free of the Dark Kiss? I didn't think anyone could pull that off, not even flunked out priests. No offense," Dave replied.

"I don't think so, either. I had given up, and then a voice was in my head, urging me to fight, to not give in. It came out of nowhere, and all of a sudden, I could."

"You're hearing voices now? Even in your line of work, that's not a good sign."

"Not voices. A voice."

"You recognize it?"

"Mary," I whispered.

"Shit."

"Yeeeeeah. Looks like we're gonna need that favor now more than ever," I said.

"What favor?" a woman's voice asked from behind me. "And where the hell do you get off not answering your phone? Mary woke up in the middle of the night in a terror over you. Demanded that I call."

My eyes went wide and locked onto Dave's, who gave the slightest of nods.

Jackie.

Fuuuuuuuuuuuuck.

I turned in the chair. "Hey. Sorry about that, but I lost my phone last night. I was looking into something for a friend and must have dropped it."

Jackie crossed her arms and settled in, popping her left hip out as she leveled a look at me.

Right. Not buying it. Still probably sounded better than 'a vampire has it.'

"Looking into something? You're back into this vague nonsense again, Jason? Look, you don't owe me anything, that's fine, but you do owe your daughter. Mary was worried about you. She woke up scared and in tears, and the only thing she wanted was to talk to you. To make sure you were okay. We called and called, and when we couldn't reach you, she spent the next hour begging me to come over here!"

"I'm sorry," I started.

"You're goddamned right, you're sorry. You're always sorry. There's always some excuse. She deserves better than that, Jason. Whatever the fuck you think you were doing, she's more important than that. She's more important than whatever game you were playing or whatever tourists you had on the hook. She's your daughter."

"I get that she's important. That you both deserve better."

"This has nothing to do with me. I told you that. I said yes to Victor. There is no more 'me and you'."

"We have Mary. There's always going to be a 'me and you,' Jackie. We just need to figure out what that's supposed to look like now," I said, looking into her eyes.

"Hey Jason, your water pressure kicks some serious ass."

Jackie's eyes tracked from me to the owner of the voice standing at the bottom of the stairs to my apartment.

I closed my eyes and let out a deep sigh before turning to see Ava paused in the middle of toweling off her hair. She was wearing one of my t-shirts (a plain black one that looked like it could fit three of her and came down to mid-thigh and the scrub pants from the night before (no way I had anything that would fit her). She was barefoot and had obviously just stepped out of the shower.

"Oh. Hi, Jackie."

"Ava," she returned, then moved her gaze back to me. "Case in point. You've clearly changed so much that you've gone and started collecting the old gang again. All you're missing are Nero, Nat, and a few hangers-on, and it'll be just like old times."

"It's not like that, Jackie. Ava was just—"

Jackie held up a hand. "I don't need to know what Ava 'was just.' Or what you 'were just.' I keep telling you: I don't have any claim on you anymore, Jason. There is no us. Clearly, at least part of you has accepted that," she spat. "But this isn't about me. Or us. Or Ava. It's about Mary. You need to be there for her. If you can't be, you need to admit that too."

"I am there for her."

"Not last night. Not when she needed you. She woke up, hysterical, and called you. Being her parent isn't a part-time job, Jason. It's not something you can fit in between running ghost tours with your groupies. She needs a father, not a tour guide. Pick up the damned phone next time."

I opened my mouth to reply, but she'd already stormed out.

I closed my eyes and leaned my head back.

"Did she just call me a groupie?" Dave asked.

"I think that was more directed at me," Ava replied with a sigh. "Gotta give the girl credit; she knows how to make an exit."

"Pfft. If anything, Bishop is your groupie," Dave replied.

"That's what I was thinking," Ava said with a laugh.

I opened my eyes and found her sitting in the chair across from me, Dave standing between us.

"Okay, boss, no matter what she thinks, for you, this is all about Mary. You get to decide if getting into her good graces is more important than making sure your little girl is safe and taken care of."

"That's a no brainer. Mary comes first," I said with a shake of my head.

"Oh, thank God," Ava breathed. "I was afraid I was gonna have to kick your ass to get your priorities in line."

"What's that supposed to mean?" I asked.

"That when it comes to that woman, you've been willing to set your whole world on fire in the past," Ava said.

"That's not true."

"How many friends did you cut off over her?" Dave asked.

"It's not like that."

"How much about yourself did you try to bury or leave behind to make her happy? How much did you try to hide?" Ava added.

"That's not entirely—"

"How often did you lie to her because you felt like you had to protect her?" Dave continued.

"That's not fair. She's not from this world. She's not capable of dealing with the problems that come with our line of work. And the Order gets cranky about leaks."

"But you never bothered to find out if it was an option for her either," Ava pointed out. "You made the decision for her. Kept a big part of your life hidden and locked away from her. Under those circumstances, no one could make it work. No relationship could possibly survive."

I opened my mouth, then closed it.

"There's probably some truth to that," I admitted. "But I didn't think she would have been able to deal with the truth. I still don't think she could."

"If that's the case, then she's probably not someone you should have been with. That's part of who you are." Dave said.

I looked at him and frowned. "I think you've taken a bit too well to the whole 'bartender advice' thing."

He shrugged. "You tip like shit anyway."

We all shared a little laugh to break the tension, then took a long pause.

"Y'know," I began. "She did bring up a great point."

"That you're delusional?" Ava asked.

"No. Nero."

Dave shook his head, and Ava smiled.

"Boss, Nero's not exactly...stable."

"No psychic is."

"Right, but Nero is less so," Dave continued.

"I like him," Ava added helpfully. "He makes me laugh."

"What about Nat?" Dave asked.

Nat. Nat had been a teenage runaway with the potential to work the same sort of magic that Papa Ivé (and apparently Mary) did. David had practically adopted her after he escaped his family, making sure she had food and clothes. She'd wanted more out of him, but the big man had very gently and very firmly turned her down. The timing had been wrong, as I'd retired less than a month later. My 'retirement' had hit her hard, and she took it as a personal rejection and vanished into New Orleans. I hadn't even heard any rumors of her since.

People get lost far too easily around here. Especially, people who walk the roads I do.

Well, we do.

"I lost track of her," I said. "When the kid doesn't want to be found, she doesn't get found."

"I know where she is," Ava replied.

We both looked at her.

"What? Someone had to make sure she was okay. Jason, you were too busy wallowing in your attempted domesticity, and David was...doing whatever it is that he does when we aren't working cases. Cleaning up your puke when you drink yourself into a stupor, I'm guessing."

"She *has* been keeping an eye on you, boss!"

I shot David a half-hearted glare, then stared at the table for a moment, concentrating.

"Wherever Nat is, I think if she wanted to see me, she'd have come by. In the meantime, I don't have anything of Evangeline's to use for any sort of tracking ritual. The spirits have come up blank, or Ivé would have found her the day she vanished. While Nero's not the most..." I paused, looking for the right word.

"Stable?" David supplied.

"Conventional?" Ava offered.

"Reliable," I said, settling on the right one. "Reliable source; he can get us pointed in the right direction."

"If you understand a damned word he says," David muttered.

"That's fine. I need you to stay here and keep an eye on the shop. The vampires have my phone, which means they can probably mine

God-knows-what kind of information off of it. So if you could report it stolen and get another one shipped to me, I'd be forever grateful."

"Gotcha. I'll get a burner phone and set up your number to forward over to it."

"That'd be even better."

Nero is the type of person that could only happen in New Orleans. His given name is Antoine Frye, but he started going by Nero so long ago that most people only know him by that handle. Said he chose it because he was gonna fiddle while he watched it all burn.

He's got a flair for the dramatic.

A gay creole man in his early 30's, Nero was what most people would call a psychic. Not one of the 99 cents a minute types or the late-night TV types. An actual person gifted with a sixth sense. In my experience with him, he's been able to touch objects, gain insight into them, reach out into the astral plane to gain impressions on people or objects, and other psychic phenomena. He stood around five foot eight and was on the pudgy side. He wore his hair slicked back in a ponytail, tended to wear foundation that's several shades lighter than his actual skin tone, and dressed like a refugee from 1790.

Today he was sitting just inside the Bottom of the Cup Tea room at one of their tables next to a sign that advertised "Psychic Readings, $10.00." A tourist couple stood up from their seats across from him after he finished regaling them with glimpses of the spirits that surrounded them while they were immersed in The Big Easy. Nero smiled, happily shaded under his parasol, while playing up every stereotype at his disposal to make himself more "part of the ambiance."

Ava and I stepped up to the small round table with the sun behind us. Nero looked up, squinting.

"Darlin's y'all gonna need to sit down if ya hope for a readin', but let me warn you, the spirits have me right now."

"That's fine, Nero, but we're more interested in chatting with you than the spirits," I replied with a smile as Ava and I both sat in the recently vacated seats. I smiled at the curious tourists and dropped my black backpack on the floor next to me.

The expression on the psychic's face went through a range of emotions within ten seconds: surprise, shock, happiness, concern, wariness, all made appearances, and in that order.

"Bishop," he said flatly, losing 90% of his drawl and sitting up from his partial swoon in his chair. "I thought you left all of us behind to go chase after some piece of ass from the Garden District and got turned down flat."

"Ouch. That's just mean, Nero."

"And Ava," he said, disappointment in his voice. "I expected better from you than slummin' with this bartender. Putting in time for charity?"

"I missed you too, Nero. I leave tickets at the door for you, but you never claim them."

"Sweetie, the crowds are just too much when you're up there doing your shimmy and shake. All their eyes are on you, and their thoughts are—"

He shuddered.

"Better I don't dwell on it. I appreciate the offer, but no. Don't think I can go through that again."

Nero made a show of collecting himself, looking at me primly before turning back to Ava.

"All kidding aside, it's great to see you both. Did he finally come to his senses and dump the normie to hit that hellion ass?"

Ava frowned, pursing her lips.

"Nero..." she said, her voice dropping an octave.

"So that's a no?" he asked, blinking in mock innocence.

"We're here about Evangeline Grey," I said, trying to steer at least one conversation away from my many apparent faults.

"Ivé's daughter. Went missing. Poor girl. Just tragic."

"We want you to help us find her."

Nero shook his head.

"Not even for you and Ava, Bishop. If I find her and don't tell Ivé, he'll have his boys skin me. If I find her and do tell Ivé, then whoever has her will skin me. Either way, the common denominator is that I end up skinned. I like my skin just where it is, thank you. I moisturize to make sure it stays that way. My boyfriend Aaron likes my skin, too. I'm pretty and have great bone structure, but even I'd have trouble pulling off the 'man with no skin' look. Nuh-uh. No way."

"Nero, I really need your help," I said

"It's important," Ava added, leaning across the table and putting her hand on his.

Nero looked down and smiled.

"Ava darlin', it has been too long if you think that woojie's gonna work on me. You know them charms only work on folks that are inclined toward you to begin with. Nero doesn't play for that team."

"Nero, it's for my kid," I said quietly.

Nero gasped, placing his right hand over his heart.

"Little Mary?"

"I nodded."

"What did you go and get her into?" he accused, glaring at me.

"I didn't do anything," I began, but he cut me off.

"No. No, sir. You don't just show up after making a grand diva exit nearly two years ago, tellin' us how you're leaving this life behind so you can be with the woman you love, and then show up out of the blue without so much as a call in all of that time with your sultry ex in tow talkin' about how your daughter is in trouble without it bein' your kinda fault somehow. So spill it."

I rubbed at the bridge of my nose in frustration, gritting my teeth.

"Look, Nero," I began.

"It's the Church." Ava spat out.

My head snapped around to stare at her in surprise.

"Mary's got talent. Probably going to be a willworker and the Church knows. They're holding it over Jason's head. Offered him a favor that could save her life if he tracks down Evangeline Grey and stops this war that's going to go off between the vampires and Ivé's people."

Underneath his foundation, Nero went paler.

"They're blackmailing you by threatening little Miss Mary?" he asked, caught between shock and outrage.

I nodded.

"Oh, sweetie, I'm so sorry. We got this. We'll find her."

I nodded and took a deep breath.

"Thank you, Nero."

"Oh, darlin'. Don't thank me just yet. I'll try to find her, but if Ivé hasn't been able to, that means wherever she is, is probably awful beyond compare. Don't say I didn't warn you."

Ava and I both sat back in our chairs as Nero took off his sunglasses, put both of his hands palm-down on the little round table, and closed his eyes. His lips moved rapidly as he spoke under his breath in a language that I always seemed to be just on the edge of understanding. I felt an itch at the back of my skull, but on the inside as his breath became erratic. Finally, his back arched, and he threw his head back, took a deep breath, then sagged back down to a normal sitting position.

"I see her. I think. Twice. Once surrounded by darkness, another surrounded by. . . chanting?" he asked.

I looked at Ava, who returned my puzzled expression. "Ignore the one in darkness. Probably some sort of reflection that threw Ivé off. The chanting sounds like a ritual. Could it be to block magical scrying?"

"Could be. My mojo don't work the same way as Ivé's, so it's hard to say. But the chanting? I can't see exactly where she is, but she's close. And alive."

"See if you can find any landmarks, Nero," Ava whispered at him.

"I'm looking. Wait. Something—no...someone. Someone knows I'm here."

"Get out, Nero!" I urged.

"He's. . . oh, God! He's...*no!*"

Nero's eyes fluttered as if he were trying to open them. He started to thrash back and forth in his chair.

Ava stood up, moving around the table to stand behind him.

I looked around, unable to find anything that might help, then tore open my backpack (don't leave home without it). Rifling through, I located the object I was looking for: a black candle. Lighting it, I held it in front of Nero's face and began to chant.

He thrashed around, but Ava was more than up to the task of holding him in place until I worked my way through the ritual, the smell of the candle mixing with the light cinnamon incense from the tea room.

"Hurry," she urged.

All I could do was nod as I ran through the ancient prayer in Latin. Priests of old had used it to cast out demons that had bound themselves to the young. I found it to be effective against psychic intrusion as well. Utility is key.

Reaching the end, I closed my eyes and placed my right hand on Nero's forehead, using my left to hold the candle near his face. There was a small flash of light, and he slumped back in the chair, boneless.

Applause broke out around us. A group had gathered at the front of the store and out onto the sidewalk, mistaking the scene for a street performance.

Ava, ever the entertainer, bowed and then gestured to me. I managed a nod to the crowd while I squinted against the sun, scanning their faces for any that I either recognized or could spot as being something *other*.

I came up blank.

"Thank you all. If you liked what you saw, please feel free to donate," Ava called out, holding out a bowl she'd swiped from Nero's table. People milled closer, congratulating us, telling us how much they enjoyed the show, and tipping generously.

I suspect that Ava holding the bowl had a lot to do with that.

As the crowd dispersed, Nero groaned under his breath. Ava and I both moved closer, she hovered over him, and I crouched down next to him.

"Nero? Are you okay, honey?" Ava asked.

Nero nodded, bracing himself.

"Oh, Bishop. I think you're in trouble. Whatever has her? It knows that we know."

I nodded.

"Good," I replied. "Saves me the trouble of introducing myself before I kill it."

Chapter
Eight

Ava and I took Nero back to Bishop's Crossing after he'd recovered enough to walk. Running afoul of whatever was holding Evangeline Grey had made him more than a little bit nervous, and he didn't want to lead whatever it was back to his place, where he and his boyfriend Aaron had no real way to fend it off.

I wasn't thrilled with the idea of leading whatever it was back to my place either, but, as Ava pointed out, I had defenses there that Nero couldn't come close to replicating. I found myself moving him through the short hallway back past the stairs to my apartment, to the locked door beyond. A door that had been closed, locked, and sealed for over a year now, in both the literal and metaphorical sense. My ritual room.

We needed a place where Nero could rest and where no supernatural forces from the outside could touch him. Sort of a Faraday cage for the things that go bump in the night. Short of setting him up at St. Louis Cathedral, which was bound to attract attention, this was the best we had.

The key usually lived under the bar, but that was just the first line of defense. If someone other than Dave or me tried to use the thing, the lock would give off a nasty shock. If I set up the runes correctly, it should deliver about the same sort of load as someone getting hit with a police-grade taser. It gets worse after that. I've never had occasion to test it, so this bit of hedge trickery rested purely in the theoretical.

I swung the door open to reveal a simple room, twelve by twelve, with a twelve-foot ceiling. There were protective glyphs and runes inscribed on the floor, walls, ceiling, and shelves stuffed with a decade's worth of books, objects of power, and general badness that needed to be kept away from the world in general. It was an odd assortment of dusty tomes, necklaces, statues, and weapons. Add in a worktable, bench, and some lighting, and you've got the makings of a nice little bunker—possibly vault.

Nero sniffed. "When's the last time you cleaned in here, Bishop?"

"Been locked up for more than a year now. Make yourself comfortable."

Nero looked around and stared at me in disbelief. "How?"

"You're a creative guy. I'm sure you'll think of something. You sure you don't want Dave to go pick up Aaron for you?"

Nero shook his head. "Nah. No reason to go and drag him out of work for this mess. He'll be home soon, and I left a message on his voicemail explaining that one of my readings went sideways. It happens sometimes."

I paused, weighing Nero's demeanor, then nodded.

"Nero, I normally wouldn't ask you for this, but I need to know what you saw."

"The hell you wouldn't. And, bitch, I told you what I saw. That girl surrounded by a bunch of motherfuckers in robes chanting, then this big ol' dark presence that got some sorta hooks into me and wouldn't let go. The damned thing tried to spin through my brain like a Rolodex."

"Right, but is there any way you can let me see it? There could be something there you missed. Something that could tell us who it is or where. Something about their robes, or the area she was being held in, the chanting. Anything."

"You and your Sherlock Holmes shit. Look, it's possible, but I can't right now. That whole thing left me wiped. I barely had the wherewithal to put one foot in front of the other to get here. It was all I could do to fight him off. The thing shook me pretty hard."

"What do you normally do? When something shakes you, that is?" I asked him.

"Go to church and pray. Stop laughing; I'm serious!"

"No, no," I replied through my stifled laughter. "I...it's just...you?"

"Oh, get out of here," Nero replied in a huff. "Y'all think just because I do this stuff, I can't be right with God? You need you some Jesus."

Shaking my head, I closed Nero into the room and headed back to the front.

"Well?" Dave asked.

"Nero feels that I need some Jesus."

Ava quirked her head. "Do you think it would help?"

"Couldn't hurt," Dave replied.

Until he mentioned it, I hadn't been considering a trip to the Cathedral, but there were worse ideas. I could find out if Father Raimond had any further information or leads on active cults in the area. The only issue was Ava and the fact that her parentage would make any trip onto consecrated ground challenging for her.

Challenging. That's a vanilla word for it.

While she wasn't a full-fledged demon, Ava was a succubus, which meant that she was infernal. I didn't think she'd quite burst into flames but being there would most definitely hurt. Possibly fatally.

"We can give it a miss."

Ava shook her head. "Don't be stupid, Jason. We need information, and your friend at the church will probably have some. I can wait here. I don't think even *you* can get yourself killed during the day, in public, in a Cathedral."

Dave laid a twenty-dollar bill on the bar. "I'll take that action."

"Mr. Bishop?" a voice called from behind the bar. All three of us turned our heads to see the girl behind the counter, holding a phone.

"What's her name again?" I whispered.

"Allison. Kid number two to you," Dave replied in kind.

"What's up, Allison?"

"You've got a call. From your daughter's school?"

"Not again. What does the battle-ax want?"

"Uhh. Battle-ax? It's Mary. She says there's a guy outside giving her the creeps, and she wants you to come to get her. She won't leave."

"Mary?" I gasped, launching out of my chair and heading toward the bar as David and Ava both looked on in evident concern. "Mare-bear? What's up?" I asked into the phone.

"Daddy. There's a guy outside. Just standing across the street and staring at the front of the school. I think—" she trailed off.

"Mary?" I called into the phone. "You still there?

"Yeah. I think he's here because of me," she whispered, her voice trembling.

My face became a thundercloud. "What's he look like, sweetie?"

"He's a grown-up. Dressed all in black with a white collar in the front."

"Black with a white-collar? Like a priest?"

"Yeah, kinda like that, but he doesn't look like any of the priests at our church. He looks more like an army man."

Shit shit shit shit. The Order. Raimond must have moved in spite of all of his flowery words about finding a better way.

"Okay, sweetie. Sit tight. I'm on the way. Don't go outside, no matter what. And don't talk to him. I don't know who he is, but I'm going to find out."

"Hurry, Daddy," she said, then hung up.

I turned around to find David and Ava standing behind me, Ava holding my backpack.

"You guys don't—"

"Stow it, boss. Nobody threatens the Princess," David replied, his normally cheery voice coming out as a dangerous rumble.

"What he said. Stop wasting time and let's move," Ava added.

I smiled in appreciation, then grabbed the bag and ran out of the bar, hearing David inform Allison that she was in charge until we got back.

The houses, blocks, and streets went by in a blur. I don't remember much between my place and the school. It's a route that I've walked more times than I can count. It's generally a short, pleasant walk. Not today.

I arrived at the intersection across from the school breathless, with Ava right behind, though much less winded. Dave had managed to keep up and showed no signs of fatigue at all due to life's inherent unfairness.

The man who had worried Mary was easy to spot. He stood directly across the street from the school, staring at the entrance. His black button-up shirt and white collar strained against his massive chest in a way that made me grateful that Dave had come along.

"Ay! What the fuck is wrong with you?" I demanded, having decided to be diplomatic about the situation.

His head turned slowly to determine the source of the vulgarity. Seeing the three of us approaching him, the man simply turned his head back to watch the front of the school once again.

"Mr. Bishop. I suspected you would be along. And with Ms. Dufresne and Mr. LeBlanc in tow. My dossier indicated that you had professed to be retired from dealings with The Gloaming. Sloppy intelligence," he tsked.

He'd referred to The Gloaming right off the bat and in public. That was never a good sign.

"I don't give a shit about any of that. Where the fuck do you get off threatening my kid?" I demanded.

He turned his head once again, calmly regarding me.

"I haven't threatened anyone. I'm just here observing. Indications are that there is an individual here who has begun to bend reality to their will. An assessment needs to be made as to the level of threat your child-I'm sorry, *this individual* presents, both for now and in the future."

"Threat? You're talking about a little girl! And you call *us* monsters," Ava spat.

"I call you a monster because you *are* a monster, succubus. Your fair visage will do nothing to sway me. The Lord protects me from your influence, demon. Hearing the truth hurts because you are, in fact, a monster. As is...whatever Mr. LeBlanc is," he continued, "Mr. Bishop and his daughter? That remains to be seen."

"You touch her over my dead body," I warned him.

"If necessary, yes. I do the Lord's work, Mr. Bishop. The Lord is demanding of those who serve His will. He doesn't quibble, and he doesn't equivocate. He expects that we will protect His children, no matter the cost. If that means seeing a child burn, so they don't kill or otherwise imperil hundreds or thousands of souls, then that is my burden. My task.

"I weep for those innocents who have needed to die through no fault of their own, but that does not change the fact that I would change *nothing* of what I have done in His name. Like our methods or no, but The Order has kept the world safe for the past five centuries."

"Killing kids is more than unfortunate," Dave rumbled in response. "I had an issue with my family when they did it, and I don't have any less of an issue with you just because you're hiding behind a cross."

"My work here is done. You'll be seeing me, Mr. Bishop. Go with God."

"Fuck off," I replied, remaining invested in my diplomatic approach.

The blonde man stared at me for two seconds longer than was comfortable, then turned and walked down the street, taking a path toward the cathedral.

"Looks like you're gonna need to have that talk with Raimond sooner rather than later," Ava said. "And if that guy's around when you visit the church, no way am I taking Dave up on that bet."

I stared at his back as he strode down the street, positive he was going to become an ongoing problem. Gritting my teeth, I started across the street to collect Mary.

My darling daughter raced over and threw her arms around me, squeezing tight the instant I walked through the doors of the office. Dr. Simmons was waiting with her but didn't offer a hug. Probably for the best.

Mary squealed with delight as Dave and Ava entered the office after me, running to each of them and hugging them in turn.

"Thank you," she whispered to no one in particular.

"No one threatens our princess," Dave reassured her while patting her hair.

"Mr. Bishop," Dr. Simmons began, only to be interrupted by me holding up a finger and glaring.

"No," I said.

She continued anyway. "Your daughter was frightened by a stranger outside who we felt could potentially present a threat. We called the police, but they didn't arrive. Do you know that man?" she asked, her voice carrying some of the concern she felt.

I shook my head. "No, but I'm going to find out who he is," I replied.

"Thank you. He made me and the rest of the staff uneasy as well. Something about his eyes."

"Yeah. Like he was dead inside."

She nodded. "Exactly like that."

The three of us ushered Mary out the door and headed back to my place as I tried to shift my opinion of Dr. Simmons away from the uncaring, cold shrew trope I'd placed her in previously. We walked the streets of New Orleans clustered protectively around Mary, her left hand in my right. If she noticed, she didn't mention it, but her green eyes lost some of the worry they'd had when we first left the school. Ushered safely to Bishop's Crossing, she headed upstairs to call home so Jackie could come to pick her up.

I'm sure she was looking forward to another visit after the virtuoso-like success of our prior engagement today. And as much as I needed to be elsewhere, Mary was here, which meant I was here.

"Guys—" I started, but Ava held up her hand.

"We know. You don't need to say it. We've all known that little girl since she was born, Jason. Like hell do we let anything happen to her."

"Not many things would make me willingly take a fight to The Order. Princess is one of them," David added. "Nothing else needs to be said."

I looked at the three of them for a long moment, fighting down a long string of emotions that hit me one after the other. I knew that I'd tried to walk away from the shadows to keep Mary and Jackie safe. To try to get a shot at winning them back so we could be a regular family, but how can anyone expect me to walk away from friends like David and Ava? Hell, add Nero to the mix too. The man hadn't seen me for over a year, then jumped to help nearly the instant he'd heard that my daughter was in trouble. He'd ignored the danger to himself and did what he could without a second thought. And I'd walked away from all of them, just like that. I'd ignored Ava and Nero for over a year. I'd made Dave walk away with me.

And still, here they were. I was a complete shit of a friend.

"Right. Well, I'm gonna go upstairs and sit with Mary. You two are more than welcome to come on up and wait. The staff can take care of the place while we're up there."

On the way up the stairs, I poked my head in on Nero and asked him to come up as well, and the four of us ascended to my living room. It was like Thanksgiving at first: full of awkward pauses and long, sideways glances while everyone tried to find their footing around the rest of the group once again. In the time since we'd been (mostly) apart, even Dave hadn't come upstairs very often, instead keeping to what he considered 'his' space downstairs while I debased and abused myself up here.

For her part, Mary was in heaven. She had a whole room of grownups that she'd known since she was little, all of whom doted on her, all paying rapt attention to her at the same time. She laughed at their stories, asked distressingly insightful questions when she thought they were hiding things, and managed to repeatedly and pointedly disapprove of my behavior in some of the tamer stories that Ava and Nero shared.

It was half an hour, but it was how I'd want to spend eternity if given the choice.

A knock on the apartment door ended that.

Nero tensed, Ava and I looked concerned, and Dave stood and lumbered over toward the door, making a shooing motion behind him as he went.

"You all relax; I got this," he assured us.

Opening the door, he revealed the worst villain I could have conceived of: Jackie's fiancé, Victor. Victor Osgood was a six-foot-tall, athletically built, slightly balding oil executive. His brown hair was combed back in a way that shows he was unconcerned about the hair loss, which made me dislike him a bit more. He could at least have the common courtesy to be ashamed of his physical defects. His brown eyes tried to peek around Dave's massive frame as he stood in the entryway.

"Hi, I'm Victor. Jackie asked me to come and pick up Mary on my way home from work. Something about some trouble with a stranger outside of the school?"

I waited a bit longer than I should have before I stood up and let Victor in past Dave. My friend had shown every indication of having my daughter's future stepfather remain standing at the door until the building fell to ruin around him.

"Yeah, some idiot was spooking the kids. I walked Mare-bear home, though, right, sweetie?"

Mary rolled her eyes. "That's a baby name, Dad. But yeah, he walked me home after the blond priest was scaring everybody."

"Priest?"

I nodded. "Whack job was dressed as a priest. Probably to make him seem creepier. It worked."

"Like those people who dress as clowns and hide in the woods," offered Nero from the couch.

Victor turned to say something but got sidetracked. He'd taken in the room, the couch, and Nero, but his eyes got stuck on Ava. She has that effect on people sometimes. Especially if you're not used to being around her and if she's not making an effort to damp her magnetism down.

"I..." he swallowed. "Nice to meet you all," he said, dragging his eyes away and wiping his forehead.

From her chair on the far side of the room, Ava rolled her eyes and mouthed "boys" with a shake of her head, drawing a loud laugh from Nero and Mary.

The laugh prodded Victor a bit. He shook his head as if trying to remove cobwebs, then looked at me, moving so Ava wasn't in his line of sight.

I've gotta give him credit. He behaved himself way better in his first meeting with the woman than I did.

"Jason, Jackie asked me to talk to you. Do you mind if we step out onto the stairs?"

"Sure. Be right back, everyone. Mary, you're in charge."

This drew a girlish giggle from Mary as I followed Victor out the door, closing it behind me.

"Look, there's no need for this to be strained or weird between us, Jason."

"I didn't know that there was any 'between us' to be weird about, Vic. We only just met."

Setting his jaw, he took a deep breath. Mary had warned me that he hates being called Vic.

"Look, I'm sure you've heard by now that Jackie and I are planning to get married. If Jackie hasn't told you, I'm sure Mary has."

I said nothing, which he took as a sign to keep talking.

"This doesn't mean that you need to hate me, and it doesn't mean that I'm trying to replace you as a father to Mary. You're her father and always will be. But I'm going to be an important part of her life too. Hers and Jackie's."

"And?" I asked, proving how helpful I am.

"And I just wanted to tell you that there are no hard feelings on my part."

"No hard feelings on your part?" I asked with a disgusted chuckle. "What in the blue hell do you have to have hard feelings over?"

"What about the fact that you constantly undermine me with Mary?"

"I only take her places and show her a good time."

"Places that Jackie and I would rather you didn't."

"I don't recall asking for permission on where to take my daughter. From you *or* Jackie. And if she's got a problem, then she can come talk to me about it herself."

"You don't like me much, do you?"

"No, Vic. I really don't."

"Why? All I've been is decent to you while you've shown me nothing but contempt."

"That's kinda what I do to contemptible people. Look, it's nothing personal—"

"It sure as hell feels personal."

"—but anyone who landed in your spot would get the same treatment. The two people I love most in the world live with you. They see *you* every day, not me. *You* get to say goodnight to them. *You*."

There was a long pause before Victor replied.

"She left you, Jason, and from what she's told me about it, for a good reason."

"And what the fuck did she tell you?" I spat back.

"Enough," he said, then looked meaningfully up the stairs. "There was a lot of drinking—"

"I own a bar."

"There were drugs. There were women—"

"I never once cheated on her."

"And there was lying. A lot of lying."

I had no reply to that.

"We're getting married, Jason. It's happening. I don't want an adversarial relationship with you, even if you continue to lash out at me like a child."

I fought the urge to flip him off. Didn't want to give him the satisfaction of being right.

"But the clock is running on how long Jackie is going to tolerate your behavior. You need to stop holding out hope she's going to take you back."

"I don't—"

"Please. Just stop. Have some pride, man. She said no. Move on. It'll only make things ugly between you, her, and Mary if you don't."

He patted me on the shoulder. I managed not to punch him in his stupid, smug, correct face. I'd say that qualified as 'polite' under the circumstances.

"Okay," he concluded. "Good talk. Now we're gonna go upstairs, and I'm going to take Mary home for dinner. No need to bother her with any of this adult stuff, right?"

There we agreed.

We re-entered the apartment in the middle of Ava regaling Mary with a story about the time I fell out of an airboat and landed in the bayou while we were out and about. She'd just gotten to the part where I'd mistaken a log for an alligator when we walked in.

"Sorry, kiddo, but it's time for you to head off with Victor," I informed her.

Mary looked up at me, then at Victor, and smiled. "Good. No one got punched. I was worried about that."

"I wasn't going to punch anyone," Victor objected.

"I was talking about Dad," she replied with a roll of her eyes. "Bye, everybody! Behave yourselves!" she called, waving over her shoulder as she and Victor headed out the door and down the stairs.

The room was silent for four heartbeats before Nero spoke up.

"Yup. I'd be willing to burn the entire world for that little girl."

After a brief conversation with the group at my apartment, everyone agreed that going to the Cathedral was a terrible idea. Dave and Ava thought it possible the blonde man might be there and wasn't sure if I'd be able to control my temper if I saw him. Nero disagreed. He was *positive* I'd have no ability to control myself if I ran afoul of the man who had threatened my daughter.

I can't say Nero was wrong, but this was something that needed to be done. Raimond had access to information, and information was what we needed right now. Something with real power was holding Evangeline Grey, and the signs pointed to a cult. It was the robes. Cults are *really* into their robes. We needed more information, but we'd exhausted the less dangerous options at our disposal, which meant it was time for the more dangerous ones.

If anyone would know about cults active in the greater New Orleans area, it would be The Order, which was, under the circumstances, the least dangerous of the dangerous options. I think. Maybe. They keep tabs on cults like cops do on street gangs, just in case one of them stumbles onto something legitimate, and they can move in with extreme prejudice. Having no other option, I ignored my friends' advice and snuck out to see if I could track down Raimond while they were all lost in the sentimentality of catching up.

I'd have loved to stay. Loved to live in that moment, but priorities are a bitch, and I've got 'em.

The October sky was splashed with red and orange as I made my way from the bar to the Cathedral. It was a five-minute walk, and as I headed toward Jackson Square Park, I could see the buskers, artists, and street performers out in full force. The clung to the last vestiges of daylight, futility hoping for a spate of final sales or donations before allowing the night to spread from the myriad of shadows cast by the dense foliage in the area and lay claim to their spaces. The foot traffic had already started to thin, the steady parade of visitors to The Big Easy beginning the transition from wandering the Quarter and taking in the atmosphere and architecture to individuals more focused on drunken revelry.

No judgments. Drunken revelers are the reason I haven't had to find a 'real' job.

I climbed the few steps to the front doors with a queasy feeling in the pit of my gut. All of Ava's admonitions about me being out of practice had come crashing down around my ears, and the lunatic priest's visit to Mary's school had served to highlight the very real danger she was in.

It was enough to cause a light sheen of sweat to cover me from head to toe as I strode through the vestibule and into the nave of the cathedral proper.

"Can I help you?" a woman's voice rasped from my left.

"I need to speak to Father Raimond," I replied without breaking stride.

"The Father isn't accepting—" the nun replied, moving to try to get ahead of me.

"I didn't ask. I'm going to go see Raimond. Now. You can call him and tell him Bishop's on the way or not, sister. Your choice."

"Mr. Bishop, Father Raimond is medi—"

I didn't hear the rest of her objection as I slammed open the double doors and headed down the stairs, retracing the same steps that had deposited me in his office the day before.

Sweet Jesus. Had it really only been the day before?

Finding his door locked, I pounded three times with the heel of my hand.

"Raimond, open the damned door. You've got some explaining to do."

I paused for a five-count, then repeated the action, "I mean it, Raimond. You and me—"

The door opened to reveal a shirtless Raimond, covered in sweat and wearing a pair of black Adidas workout pants. I'd interrupted some sort of exercise session.

"—need to talk," I finished, ignoring his state of undress and shoving my way into the office and stood, facing the wall, leaving my back to him as I attempted to reign in my temper. Three deep breaths. Then three more.

"Jason, while I appreciate you stopping by, I must remind you this isn't your bar. Obscenity is tolerated, if not appreciated. Blasphemy is not."

I waved my hand, dismissing his objection.

"You're lucky it's only words at this point, Raimond. I've been playing by your rules and chasing down the kid, just like you asked."

"And you'll be rewarded for it, as agreed."

"So why the fuck did you send a Nazi-wannabe to Mary's school?" I demanded, turning to face him once again. I was unprepared for the look of surprise on his face.

Did he really not know?

"Nazi wannabe? I sent no such person. Can you describe him?"

"Big, square-jawed motherfucker—"

"Jason," he warned.

"—yeah yeah. Built like a football player. Blue eyes. Hair in a crew cut. Dressed like a priest. He was at Mary's school today, waiting outside and creeping out the kids, faculty, and staff."

Raimond sighed, walked over to his battered wooden desk, and picked up a black t-shirt off of it, pulling it over his head.

"Jason, I'm very sorry, mon ami. The man you saw today is likely Father Harlan Chase."

"Harlan? With a name like that, no wonder he's a sociopath."

Ignoring me, Raimond continued, "He's a former Army Ranger. From what I know about him, his personnel file is full of commendations. He considered joining the Chaplain corps but declined due to its non-combat role. From what the higher-ups have told me, he is fervently dedicated to the letter of the law regarding The Gloaming. He would happily remove anything that is a party to the Liturgy of the Forgotten. He feels they are an abomination in the eyes of God."

"Jesus, Raimond. What the hell is he doing in New Orleans?"

"I didn't know he was here, Jason. You have my word."

I pulled out the chair and slumped into it, leaning my head back and staring up at the ceiling. Raimond moved to the other side of the desk and sat in silence, his dark eyes watching me. Content to wait.

He's infuriating that way.

"I've chased some leads, but signs are pointing away from the vampires," I said without bothering to look at him.

"You're sure?"

"Positive. Not that it'll stop Conrad from using the situation to his benefit. Fucker *wants* a fight with Ivé. Seems like he's spoiling for it. Ivé has had his fingers in every piece of the pie in this town for a lot of years. He's the big fish. If someone wants to take the top spot, then that road leads through his front door. Even if Ivé gets his little girl, if Conrad stays around, you're gonna have that open warfare in the streets that you were worried about."

"Then we'll need to collect this, Conrad."

Now I looked him in the eye, sitting up from my slouch. "Gonna be easier said than done. The leech almost got me. Had me dead to rights before I managed to weasel out of it. But in the process of doing it, I think I mighta put a scare into him. Chances are that he ran down a hole and pulled it closed after him. But that's not why I'm here. *Something's* got the girl. Just about blew the brains out of a psychic I used to track it."

"You've tapped your old network for this?"

I stared flatly at him for a moment, then chose to ignore his question and continued. "Something with power. My initial thought was that there might be a cult operating in the city that has managed to stumble onto something. Do you have any information on that?"

Raimond shook his head.

"The last cult we were watching ate itself six months ago."

"Ate itself? Internal power struggle?"

Raimond shook his head. "No, I was being literal. The Order planted a ritual they located and enacted. It drove them all to self-cannibalism. Horrible, but very tidy."

I fought to suppress a shudder.

"Then, a rival willworker?"

"None that could repel Ivé if he scryed for the girl, which he certainly has," Raimond replied.

I shook my head in frustration.

"It doesn't make any sense. Anything that could have nabbed a psychic of that skill level—"

"There's no need to be coy, Jason. I know you're referring to Nero."

"—wouldn't be something that could fly under the radar for long," I finished, ignoring his observation.

"If it were obvious, it would have already been dealt with. I wish I could offer you some insights, but we have nothing."

I muttered a curse and came to my feet.

"You don't make things easy, Raimond. The only help I get from the 'all I need' offer from The Order is news that a PTSD-riddled Army Ranger wants to kill my kid, and you've got no clue what's going on in the city right now."

Raimond sighed, then leaned back in his chair.

"All I have is rumors from our soup kitchens. Fewer young people are coming in lately."

"Fewer young people? You mean homeless kids and runaways?"

He nodded, sending my mind racing down a number of different avenues, none of which were pleasant.

I offered a grim smile.

"I know it's not much—" he started, then stopped when he saw my expression. "What? It could mean anything."

"It could," I agreed. "But I think I might know how to narrow that 'anything' down a bit."

Ava was waiting outside of the Cathedral when I emerged, her arms crossed and her eyes flashing. Not a good sign.

"That was damnably stupid," she spat.

"Not completely," I objected. "I got a bio on our blonde man. He's Order, former military. Pretty much as badass as badass can be. The fucker."

"That's nothing you couldn't have gotten on the phone, asshole. You took a huge risk walking in there the way you did. This isn't a game, Jason. People are counting on you, and not just Mary. Whatever's going on with Evangeline Grey is the real deal. No part-timer could have done that to Nero."

I nodded in agreement, then motioned for her to walk with me.

"I know, but I was hoping for word on cults from Raimond," I said, repeating my reasoning from back at my apartment. "And like I said before, that's not information he's likely to share over the phone. Face to face works with him."

Ava grunted in irritation.

"Well, *did* you get anything?" she asked.

I grimaced.

"Maybe. If I did, it's slim. Raimond ruled out a bunch of stuff, but there are rumors about fewer kids showing up in the soup kitchens lately."

"Slim is an understatement," Ava replied, shaking her head.

"It's what we've got," I paused, bracing myself. "I don't suppose Nat's still plugged into those groups, is she?"

Ava let out a low whistle. "You're treading on dangerous ground there, Jason. Nat didn't take your 'retirement' as well as the rest of us. If you want her help, you need to understand a couple of things. First, you need to treat her with kid gloves. Your regular 'full speed ahead and other people's feelings be damned' won't get her on board."

"Yeah," I agreed. "I sorta figured."

"And second, if you're bringing her back in, she'll see it as you being back. Period. Not on a trial basis. Not 'just till Mary's safe.' She'll think it means you're back, with everything that comes along with it. That kid's been through too much for you to play with her emotions on this. If that's not your intention, you need to be upfront and tell her. Lying isn't an option. Not with her. Not on this. It's too important to her. She's too fragile."

We walked on in silence while I weighed what she said, our footsteps eating pavement as the distance between us and our destination dwindled with each stride. I walked mindlessly, following Ava's lead as we took turns seemingly at random until finally, I nodded.

"Yeah. Now I just need to figure that out for myself," I muttered.

Ava quirked a crooked smile at me. "You'll do fine," she reassured me. "But let me talk to her first."

I took a deep breath and came to a stop. "Yeah. Wait. What?"

Ava and I stood outside of Big Easy Voodoo and Gift Shoppe.

I blinked, then shot a glare at Ava. "Slick."

She shrugged. "She's going to bark at you. You know that, right?" Ava asked, her brown eyes almost black in the early evening light.

"Yeah."

"You've gotta just take it if you want her help, Jason."

"Yeah."

"She was really hurt."

"Yeah, you said that," I replied, taking a deep breath. "Okay. Let's do this."

I think Ava knew where we were going before I even came out of the Cathedral. I know she'd been in touch, but she seemed positive we'd need Nat and that Nat would be here. Natalie "Nat" Jenkins was a petite, Filipino American girl of the goth variety. She had been a teenage runaway we saved from a cult back in the day, then proceeded to hide from The Order.

Nat has the potential to be a willworker, which, as you've seen from their approach to Mary, isn't something The Order is too keen on. After that job, she latched on to us, no matter how many times we tried to put her someplace safer, and eventually, she became part of the group.

Then I retired.

Moving past the displays at the front of the store, I stopped in the middle of the aisle, facing the back of the store, where Nat stood, talking to a kid that was taking over the register for her. She hadn't grown any, but not many women in their early 20's do. She'd cut her hair shorter and straightened it, adding bangs to the heavy black lipstick and eyeliner she'd always sported. Nat gave some instructions, then turned to leave, and nearly bumped into Ava. Her face lit up, and it broke my heart just a little bit. The two exchanged a few words, a big hug, and then Nat froze before her eyes darted over Ava's shoulder and locked on to me.

Then moved away as if they'd been burned.

Oh, this was going to go well.

I walked slowly down the aisle.

"No," she said before I could say a word. "No, Bishop. This is where I work. You don't get to do this to me. Not here, not anywhere. No. You made it clear I wasn't important to you. So, no," her voice was trembling with barely contained rage as she shouldered by me, storming out the front of the store and onto St. Ann Street, walking quickly past the other pedestrians.

I looked at Ava and shrugged. She returned a stern look, pointing after the girl, and mouthed the word "Go."

Shaking my head, I hurried after her.

"Nat! Nat! Wait!"

"Nope," she replied. "You didn't feel like we were important enough to have around you, so you don't get to take it back now, you self-centered motherfucker."

"Nat, it wasn't like that."

"Yeah, it was, Bishop," she said as she continued to power-walk ahead, refusing to look at me, her voice still trembling. "That's *exactly* what it was like. You were the thing that held everyone together. The one that made everything make sense. One word from Jackie 'Yoko-fucking-Ono' Beaumont, and you tossed us all aside. *After* she'd already dumped you, you stupid asshole."

Okay, that stung a bit.

"Nat, you have every right to be upset."

"Upset?" she squeaked, her voice raising an octave as tears formed in her eyes. "I'm not upset, you dick! I'm pissed! You fucking tossed me aside like I was garbage. Like I was unimportant. Like I was used up, and you were done with me!"

"Miss, is this man bothering you?" an older white woman asked.

Nat whirled on her. "Fuck you, lady! We're having a private fucking conversation! Go back to your hurricanes!"

The venom in Nat's voice brought a startled flinch from the tourist and the slightest hint of a smile from me. The lady missed Nat's next barrage as she beat a hasty retreat.

"No! You don't get to be happy about anything I do!" she shouted, punching me hard in the shoulder twice, her voice trembling more. "I promised myself you weren't gonna make me cry anymore, Bishop. You made me cry enough when you said you were done. When you sent us away? When you told me we weren't enough for you."

"I never even thought that, Nat."

"You did! You didn't use those words, but it meant the same thing!" she sobbed. "You told us you had to give it up to have a chance with Jackie. That meant all of The Gloaming stuff had to stop. That you couldn't be around Ava anymore. That if we were gonna—"

She lost her coherence and started to cry, immediately sending rivulets of black down her cheeks. She looked up at me, then collapsed into my chest, heaving big, ugly sobs.

I closed my eyes, ignored the crowd, and put my arms around her.

"Nat, I'm so sorry. I wasn't thinking when I made those calls. If I'd realized what it would have done to you, I'd have done it differently. I never wanted you to get hurt, kid."

"I did. I hurt, Bishop. Dave was the only one you'd let stay near you. The rest of us might as well have not existed anymore," she said, fighting sobs all the while.

"Nat, I'm back in."

"For now. Because you need something. Ava told me. Mary's in trouble with The Order. But once it's done, what then? Yoko's engaged to some banker, and you're still the same asshole," she sniffled.

"Oil exec," I corrected.

She shrugged, "Whatever. Point is that for you to have a chance, you've gotta stay legit. We're not wired that way. Not even Dave, really. He just tries to pretend for you."

I paused for a long moment, unsure how to answer, which prompted Nat to step back and look up at me. Her makeup was a mess, ravaged by tears. It left long streaks down her face. She took a pair of shuddering breaths, trying to bring the crying under control. She wiped at her eyes and shook her head. "Are you at a loss for words? Jason fucking Bishop doesn't have a snappy fucking comeback for something?"

"I don't know what happens after," I admitted. "I'm just trying to get this taken care of and clean up the messes I left behind."

She laughed, shaking her head. "Well, if I didn't qualify before," she trailed off, gesturing vaguely at her face. Sniffling loudly, she again wiped at her face with the sleeves of her dress (black, of course).

"I really am sorry, Nat," I said.

"Whatever. I'll help. For now. I don't know what happens after."

I grimaced, then took a deep breath and let out a slow sigh.

"Fair enough," I replied. "Because neither do I."

She leveled her gaze at me and smiled sadly. "What the fuck, Bishop? You *have* gone soft."

The amount of hugging that had occurred in my apartment upon our return may have set a world record.

Nero could barely contain himself when Nat came through the door. Once he recovered, he had some pointed comments regarding the current state of her makeup, which drew an embarrassing trip to the bathroom to 'fix things up' once her eyes found Dave smiling at her from across the room.

So, *that* was still a thing.

The raucous, cheerful banter flowed from the four of them as they caught up, lounging on my chairs and couch, trading spots as the conversation ebbed and flowed. It was like everything else had been wiped away, filling a hole in my life I hadn't realized was there.

I turned to look out the window, ostensibly at the foot traffic on the street below, but really just staring away, when Dave's massive hand clapped on my right shoulder.

"No need to beat yourself up, boss. I knew you'd get there eventually."

"Get there? My kid's in trouble, Dave. I love the reunion as much as any of you, but right now, the clock's ticking on Mary."

"But now you've got family. You got this."

I looked up at the big man, his mismatched eyes and fearsome features giving lie to the gentle soul inside. Then to each of the others: Ava, supposedly demonic, but currently making sure everyone in the room was okay; Nero, previously aloof and apart because of his gift, throwing himself into the camaraderie with abandon; Nat, the youngest and most hurt, stepping back in and embracing us like we were the family she'd never really had. Because we were.

Dave smiled and put his arm around my shoulders.

I smiled, then nodded and moved closer to the rest of them, taking a seat in the chair across from the couch.

"Okay, what've we got?" I asked.

"Nero's got a *boyfriend* he hasn't introduced me to," Nat replied with mock venom, glaring at Nero, who held up his hands in surrender.

"It's fine, it's fine. We'll do dinner soon, I promise. I'm just upset that neither of you got one to report to me."

Nat shrugged. "I've got my eye on somebody, but we'll see what happens," she replied with a dismissive wave of her hand, while Ava simply smiled in response.

"Kids," Ava announced, trying to drag everyone back on topic, "What've we got are *leads*. We're on the clock on this one. The Order's got Mary in their crosshairs."

"Fucking zealots," Nat muttered.

"Right. They are. Which is why we know they won't hesitate to burn your little girl at the stake if they get the chance. 'Untrained,' 'dangerous,' blah blah blah," she continued.

I nodded. "Yeah, but our leads are thin. Raimond tells me he's gotten word there are missing kids from the soup kitchens. Like someone might be putting the grab on teen runaways."

"More than just regular vampire trafficking?" Nat asked, her brows knitting together and chin going rigid. "'Cause we all know that for all their posturing, The Order just lets that shit go."

"It'd have to be. And whatever's doing it isn't your run-of-the-mill human traffickers," Nero added. "Those bitches just about dry cleaned my brain when I went peeking in on their dirty little deeds. I don't care what Mr. Man said over at that church, Bishop. That was a damned cult."

"Church says it ain't," Dave replied.

"Then Momma Church is wrong," Nero insisted. "You don't get to dress up in robes and kidnap teenage girls and not be a cult. Nuh-uh. It's practically in the handbook."

"Cult or organized crime, the approach is the same, isn't it? We're gonna need to find out who the players are so we can catch them in the act and track them back to wherever they're holding the kid," Ava asked.

"I can try to get impressions off of anyone that seems like a good target," Nero offered. "Whatever bastard that was can't cover all of his worker bees when they're out gathering kids."

"Are you gonna be okay in a crowd?" Ava asked Nero. "That's not normally your scene."

Nero sighed, then nodded. "People are loud. Louder than the sound system when you pile 'em all in close and liquor 'em up, but I'll manage. What other choice do we have?"

"We're making an assumption," I pointed out.

Four pairs of eyes looked at me, asking what I was talking about.

"So far, we're operating like whoever grabbed Evangeline swept her up as part of a larger scheme."

"Yeah?" Nat said, prompting.

"What if the other kids are just cover? Or even worse, ritual components?" I asked. "What if she and her dad were the targets all along?"

My question was met with absolute silence in the room. The ambient noise of the Quarter's eternal party filtered through my windows and up the stairs from the bar below as the five of us exchanged uncomfortable glances.

"You mean," Ava offered, "What if someone wanted Evangeline Grey not because she was a teenager, but specifically because she was Ivé's daughter?"

"They'd have had to, wouldn't they?" asked Nero. "You said she disappeared out of her bedroom like a ghost."

"Ivé has security on his place that would make a dragon think twice about tackling him," Dave observed. "Don't know how anyone could have possibly pulled that off."

"That's not a thing, is it? Dragons attacking?" Nat asked.

"It's a thing," Ava and I replied in unison, drawing a giggle from Nero.

"The stuff that must go on when I'm not around. Anyway. They had to have her help," Nat continued with a shrug, "it's the only thing that makes sense. Girl gets kept in an ivory tower for her entire life. Dad won't let her do teenage things with teenage people. She rebels. She probably met someone online, or one of the times she was allowed out. She used to go to the clubs with a big escort of his bodyguards surrounding her. I saw her a few times. Nice girl. Sweet. A bit dumb."

"How did I never hear about this?" Ava asked.

"Because Ivé was really careful about who knew what, and those of us that found out got told what would happen to our ships if we got a case of the loose lips. She liked to dance. *Loved* dancing with one of the bodyguards - Marcus, I think his name was. I guess he got too close with Ivé's pride and joy 'cause he got cut loose a couple of months back."

"Cut loose permanently?" I asked.

Nat shrugged.

"Dunno. I haven't seen him around lately, and he was around *all* the time, even if Little Miss Thang wasn't. I figured Daddy caught him with his hand in her cookie jar and introduced him to the bottom of the Mississippi or something."

"But..." Ava said, pausing. "He'd be a great way to draw her out, wouldn't he? If someone *did* know about the two of them, *and* they had the sort of power it would take to try to brain fry poor Nero—"

"Don't remind me," he groaned.

Ava made a 'poor baby' face at him and continued. "Wouldn't some sort of illusion of Marcus be the perfect way to draw her out of the house voluntarily?"

"It could work," Dave offered. "If she wanted to leave, she'd probably know the way 'round any sort of security measures Papa had in place. Kids are resourceful like that."

I nodded. "And the fact he's a fake explains why they need to keep her under guard now. Whoever has her probably has some sort of plan on how to use her as leverage against Ivé."

"I've heard worse plans," Ava said.

"You've *had* worse plans," Nat corrected, looking meaningfully at me, which prompted an eruption of laughter.

Once they'd all laughed themselves out a bit, I continued.

"Okay, so we've got some ideas on how they could have gotten her out and a vague idea on what they're trying to do. Now we figure out how to break into their circle."

"Isn't it obvious?" Nat asked. "I go into the clubs and start moving around with the runaways again. Most of them know me, and me being there won't raise any eyebrows like it would with you old farts. Nothing personal, but only Ava goes to the dance clubs around here at all, and when she does, she definitely draws a lot of attention."

Ava shrugged, offering a seated curtsy and a mischievous smile.

"So it's gotta be me. I can change up my makeup and make myself look like jailbait, then find the wrong people to talk to and see if they're willing to whisk the disaffected, jaded teenaged Nat away from this humdrum life she's living."

"I'm not crazy about—" I started.

"No," Dave said. "It's too dangerous. You'd be putting yourself in the line of fire."

"—this idea. Or what he said," I finished.

"I will, but I'll have you strong, clever bastards ready to come in and rescue me. Easy peasy. Besides," she said, tossing a wink at Dave and me, "neither of you can stop me from doing this if I want to, so I guess you'll just have to make sure I don't get dead in the process."

"You've been spending too much time with Ava," I accused.

The two leaned cheek to cheek and flashed wide, matching, disingenuous grins.

"God help us all," groaned Nero.

We all agreed we weren't prepared to move that evening, so we marked tomorrow night as our first attempt.

The night continued with talking and drinking. With stories and laughter. It was the type of night that doesn't seem like a big deal at the time, but one you look back on later and realize it means everything to everyone there. It was more than friendship. It was like Dave said: it was family. Not the kind that's linked by blood. That sort is just genetic happenstance. This was the more adult, more deliberate sort of family. It's the family you choose once you're a fully formed person. It says a lot about who you are and what you care about, this family, and as Nat reminded me, you don't walk out on that sort of family.

Even after you do.

After the warmth of their bodies had faded from their chairs, and their voices and smiles had all faded beyond echoes, I found myself standing alone in my living room, looking out the window at the street below with a glass of whiskey in hand. Strangers walked by, arm-in-arm, fortified against the chilly October air by a combination of booze and endorphins, all of them oblivious to the horrors that lived just at the edge of the flickering lights, waiting for them. Hungering for them. I'd been ignoring those horrors. Convincing myself that if I didn't pay attention to them, they'd leave me and mine alone. I'd tried to pretend if I just ignored them hard enough, it wouldn't matter. That I could be honest and open with Jackie about all of the parts in my life that I'd kept her away from, and that I could be enough for her if I did. Knowing that me telling her was never an option.

It didn't work. The horrors had come anyway, and now they were threatening Mary. Part of me kept saying that I needed to tell Jackie. To warn her. Make her understand. Make her believe. But even after the shock wore off, even after the disbelief faded, what would it do other than open her up to a world she was ill-prepared to face? As satisfying as it would be for me to shatter her preconceived notions about the world and to shout to the heavens that this was what had kept me from being completely open with her, she didn't deserve that. All it would do is make me feel self-righteous and make her scared.

Most importantly, it wouldn't do anything to help Mary, and as much as I loved Jackie, Mary was my daughter, and there was nothing I wouldn't do or endure to protect her.

Taking a long swig of my drink, I grimaced, then leaned forward, pressing my forehead up against the glass and closing my eyes. I let the weather's cold fingers work their way into my forehead, wishing things were different.

I stumbled to my bed, wishing *I* was different. Wishing I didn't know what I did and couldn't do what I do. Wondering if who I was caused Mary to be what she is and wishing I could do something to fix it. Wishing...wishing...wishing.

Just wishing.

And then came the nightmare.

My chest burned as I ran.

The stiff white collar worn by seminary students cut off my breath as I gasped. I clawed it off as I rushed through the darkened, misty streets of New Orleans. The damp air was clammy against my skin as I rounded the corner to my childhood home. I threw open the wrought iron gate and scrambled for the front door as dark storm clouds gathered overhead.

I felt my shoulder impact the heavy outer door as my hands fumbled with the doorknob.

I smelled that terrible, sickly coppery odor as I burst into the foyer and heard the chanting voice coming from the study.

My father's voice.

I heard a gasp and wet noise as metal bit into flesh. Then again. And again. And again.

I saw my father's eyes, filled with regret. He stared at me for a heartbeat. Then another.

"Jason, you weren't—I'm sorry you had to see this," my father said, oblivious to the incongruous image that his tone portrayed with the abattoir he'd created.

"Jason. Please..." my sister whispered, pleading. "Help...me..."

I saw her pleading eyes as blood welled from her mouth. Her hand reached out for me, trembling.

I saw my mother's body lying on the floor like a discarded puppet. Limbs askew and unmoving.

"Look away, son. You were never supposed to be here for this," my father pleaded. "This is for you. A gift for you to do His work. Just look away."

I heard the roar coming from my throat, then, mercifully, oblivion.

I jerked awake to the stabbing pain like an ice pick through my right eye as the bottle I'd been drinking from last night made a solid impact into a metal trash can.

"Rise and shine, boss!"

I groaned loudly, then buried my face in my hands.

"It's eleven, in case you were wondering. Figure that people will start coming by soon to prep for tonight and didn't nobody need to see you laid out like this. Had yourself a nice pity party after everyone left, did you?"

I took a deep, shuddering breath.

"The dreams again?" he asked, his tone shifting from mockery to concern.

I nodded, eyes closed, then ran my hands through my hair as I lay prone.

"There are charms you could get to handle that," he suggested.

I gingerly sat up, then cracked my eyes, squinting hard against the morning light. "Not interested," I croaked.

"Was it the family thing again?"

I nodded a second time. "Y'know, over the years, I've collected some prime fodder for nightmares, Dave. I've almost been killed by vampires, demons, and shapeshifters. I've seen a dragon reveal itself in all its terrible glory. I've stood up and confronted more types of ghosts and spirits than I can care to think of. Been the target of voodoo curses and pissed off wizards. But it's always the same dream that comes back. Always Catherine begging me..." I trailed off, shaking my head.

"Family is where the hurt lives, boss. Where we're happiest. That's what makes us vulnerable there. That's why when a family cuts us, they cut deep."

I glared up at Dave, who blinked.

"Shit. Bad choice of words, but you know what I mean."

"Yeah," I spat through clenched teeth. "I get it."

"Good, because that's what's at stake tonight with Nat. She's still raw, feeling like we abandoned her. She's lettin' us back in and helping, but—"

"But tread lightly. I get it. Between you and Ava—"

"You might just listen to someone's advice," Dave finished for me, even if it wasn't what I was originally going to say.

I leveled my gaze at him before sighing. "Yup. Exactly that."

I lurched to my feet, staggering into the kitchen to start some coffee, then discovered that Dave had already done so. I poured a cup, then turned, leaning hard against the counter.

"Everyone will be here a bit after five. Seems that some of your friends lacked the foresight to be independently wealthy, so they needed to do things to earn money. That should give you plenty of time to shower, 'cause, *damn*."

I sighed. "Anything else?"

"Yeah. You should see the Princess before you go. Try to keep things normal for her. Yesterday was scary, and you being around makes her feel better."

I started to say something unfair and acerbic but bit it back and nodded instead.

"Yeah. Probably a good idea," I agreed.

"Plus, seeing her makes you less of an asshole, and that's always a nice side effect," he said.

"Every little bit helps. People coming back here?" I replied.

Dave nodded. "You've got the biggest place and the most central. No one else can afford to live in the Quarter, except Ava, and no one gets to see Ava's place," Dave chuckled.

It was a long-standing joke. In all the years we'd known Ava, we had only seen her apartment two or three times, and she generally moved shortly afterward. The woman liked her privacy.

The early afternoon passed in the sort of domestic fervor that everyone goes through from time to time: Dave went downstairs to mind the business while I addressed my apartment. Dishes and clothing were washed, the living area was cleaned, I showered. It's the sort of minutiae that doesn't make it into movies or get a mention in a stirring narrative, but it's what makes up the majority of our lives. Those moments in between the big tent poles where we just...live. It's not compelling. It's not exciting. It's just life.

It's all Jackie had ever wanted me to offer her while we were together: a normal life. How the fuck could I do normal? Talk about a rigged game.

But I tried. After all, it's compelling in its own way, and I needed something - anything to chase away the remnants of the horrid dreams from the night before. I imagined what it would be like to have her here with me while I cleaned. Thought back to what it was like when she was. There wasn't anything eventful about it. Not even anything, particularly sensual. It was just two people doing what needed to be done while enjoying one another's company.

I picked up Mary from school. We chatted and stopped in Jackson Square park to watch the street performers under the cathedral's watchful eye. An acrobat in a huge steel hoop delighted Mary, drawing squeals of laughter from her, but the shadows from those steeples felt like long, cold fingers reaching for her, and that thought killed my smile before it had a chance to fully form. I frowned instead, wondering what being a normal parent would be like.

Jackie was a normal parent. Jackie was probably down at the art gallery a few blocks over, and after she finished there, she'd be going back to the house she shared with Victor, another normal parent. The man she'd decided to marry. The man who wasn't me. The man who could give her the life I couldn't. That could let her see into his dark corners. The man who didn't have literal monsters waiting in his dark corners. Monsters are only normal for people like me.

I kept trying to ignore that part. Kept succeeding at it too, which was a dangerous trap. I needed to accept the here and now: Mary was in trouble. Jackie was moving on, and I needed to focus on the former because it meant my kid's life.

And possibly Ivé's kid too. That was also important, but not nearly as personal.

And I'd learned long ago: personal is everything.

The sun set all too quickly.

After my orgy of domesticity, I dropped Mary back off and spent the remainder of the day downstairs in my workshop. I knew what Nat had planned, and as much as she was trying to play it off, we all knew what the stakes were. I'd be damned if she was going to go in without a card up her sleeve.

I decided it was better to be the dealer than to play the game straight and got to work on stacking the deck.

A few hours later, we had a tracking spell consisting of two pennies. I'd found a few matched pairs, minted at the same place and time years before. This link made them symbolically and practically bound to one another. Following the right instructions in an old, dusty tome, applying the right ingredients, and saying the right words accompanied by the right gestures removed the "symbolically" from the previous sentence. To be honest, ritual magic is a bit like baking a cake. Just follow the directions on the box.

I emerged from my workroom to find David, Ava, Nat, and Nero, waiting in the bar area for me. All dressed to the nines.

"No," Nat declared.

"No?" I asked.

"No. You're not going out to a club dressed like that. Ava, can you fix ...?" she asked, waving a disgusted hand in my general direction.

With all their eyes on me, I looked down at myself and didn't see the issue—a pair of khakis, black sneakers, and a plain black t-shirt.

"Yeah, this isn't gonna work, Jason," Ava declared. "Let's go."

She stepped forward, grabbed my hand, and led me upstairs. I objected about a lack of time. Reaching the door, she threw it open and hurried me into my bedroom.

"You're right; there's no time for this, so move your ass, Jason," she said. "Right now, you're wearing *nothing* that works. We need to try to blend in at least a little bit for this to work. You look like someone's dad."

"I *am* someone's dad," I objected.

"Right, but let's not advertise it, 'kay? Dads don't go to these clubs. Strip."

Ava busied herself rifling through my closet, making odd noises at the various pairs of pants and shirts she came across while I slid the offending t-shirt over my head and tossed it into the hamper.

"What about the blue one?" I asked.

"I don't see a blue one."

Moving over to the closet, I reached over her shoulder for the shirt, only to discover its absence.

"Oh, right. Dirty."

Ava shifted to the side, and I stepped in, each shuffling through my available wardrobe, each working from the outside in until we turned to face each other and met in the middle.

"What about this one?" Ava asked, reaching past me, then pausing as we pressed up against each other. We froze. The air in the room suddenly felt very heavy, scented vaguely of vanilla. I could feel her breath in the enclosed space, and the hairs on my arms stood up. The little black dress she wore accentuated the...well...the Ava-ness of her, its thin material painfully obvious as she brushed up against me. Her heels brought her height up to only slightly shy of my own, putting our lips in close proximity.

I held my breath. Ava's came out in a shudder.

"Your hand, Jason," she said softly.

"Yeah?"

"It's on my hip."

"Is it?"

It was. I had no recollection of putting it there, but it seemed like the most natural place in the world for it to be.

She looked up at me, her dark eyes meeting mine. I leaned closer.

"Now it's on the small of my back," she whispered, her breath warm and moist against my lips as my hand traced further down.

"It is. Was," I confirmed, then corrected, feeling her delicate hands come to rest on my chest in response. Her fingers flexed slightly. I could feel her fingernails on my chest, bringing an involuntary shiver.

Her eyes met mine, then closed as she parted her lips.

I leaned closer, brushing my lips against hers. Her breath, warm against mine, tasted slightly of cinnamon and sent an electric jolt through me. Ava drew back a hair's-breadth, then nipped at my bottom lip before hovering her lips over mine. Her hands balled up in my chest hair as she held her breath.

"Jason...I... we...NO!"

And like that, the moment was over. Ava sent me airborne with an abrupt shove. I landed six feet away, bouncing off my mattress, into the wall, and then back onto my mattress again in a tangle of limbs and blankets.

"What the hell is wrong with you?" she demanded. "You spend all of your time telling anyone who will listen that you're going to get back together with Jackie, that you're gonna win her back. Make a family with her and Mary, then every time you're around a woman, the first thing you try to do is try to fuck her?"

"I—"

"Shut up! Just shut up, you fucking *moron*!" she spat. "You made it crystal fucking clear how things were between us, Jason. You made that call, and I respected it. You rejected *me*, and I fucking well gave you distance, ignored anything that I—and the second we start working on something together, you—*argh*! And *now*? When we're about to—I—no. Just no."

She balled up her hands and turned away, facing the closet.

"I-I'm gonna go downstairs," she muttered, not looking at me. "Find something that works for a club and come down when your head is clear, and you're ready to work. We're on the clock, remember?"

I sat on the bed in a mixture of confusion and shame as Ava walked out of the room, her arms wrapped around her and her face averted.

"Fucking genius," I muttered to the room as I rubbed the back of my neck. Glancing over my shoulder, I winced, first in pain, then at the dent, my body had made in the wall's plaster. I wallowed in the fact that Ava was right.

It took longer than I'm happy to admit to quiet the chaos roiling around inside my head after her exit. It's possible that I meandered through a couple of the phases of grief while I stormed around my room, hunting down the passable articles of clothing and tossing them onto the bed. The act of clothes hunting was enough to remove the irritation from my chest, but in its absence, hollowness set in.

What was I doing?

The shit I was pulling in my personal life just made it easier for Jackie to say she'd made the right decision. If I was serious about getting back into the game with her, I needed to make some serious changes, or accept the situation for what it was and own my role in it.

But tonight, I needed to be the old Jason Bishop. The ruthless bastard with a well-deserved reputation for doing whatever it took to finish the job. The guy who made the monsters tread lightly, not the bar owner. Not the Jason Bishop who pined over Jackie. Not the Jason Bishop who'd just complicated his relationship with Ava. I needed the old Jason Bishop back, and I was determined to be the person my friends - my family needed me to be.

I gave myself a full five minutes for my pity party before I settled on some clothes I hoped would be minimally acceptable. I changed into a white button-up shirt, black jeans, and combat boots and joined the others downstairs.

"Let's do this."

I'd suggested Nat put one of the pennies in her shoe, but she shook her head and deposited it in her bra instead.

"I'm pretty sure I'll notice if anyone goes rooting around in there," she quipped.

I nodded. Seemed like a good place to escape cultist detection, which would give us a near-foolproof way to tail her.

Forty-five minutes later, Ava, Dave, Nero, and me were scattered around the club. I took up a spot at one of the tables and ordered a rum and coke. Whiskey's my drink of choice, but I needed to stay sharp.

I chatted with people as they wandered by, the traditional lean-in-and-shout pantomime when you're at a club.

You know, the classics.

Dave placed himself near the bathrooms at the back door to the club. Nero and Ava moved around the dance floor like the pros they both were, and Nat was being Nat.

In a way, it was like seeing Ava perform earlier. The kid was a natural. She commanded the people around her, brought in a crowd, and held court. And she did it without saying a word.

Hell, I think she even did it without bending reality to her will, but don't quote me on that one. Like I said, she was that good.

As minutes turned into hours at the club, we each settled into our roles. Nat commanded the knot around her like a benign dictator. People fell over themselves to do her bidding, retrieving drinks, locating other people to bring in, and generally falling into step with her whims.

Nero set up shop on the back right-hand side of the dance floor, near the door that led to the storage rooms. It was brilliant placement: Nat had warned about a service exit there, so it would be impossible to get out without going directly through the small group he'd accumulated.

Dave didn't seem to have much interest in the dancing part. He meandered over near where the bouncers had stood and appeared to be talking shop with them. Or at least, he was talking to a small group of big guys with varying degrees of "no neck" and a tendency to wade into the crowd and put a stop when the patrons went from an R rating and into NC-17 territory.

Ava danced as if she didn't have a care in the world, never wanting for partners as she slithered from person to person, leaving broken hearts in her wake. For my part, looking disinterested, world-weary, and mildly depressed seemed to be working as a beacon. A parade of damaged women made their way to my table, like moths drawn to flame. Each left with a look of disappointment on her face. What can I say? I apparently wear my pain and dysfunction like an armband.

From time to time, my eyes found Ava's as she made her way around the dance floor, which led to an exchange of sad smiles or shrugs.

Life never gets less complicated, does it?

I stayed at my high-top table near the front door, nursing my drink like a pro and fighting the urge to self-medicate with more. Dave would *not* have approved if I ended up sheets to the wind tonight. It was too important.

By the time the clock moved past midnight, I had begun to get worried we were in the wrong place. Nat had assured me before we left that it would take a little time for word to spread but that everyone would talk eventually. I had just hoped "eventually" would happen sooner.

I shouldn't have doubted her. At just after one in the morning, a trio of people who belonged even less than I did entered. They were in their thirties or forties and dressed for business, not clubbing. The one in the lead wore a white suit and had a used car salesman sheen about him, while the two behind him screamed 'muscle.'

For the first time all night, I slid off the stool as they passed by.

Dave was the next to notice, locking eyes with me and giving a nod. Then Ava and Nero. Our suspects moved around the dance floor, focusing on the kids on the young end. Anyone with a black X on their hand (indicating no booze for them) got approached. Cards were handed out; then, as if saving the big prize for last, they approached Nat and her court.

Nat's court didn't grant access to their queen, as the fringes shifted to block our suspects' paths. But gradually, they exerted pressure, whether physical or otherwise, I couldn't say, and a path opened to Nat, who smiled broadly at them, her eyes staying on the new arrivals.

I nodded in approval, smiling grimly.

"Good job, kiddo. Don't look at the backup is the first rule of playing bait," I muttered, downing the last of my drink and sliding out from behind my table. I gestured to Dave and saw him move toward the back door before I turned on my heel and headed toward the front, where I'd merge with the foot traffic outside.

Nat was in their jaws. Dave and I had moved outside. Nero and Ava were keeping an eye on the club.

Now was the hard part. Now we waited for them to take her away.

What could possibly go wrong?

Following a person through the bustling streets of the French Quarter presents a unique series of problems. First, if you're close enough to actually see them, it means you're practically touching them. Second, if you hang back at all, there is an excellent chance you'll get scraped off by a knot of tourists and drunken revelers frequenting Bourbon Street. Third, many of the non-Bourbon Street portions of The Quarter are relatively clear of pedestrian traffic after regular business hours, making it painfully obvious if your target happens on one of those. It's pointless to try to get a cab or climb into a car until you're well away from the busier portions. The roads were laid out and paved well in advance of the advent of automobiles, so traffic doesn't so much flow through this portion of the Crescent City as it meanders, stagnant as the bayou that bordered the city. Don't get me wrong; there are portions of the city where a car chase is completely possible. The Quarter just ain't those.

Which is why I'd spent the day on that matched pair of pennies. Keeping mine firmly in my hand, I followed the trio as they left the club, giving them between thirty and fifty yards as a cushion. Combine that with the GPS app that all of us put on our phones, and the rest of our little group knew exactly where I was.

Magic is nifty, and all, but modern technology has something to be said for it.

I wove my way through the crowds as the trio took Nat onto Bourbon Street and turned toward Canal, which could be a problem: Canal *was* a street that could allow a car to move much more quickly than the flow of foot traffic. I started to walk faster, closing the distance as I pulled my cell phone out and shot off a quick text to Dave, Ava, and Nero, telling them to move as quickly as they could to Canal and get us a car.

I was less than twenty feet from Nat now. Close enough to see her leaning into the idea that she was too young to drink. She was acting like she was wasted: stumbling, giggling, and trying to wander off to delay their progress. If the would-be kidnappers didn't want to make a scene by forcibly picking her up in the middle of a crowded street, they had to humor her, if only slightly.

Everything was going according to plan, right up until they made a right-hand turn onto Conti, taking them parallel to Canal and toward the much larger North Rampart Street.

"Shit shit shit shit," I muttered, sending the new information to the rest of the group.

Nat giggled loudly and tried to 'boop' one of her would-be abductors on the nose. The used car salesman wasn't amused. He motioned to the muscle, grabbed Nat under the arm, and marched her toward North Rampart at a pace that could be considered downright brisk.

I cursed under my breath and picked up my pace, hoping the shadows would provide some cover since I'd completely abandoned subtlety. I fired off another text to the crew on where to rendezvous.

My fears were realized as I saw a black SUV's rear doors open, and Nat immediately vanish inside. I saw her face, eyes wide as one of the two goons climbed in behind her and managed to give her a nod before the door closed as I emerged onto the main thoroughfare. I could smell the exhaust from the car as it pulled away and was reduced to staring helplessly at the taillights as it rolled up the avenue.

"Where the fuck *are* you guys?" I spat; my jaw clenched.

I saw Nero's car taking a corner entirely too quickly and breathed a sigh of relief. We could still make it. We could still make sure we were there for Nat.

Then my phone rang—Jackie's number.

My eyes narrowed. There was no reason for this call. Not right now.

I picked it up and hit the answer key.

"Hello, Mr. Bishop. I can understand why you're so protective of them. You have such a lovely family."

My stomach dropped.

"Chase," I growled as Ava hopped out of the open door before Nero had even stopped. "I swear to God if you've so much as touched them--"

"The idea that you would swear anything to the Almighty is laughable in the extreme, apostate, but your adulterous ex and your bastard are both whole. For now. How long they remain that way is entirely up to you."

I put him on speaker as Ava made a questioning face, which immediately slid into horror as she recognized Father Chase's voice.

"Oh, no. Not Mary...no no no..." she whispered.

I nodded, then closed my eyes. I needed to concentrate, and my brain was screaming, filled with static.

"What—what do you want from me, Chase?"

There was silence on the other end of the phone for a moment, and I feared the worst. Then he spoke.

"I want you, Bishop. You and your demonic whore. Both of you. Here. Within the hour." There was another pause. "I"m not a complete monster, you know. I don't relish the idea of taking your daughter's head. It is my burden and one I willingly bear for Our Heavenly Father with clear and open eyes. But executing children is...taxing. There may be another way. She may be able to be cleansed. You and the whore will both need to die for your daughter to live."

I stared in abject horror at Ava, then opened my mouth to refuse...to find another way. Any other way when she stepped forward. "Fine," she said. "Just don't hurt her."

"With the demon, I see. I'm not surprised. You're not half the man Raimond thinks you are. You're flawed. Comprom—"

"Yeah, whatever. We'll be there," I said, cutting him off and hanging up the phone. Looking at Ava, we met each other's eyes.

"Whatever it takes," she said quietly.

Swallowing, I reached into my pocket and took out the penny.

"Okay. Dave. Nero. New plan: You guys are following Nat. Don't let 'em get too far. They've already got a hell of a head start..." I shook my head. "Don't let *anything* happen to Nat. You think shit's about to go sideways, do whatever it takes to get her out."

"What can we—" Nero started to ask.

"*Whatever* it takes," Dave agreed, nodding, then patting Nero on the back. "We got this, boss. Go get her."

The pair took off without another word as Ava hailed a cab.

Looking over her shoulder, she gave me an encouraging smile.

"What? It's too far to walk in these heels, and I'll be damned if that bastard lays a hand on my baby girl. You may be her dad, but we all helped raise that kid."

The cabs nearly crashed into each other to pick up Ava. Who could blame them? Ready to drive headlong into a kill zone as long as they got to do so with her.

I could relate.

We just needed to figure out what the hell to do once we got there.

Chapter
Twelve

The cab dropped us off in a dark patch of the New Orleans night around the corner from Victor's house. We moved as quickly and quietly as we could, seeing sinister priests lurking behind every planter and fearing a laser sight with every stray beam of light. I could hear my heartbeat pounding in my ears, but I tried to fight my way through it. I needed to be sharp. Cold. I needed to feel the thrum of the city, to immerse myself in its pulse. It was the only way I could hope to—

My cell phone's ringer shattered my reverie, reminding me that I was not, in fact, a thing that went bump in the night.

I didn't recognize the number, so I sent it into the limbo of voicemail. As night stalking terrors do.

As we reached Victor's neighborhood, Ava's eyes narrowed while she scanned the street, then locked with mine in confusion as she shook her head.

"Nothing. I've got nothing."

I frowned in response, then nodded. I had the same.

"The call came from Jackie's number. The landline," I whispered, my lips close to her ear to limit the chances of being overheard.

"Bastard might be in the house with them, holed up," she agreed.

We locked eyes, then nodded.

I stood up straight, then reached out, taking Ava's hand and placing it on my forearm, putting on my best cocky smirk and walking with my back straight (and the area between my shoulder blades itching) directly to the front door.

Victor answered the door almost immediately.

"Bishop? What are you—and who's this? Ava wasn't it?" he asked, his eyes going to my partner in crime.

I've seen a lot of men (and women) interact with Ava. Even when her supernatural charms aren't firing, she's hard not to ogle. The way her smile quirks at just the right angle. The way her hair caresses her neck. The smolder and promise of mischief in her eyes.

She's downright hypnotic.

At only their second meeting, Victor managed with hardly a glance.

I desperately wanted to hate him for it but had to admit to being impressed.

"Vic! We were just in the neighborhood and thought we might drop in and invite the three of you out for dinner," I lied, glancing over Osgood's shoulder and into the house. No sign of Chase.

Shit.

Ava nodded, picking up on my bullshit and adding some flavor of her own. "I've heard *so* much about you from Jason, and I just *had* to meet you. He speaks highly of so few people, and I just adore Mary and Jackie. We go *way* back."

As she spoke, I got more nervous.

"*He* spoke highly of *me*?" Victor asked, clearly skeptical.

Something wasn't right here. Osgood wasn't the sort of guy who would seem confused if a killer like Chase was inside of his house. He'd be scared. There'd be tells. He'd be sweating.

Which meant Chase wasn't inside the house; he was behind us.

Hearing my voice, Ava's voice, and her name, Jackie appeared at the corner to the entryway and the living room just in time for things to go to hell.

"Jas—"

"*Down!*"

I shouted and grabbed Ava's arm, diving forward and driving my shoulder into Vic's midsection, yanking Ava toward me and into the house as my legs pistoned forward.

A split second later, the planter Ava had been standing in front of exploded in a shower of terra cotta as Victor, Ava, and I all ended up in a pile of limbs, flailing about while gunfire traced a path through our previous positions and around us.

Jackie, being the sensible sort, screamed.

There was no purchase for me to use on the tiled floor to force us forward. Victor, unaware of the danger he was in, was wrestling with me in an attempt to get me off of him while I struggled to get free and get the door closed. Ava was on top of me, sandwiching me between her and my ex-lover's fiancé, and decided that safety was more important than secrets. Her left arm grew improbably long, reaching out from her position and slamming the door behind us.

Then I saw stars as Victor hit me.

He growled, trying to wrestle free. "This isn't funny, you sick son of a bitch!" he snarled. You come to *my* house and—"

"VICTOR! SOMEONE'S SHOOTING AT US!"

Jackie's voice cut through his rage, bringing his attention to some of the peripheral details around him.

The odd holes in the tile of his entryway. The matching holes in his door. The blood coming out of Ava's left shoulder.

"Oh, God! Miss?" he asked, his rage evaporating.

"Mommy?" Mary's voice called from the top of the stairs.

"Get under your bed, sweetie! Hurry!" Jackie ordered.

"What's happening? Why are Daddy and Miss Ava here?" Mary asked.

"Sweetie! Please!" Jacki cried.

Something about the insistence, the fear in her mother's voice silenced the normally strong-willed and inquisitive child, sending Mary scampering back toward her bedroom. Satisfied with her daughter's safety, Jackie burst into motion, moving toward the three of us in a crouching run.

"Bishop, what the hell is going on here?" Victor demanded.

"Stay down and get into the living room," I barked, rubbing my jaw. Turns out, Victor threw a good punch. Who knew? I decided to ignore his questions for now.

"Ava?" I asked, sliding over to check on her.

She was pale. Well, paler than normal, and her jaw was clenched in pain that haunted her eyes.

"This—was one of my favorite dresses," she hissed, then offered a lopsided smile that never reached her eyes.

"You can still make it work," I reassured her, looking around for something, for anything, to help.

Jackie, thinking more quickly than the rest of us, promptly reached up and killed the lights, then locked eyes with me and nodded. She took

Victor's hand and guided him to the living room as I helped Ava make the same trek. Killing the lights there as well, we took shelter behind the thick, stone walls of the antebellum splendor that was Casa de Osgood.

We all leaned against the wall, breathing heavily as I tried to angle myself so I could see out of one of the two large windows in the room.

"Bishop. Talk," Jackie barked, her voice high and on the verge of panic.

I looked at her, dread contracting my heart like a vice. This was the moment I'd dreaded for a decade. This was what I'd worked so hard to avoid. My nightmare come to life. My two worlds crashing together. The end of any illusions about who I was.

I opened my mouth to reply, ready to tell her. Tell her everything. Admit what I'd been hiding all of this time. To unburden my soul.

But then my phone rang. Sighing, I reached into my pocket and pulled it out.

Jackie's number.

Chase.

"Fuck you," I answered.

"I see I've hit the demon. It's only a matter of time now. Don't make this harder than it needs to be. Think of your former lover and your bastard."

"Piss off. It's just a flesh wound," I said, playing off Ava's injury. "She's walked away from worse. Be jumping rope in a minute."

"You should say your goodbyes to her, Mr. Bishop. Her unholy flesh will not endure the presence of the divine, and the arsenal of the Lord that is carried by his servants in Ordinis Templi Erinnys—"

My heart sank, and I felt sick to my stomach.

"Is blessed," I whispered.

"Is blessed," he agreed. "It's burning its way through her body as we speak. Purifying her. It would be a mercy to finish her. I'm afraid her suffering will be substantial."

"Fuck you, you sick mother—I'm gonna shove my fist so far down your goddamned—"

"*No.* You will *not* blaspheme. I have stood by and watched you defile all that is—,"

In response, I hung up.

Jackie and Victor looked at me, confusion plain on their faces. Ava leaned against the wall, her eyes closed, and her skin covered in a fine sheen of sweat. This was bad. I could feel panic starting to creep around the edges of my brain, robbing me of the ability to think. That was a good way to get Ava killed.

Think. I needed to think.

I looked at Jackie and Victor, then took a breath.

"I haven't been entirely honest about what it is that I do, not when we first met, not ever," I said to Jackie with a sad smile. "And I'm not going to tell you now. Right now, what you need to know is that a very bad man with a very big gun is out there, and he would really, *really* like to kill me, Ava, and Mary."

"Mary? Why Mary? Jason, if you involved her in—"

"Jackie," I snapped, talking over her, raising my voice.

I closed my eyes. Made a fist. Gritted my teeth. Took a deep breath, then let it all go.

"If we don't get Ava help, she's gonna die. We need something to remove a bullet. Now. What do you have?"

"First Aid kit in the kitchen. My EMT kit in the closet back that way," Victor offered, once again surprising me by smoothly moving into crisis mode and putting the personal shit on the back burner.

He was a volunteer EMT? Of course, he was. If I didn't hate him so much, I'd sorta love the guy right now.

I nodded.

"Go get it. Maybe if we get the bullet out, it'll—" I trailed off, looking at Ava, who shook her head, a tear rolling down her cheek.

"'Fraid not, hero. I can...feel...something. It's not just a bullet. Probably had something in it. Maybe liquid. Maybe something that splintered. It's—it *burns*—"

She tried to take a deeper breath, but gasped in pain, then closed her eyes tighter.

And my heart sank even further into my chest. I recognized the munition she was describing. The workings of the Order weren't exactly cooler-level talk while I was in seminary, but I'd been on a list. Before my incident, I'd been identified as a potential recruit.

You tended to learn things as a recruit.

I don't know how to make the damned things, but I know they break apart inside of the target, exposing a center that contained blessed Eucharist. For something with an infernal background, it might as well have been napalm.

The three of us moved forward, crouched low around Ava with Victor working on her shoulder, probing for the bullet with some sort of pliers. Jackie supported her head, and I held her hand and a flashlight for Victor to work by. Ava's skin was too warm and drenched with sweat. Her breath came in shallow, ragged gasps.

I had no doubt that I was losing her and found myself doing something for the first time in more than a decade. Praying.

Sort of.

Dammit, Gabriel! I've held up my end of bargains with you bunch of bastards. I've stood on the line between humanity and the monsters. I've sacrificed my blood, my sweat, and my tears for your causes. I've lost Jackie, I'm losing Mary, and now you're going to stand by and let Ava get killed by someone who literally works for you.

You owe me Ava, Gabriel.

I've never asked for anything from you before. I didn't ask for the angelic flame thing. I didn't ask for anything. I'm asking for this. I can't lose her.

Please. I'm begging you. I need her to be okay. It's too much. I can't lose another person that I—

"What happened to Miss Ava?"

Mary's voice from the entryway to the living room cut through my bargaining/prayer session.

I quickly wiped my eyes with my arm, trying to clear the tears.

"There's a bad guy out there, sweetie, and he shot her. Stay low and get over here!"

Jackie looked at Mary in shock.

"I told you to hide."

"Yeah. I know. I'm sorry. I wanted to see Daddy," Mary replied as she scooted across the floor on her hands and knees, sliding up next to me and looking at Ava, her green eyes scanning the wounded woman.

Victor grunted as he managed to lock onto a piece of bullet and extract it, which tore a cry from Ava and forced me to stop holding her hand and to try to hold her still instead, as she squirmed away from the pain.

"There's still some in there," Mary whispered.

Victor and Jackie both looked at the small girl, their eyes wide.

"Y-yeah," Victor agreed. "There is, but it's soft. Malleable. It's not—I can't get a decent grip on it, and the tissue around it is swelling. It's—she's not doing well, sweetie."

Jackie's gaze had shifted from Mary to Victor, then to me. Her million unasked questions hung thick in the air between us. I shook my head in response.

Not now.

"Sweetie," I asked. "How did you know there's more in there?"

Mary shrugged. "I dunno. I can feel them. Like a humming."

I swallowed, then nodded.

"Okay. Jackie, Victor - can you back up a bit?" I asked, shifting so I was sitting knee to knee with Mary. "Sweetheart, we're gonna play an imagination game, and I think...I think...it'll help Miss Ava. Do you want to try?"

"Jason, what the hell is going on here?" Jackie demanded.

"Not now, Jackie," I said.

I looked from Mary to Ava, then shifted, so I was holding Mary's left hand, and her right was free, hovering over the wound in Ava's shoulder.

"Right. Close your eyes. You can feel the hum in Miss Ava's shoulder from the parts we couldn't get out?"

She nodded.

"Good. Now I want you to think about how the hum feels. Feel the way it moves. Imagine if your hand felt that same way. Imagine that's the *only* thing your hand could feel. It couldn't feel air. It couldn't feel the floor. It can just feel that hum. Can you imagine that?"

Mary's face contorted in a frown, then she nodded. Her little face was the very picture of concentration.

"Good. Now, reach down next to Ava's shoulder and into the floor."

Mary's hand lifted three inches above Ava's shoulder, lowered slowly, then passed through the tiled floor effortlessly, as if it were made of smoke.

Score. It worked.

Jackie and Victor gasped, earning a furious shushing motion from me.

"You're doing great, sweetheart. You're doing perfect. Now I need you to take your hand and reach out to where you feel the hum and grab those bits, okay?"

Mary's hand moved slowly, entering Ava's shoulder like a plane disappearing into a cloudbank. Her hand made several passes as she daintily collected pieces from where they'd dispersed inside of Ava's flesh, and with each piece that Mary successfully collected, Ava seemed to improve.

It took the eight-year-old nearly five minutes before she was sure she'd gotten everything, including a time when she stopped, removed her hand, then frowned and sat stock-still for nearly a full minute before reaching into Ava's torso and fishing out other pieces.

"Okay, now imagine you're back to normal. That the hum and your hand are different. That your hand feels like the rest of you. Can you do that?"

Mary took a breath, then opened her eyes, putting both clenched hands in front of her and staring at them intently. Sweat stood out on her forehead and was starting to show on her superhero t-shirt, but after a moment, she exhaled and slumped, opening her right hand to show numerous gooey bits of doughy material.

"Did we save her? Did we save Miss Ava?"

"You saved her, kiddo. It was all you," I replied, sighing a breath of relief and closing my eyes.

"She's not out of the woods yet, Bishop," Victor muttered from where he leaned over Ava. "She's lost blood. More than she should have from that wound. I—I can't explain it."

I bit back a curse because I could.

The damned ammo Chase had used burned through the blood it came into contact with.

I met the other man's eyes. "How bad?"

He shook his head. "She needs a hospital, a couple units of blood, and to away from this shooter," He shook his head. "And where the hell are the cops? Shouldn't they be here by now?"

I sighed.

"Vic, there aren't going to be any cops."

We had a more immediate problem: Ava had lost too much blood.

She needed a transfusion, and we were pinned down.

She'd donated blood to me after the vampire chowed down on me, so—

"Victor, if she donated blood for me not too long ago, does that mean we're compatible types?"

Victor's eyes shot up. Then he shook his head.

"Not necessarily. What's your blood type?"

"O Negative," Jackie chimed in.

I looked at Vic with naked hope in my eyes. He looked at me, down at Ava, over at Jackie, then finally Mary, and nodded.

"It's not safe, and I don't like it, but—" he trailed off but was interrupted as Mary flung her arms around his shoulders and enveloped him in a grateful hug.

I've been on the receiving end of those, and even when you're prepared, they're devastating. Victor hadn't been prepared. I suspect he'd have handed over both of his kidneys if Mary had asked him to.

"It'll work," I said, refusing to accept any alternative. I rolled up my sleeve, then leaned back against the wall as Victor set up tubes and needles, ready to do his thing.

As soon as Victor had the IV hooked up to my arm, Mary slid over and leaned against me. She rested her head on my leg as she lay down, watching the rise and fall of Ava's chest until her eyes drifted shut. Jackie took up position across from me, sitting next to Victor. The two of them watched warily, their eyes moving from point of interest to point of interest.

The window.

The hole in Ava's shoulder.

Mary's hand.

And finally, me.

"Spill it, Jason," Jackie demanded.

One of the drawbacks to giving blood is that you really can't *go* anywhere while it's happening. There was no possibility of wandering off, and Jackie didn't look like she'd accept just changing the subject. No chance to deflect, and after a moment, I'd be feeling light-headed, making subterfuge a dodgy proposition, at best.

Accepting the inevitable, I nodded. "What do you want to know?"

"Everything," she said.

I shook my head. "There's too much. I can fill you in on what's going on right now."

I took a deep breath and dove in. "The world most people know is a lie—a facade. A Potemkin Village whose foundation was laid way back at the Council of Trent in 1545," I began.

Victor raised a hand.

"Wait. The Council of Trent? Isn't that the Catholic Church's response to the Protestant Reformation?"

I nodded. "Mother Church was responding to that, but Protestantism was suspected of being organized and fanned by occult forces, which are very much a real thing. Pope Paul III, Pope Julius III, and Pope Pious IV each worked with both members of the clergy and representatives from various supernatural factions. You name it; they were there: Vampires, The Fae from both the Seelie and Unseelie Courts, willworkers...you'd call them wizards...dragons—"

Jackie and Victor exchanged highly skeptical looks with one another.

"Don't laugh," I replied. "They're out there. Real. A vampire damned near killed me two nights ago, and you just saw Mary push her hand through the floor, then through Ava's shoulder and ribcage like they weren't there."

Jackie nodded, eyes wide as Victor sat, his face pale as he stared at the little girl.

"How did she do that, Bishop?" he asked. "How *can* someone do that?"

I leaned back and closed my eyes, sighing deeply. "No one really knows, but there are some people...not many, but some...who have some sort of spark in them. Something inside of them lets them rewrite how the world works based on what they believe...what they want. Mary's one of those people."

The words hung in the silence in the room for far longer than was comfortable.

"How long, Bishop? How long have you known? How fucking long have you known and not told me?" Jackie demanded.

"Known? Not long. Maybe a couple of days. It's always been possible, but she never showed any signs."

"*Always been possible, and you didn't think to say anything?*" Jackie said, voice rising.

"Jackie..." Victor cut in, his voice carrying a calming warning.

Jackie took a deep breath, gritting her teeth, then motioned for me to continue.

I sighed. "But I only *really* knew after the meeting with her principal. That was the final piece - and the reason I got back into the supernatural scene."

"Got back into?"

I nodded, my voice catching in my throat. I struggled to find the right words.

How do you explain something like this? How do you explain to someone that you threw everything out of your life for them without them asking you to? Without them wanting you to? Because you thought it was what they wanted, what they needed?

How do you tell them you made this decision on your own? That it never occurred to you to discuss it with her or tell her the truth to begin with? That you were trying to protect her from something you were afraid was too big, too strange, and too dangerous for her?

How do you do any of that without coming off like a patronizing ass?

You don't.

"I left it all behind. All of the people from my old life. All of my old responsibilities. Everything I was doing. Dropped it like a bad habit and decided I was gonna stay on the straight and narrow for Mary and you. No offense," I added, looking toward Victor.

He shrugged and replied, "None taken."

"And the amazing thing? I did it. I mean, I really, *really* did. No more late-night hunts looking to root out a rogue vampire nest. No more answering calls about needing an exorcism. No more clearing hauntings. No more freeing people who fell into bad deals with the fae. No more demons. No more angels."

I trailed off, trying to focus on the here and now. Or the distant past, as it were.

"That meeting was made up of the hidden remnants of the Knights Templar, as well as representatives from the Vatican proper, the vampire bloodlines, the werewolf nations, the Seelie and Unseelie courts, several dragons and the Order of the Enlightened...the wizards I talked about earlier. The Catholic Church agreed to cease Inquisitorial operations against the supernatural in exchange for the Liturgy of the Forgotten. No supernatural creature was to reveal itself to mundane humanity in any way, shape, or form. The supernatural creatures were expected to help with enforcement of this stricture, but the Templars...the Erinnys were the final arbiters of justice, working from the shadows to safeguard humanity from the Forgotten...that's what the supernatural creatures started calling themselves, and the Forgotten from each other.

"The final deal can get put at the feet of Pope Pious IV. Growing up as a de Medici taught him how to push buttons and manipulate with the best of them, and man did he ever. He convinced an entire conclave full of some of the world's most powerful entities to self-limit their power and influence. He played factions off of one another, manipulated immortal and near-immortal creatures, and eventually wrangled concessions out of the lot of them—"

"Jason? You said you were going to tell us about things that are pertinent. It's not that it's not an interesting story, but it's like six hundred years old," Jackie said, interrupting.

I grinned, then nodded.

Focus, Bishop.

"Right. Sorry. I got approached by someone who works in a different faction inside of the Erinnys from Chase—the man outside with the gun. He wanted my help to stop a war between a powerful voodoo wizard and the vampires of New Orleans. We have an awful lot of them, and they've got quite a bit of influence in the city. I heard what he had to say and told him 'no thanks. I'm retired.' And I meant it."

Jackie looked unconvinced, but I shook my head.

"It's true. But then we had our meeting at the school. I heard what the principal said. What Mary could do, and I knew that if word got out about her, people like Chase would show up, and they'd try to either take advantage of her or they'd kill her. Untrained, unaffiliated people with power like hers are a threat to them, so they work to eliminate them."

"Eliminate?" Jackie asked.

Victor put his hand on top of hers. "Kill. He means they were going to kill her."

I nodded. "Yeah. So after that meeting, I got in touch with my contact and told him I'd do it. I'd get back involved and help in exchange for them owing me a favor."

"...to protect Mary?" Jackie asked.

I nodded again. "And since then, I've got back in touch with people and poking my nose into places to find out what I can. The wizard thinks the vampires have his daughter. I met with their leader, and there's no way he does, but that didn't stop him from nearly killing me."

"But Ava saved you?" Jackie asked.

I nodded.

"Why is she helping? What's in it for her? I thought you broke off your friendship years ago. After…"

"…you accused me of cheating on you with her. I never did, but we did limit contact until I walked away when you left. As to why? Mary. She loves the kid. All of the old gang does. Dave, Nero, Nat - they're all back in and involved, trying to help. Nat's…well…this can't go too much longer. Chase's phone call pulled me away from something important."

I paused, trying to steal a glance out the window, but fearful of presenting a target to an expert marksman. I gave up.

Jackie nodded slowly, turning over what she'd heard in her mind.

And then my gears started turning as well.

Anything for a kid they love.

"Victor? Jackie? Can I borrow one of your cellphones for a minute? I think I know how to get rid of Chase. Just gotta send a few texts and make a post or two to some social media sites."

Victor frowned in confusion but handed over his phone as he cut off the flow of blood from our makeshift transfusion.

"I don't want to risk having you go into cardiac arrest," he said, then paused, looking at the pile of yuck Mary had pulled out of Ava and left on the floor. "What *is* that, Bishop?" he asked, almost in a whisper.

"Eucharist," I replied as I plugged away on the phone.

"Eucharist? Why would that hurt her?"

I nodded. "Blessed Communion wafers, trans-substantiated into the Body of Christ. Divine power given form. Absolutely fatal for anything or anyone with an infernal pedigree like Ava."

"Wait," Jackie cut in. "Ava has an infernal pedigree? What's that even mean?"

"She's part demon. A succubus. Her mother was human and her father...wasn't."

"Jason, that's a lot to take in...I mean..." Jackie said, struggling. "This just isn't something that happens. Half demons and assassin-priests."

I nodded in agreement. "You're right. The entire point of the Conclave was to set up the Shadow Accords to keep monsters out of the way of regular people...to control the predation and keep limits on things. For all that he's a lunatic, Chase works for people that...they're not *good*, but they're *necessary*. He just takes it too far. Turns it up to eleven and doesn't believe in gray areas. But you can't believe that something like this happens? That's where you draw the line? Organizations and agreements? You saw what Mary did. How is what I'm talking about any harder to believe?"

Neither Vic nor Jackie had an answer, and my question remained echoing through the living room for a short eternity as I typed away on Vic's phone, sending message after message out into the ether and hoping that it ended in front of the right eyes. Or wrong eyes, depending on your perspective.

"So, what now?" Vic asked. "Ava's not in any shape to run across the city fighting monsters, and you're only marginally better with the amount of blood you just gave. How are we going to get rid of this Chase guy if the police won't help and the monster hunters are down?"

Jackie put a hand on his, which somehow didn't upset me this time. Must be light-headed from the blood loss.

"Well, I have a plan," I admitted. "One that I hope involves very little running, jumping, or generally being athletic. We have to sit and wait for a while. And hope."

So we did.

It was about half an hour before Papa Ivé's people started arriving, the first group in a pick-up truck whose bed was filled with armed, angry men. Their unruly shouts and challenges split the night just before the dual searchlights on top of the truck did the same.

"Bishop, what have you done?" Victor asked, his eyes wide as he attempted to glance out the window.

"Evened the odds a bit," I replied. "Chase has us outgunned and is in a better position to take advantage of it. I put the word to members of Papa Ivé's organization telling them Evangeline had been seen across the street from this address."

"And Papa Ivé is...the man whose daughter is missing? The voodoo wizard?" Jackie asked.

I nodded, then smiled as more cars rolled up.

"EVANGELINE!"

My smile vanished.

"Shit."

"That's him, isn't it?" Vic asked.

I nodded, then muttered a curse under my breath.

"He never goes out on calls like this."

"But it's his daughter," Jackie reminded me.

Fuck. She was right.

"Screwed the pooch on this one, Bishop."

We all started as Ava spoke, one of her hazel eyes slowly opening, and a smile curling its way onto her lips.

"Didn't have you to keep an eye on me. What do you expect when you go and take a nap in the middle of a job?"

She laughed, low and hoarse, but still Ava's laugh.

"Be more interesting, and I'll stay awake longer, jackass."

I opened my mouth to banter back when Ivé's voice thundered from the street outside.

"JASON BISHOP! I KNOW YOU'RE HERE. I CAN SMELL YOUR STINK! SHOW YOURSELF AND ACCEPT MY ACCOUNTING!"

I blinked.

"Well, that's not good."

I started to pull myself to my feet, fighting vertigo the motion caused, only to have Vic and Ava both reach out to stop me.

"You're in no condition to go out there," Vic warned.

"He'll kill you, Bishop," Ava added, her voice severe and her grip on my arm vice-like. "I know you and Ivé have a weird thing, but that won't help. Not this time."

I looked down at her arm, then met her gaze, holding it for a pair of heartbeats until she let go, then looked at Vic and nodded.

"Ivé knows I'm here, and he's calling me. This isn't a dick-measuring thing. Me and Ivé's members were measured a long time ago, and that guy's got a throbbing log as far as I'm concerned. But, the man can literally collapse this house down around our ears with a flick of his finger. I know I'm out of my league, but it's gotta be me."

"Why?" Jackie asked, her eyes wide and shining.

"Because it's always him," Ava said, her voice barely above a whisper.

I grimaced, then steadied myself against the wall before moving to the door and throwing it open.

The sudden movement brought one of the floodlights to bear. In response, I held up both hands, my left one slightly in front of me to shield my eyes, then started shuffling blindly forward. For every step I took, I could feel the gaze of every one of Ivé's people, as well as that of the man himself. They were a pack of angry, hungry predators, and they'd just been played by a couple of texts, a few social media posts talking about a young woman's current party location, and a hedge magic spell that brought them to the right people.

In retrospect, the spell was probably a bad idea. Once it was out there, a guy like Ivé was able to pinpoint who'd cast it almost without effort. Stupid of me. It's almost like I'm operating with severe blood loss or something. Ivé's lanky form unfolded from the passenger seat of the lead truck. His face was a thundercloud as he strode toward me.

"Tell me why I don't kill you where you stand, Bishop?" Ivé demanded. "You come into my home and disrespect me. The next day you thumb your nose at my loss with this - this stunt! Killing is too good. Too clean. You'll suffer for this, dying for days, and none of your tricks can save you."

"I'm looking for her, Ivé," I whispered. "Just like I said, I was going to, and I've brought *my* people back together. Nat. Dave. Nero. Ava. And we've got a lead."

"What?" he demanded, stepping forward, only to pause as I held up my hand.

"No. Nat's in there, and I know you and yours. This needs a scalpel. You're getting ready to use a chainsaw."

The Voodoo King's eyes met mine, his nostrils flaring.

"Protected yourself from the loa trying to pry into your mind, Bishop? Clever. It's refreshing to see you thinking again. Fine. You may know where she is. Why call us here?"

"Father Harland Chase."

"The Erinys? Is he hunting you for some reason?"

I shrugged.

"And Ava. And it looks like Mary. He's...the man's unhinged."

Ivé nodded.

"That he is, charlatan. But dangerous all the same. Your friendship with Raimond won't save you from him."

"I don't plan on asking Raimond to save me from him. That bastard threatened my daughter. I'm going to end him."

Ivé looked at me, then cracked into a wide grin, his teeth gleaming.

"Good. When we met yesterday, I was concerned you were trying to step halfway back into the world. There *is* no halfway. No part-time. Either you walk in The Gloaming, or you stay in the light."

He looked at me, then to Vic's house, then back to me, raising his eyebrows. "No one gets to have both, Bishop. No one."

I looked at him, refusing to look away. Refusing to admit he was right.

"I keep hearing rumor the vampires have her—"

I shook my head, causing another bout of vertigo that I wrestled back under control.

"No, Ivé. I'm telling you; Conrad's people don't have her."

"At a certain point, the truth matters less than the perception. Too many people think he's taken Evangeline from me, and he has done nothing to quell those thoughts. If I don't respond, it weakens me. It opens my people up to further predations. I can't allow that."

Ivé's dark pronouncement didn't surprise me, not really, but it wasn't what I wanted to hear.

"I need more time, Ivé. I can find her. Will find her. I'll bring her back to you, but I can't do that if there's a shooting war between you and the vampires. The second that happens, whoever's got her pulls up stakes and buries themselves in the deepest, darkest holes they can find to avoid what The Order is going to do."

"It's been too long already, Bishop. I am coming to terms with the fact that I will never see my daughter again. Not alive."

The words tumbled out of Ivé, painting him as surprisingly human. Vulnerable. Normal. Not words I would have ever associated with the man. I looked at him closely, concentrating hard, and took in the nimbus of energy that danced around him, watching the ebb and flow of it, pulsing with his emotions: Fear. Anger. Soul-crushing grief.

This was a man who had lived far beyond the span of his mortal years through his abilities. A man who fell in love and lost his wife despite all of that massive power. A man whose only child, all that remained of his beloved, had just been taken from him. A man who felt that without her, he didn't have much of a reason to live.

My heart bled for him, and his fatalistic outlook terrified me.

All I could do was shake my head. "You're jumping the gun. I'm bringing her home. I just need time to make it happen."

After a long moment, he gestured for his posse to head out. The floodlights vanished as abruptly as they'd appeared, opening the door for the darkness to come pouring back into its rightful place.

Ivé had stood down, but for how long?

Taking a deep breath, I fought off the feeling of vertigo that threatened my consciousness and stumbled back toward the house, where Mary, Jackie, and Vic were attempting to convince a now standing Ava that she needed time to recover.

Her voice came drifting out toward the front door as I entered. "He needs me, even if he doesn't know it and won't say it. He needs me, so I'm going to be there."

I paused in the doorway as gray started to invade from the sides of my vision.

"You're gonna get yourself killed, Ava," Jackie objected. "And if anything happens to you, it'd break him."

"Pfft. Bishop's only got eyes for the two of you, but he'd do the same for me," she replied. "For any of us. It's just how he's wired. How can I offer him anything less in return?"

The spinning started to subside, and my vision started to pull back to its regular range.

"You and Daddy need to take care of each other, Ava. He'll protect you, and you'll protect him, right?" Mary asked.

"I'll keep your dad safe for you, Mary," Ava promised.

"This is a bad idea. Both of you are beat to hell," Vic objected.

"Must be Tuesday," Ava shot back, her lopsided smile and wry amusement giving color to her voice. "Back against the wall, and everything looks hopeless? That's when he does his best work. Always has."

I walked in and smiled.

"That way, I can make the best entrances," I said, offering what I hoped was my best rakish grin. "I got Ivé to back off for a bit to give us a bit of time to find Evangeline, but if we don't put hands on that kid soon, he's going to war with the vampires."

"War?" Vic asked.

"Perfect," Ava muttered. "We gotta get to Nat."

Ignoring Vic, I nodded to Ava. Grinning, I turned to Jackie and Vic.

"So, I'm gonna need a car. And I'm not sure what sort of shape it's gonna be in when I get it back to you. Averting a city-wide catastrophe and all that."

They looked at one another, Jackie appearing worried, while Vic took a deep breath, then strode toward the kitchen, grabbed his keys, and tossed them to me.

"Just filled it up. Go. Do what it is you both do. Call if you need us."

"It's not safe for you here. Ivé probably ran Chase off, but nothing is stopping him from coming back."

"What about your place, Daddy?"

"You have your key. Pack an overnight bag and go. Chase can't get into my apartment."

"Why not?" asked Jackie, only to get a flat stare and a quirked eyebrow from our daughter.

"*Magic*, Mommy," she said with an exasperated sigh. "Don't worry; we'll leave right after you, Daddy."

Mary hugged me, then Ava, then me again, her tiny arms wrapping around my neck and her rosebud lips planting a kiss on my scratchy cheek.

"Please come back. All of you."

Ava looked at me, then her, unformed tears hanging in her eyes.

"We promise," I replied as Ava nodded for good measure.

"Good. Then go save Nat."

And so we left the three of them to gather belongings and flee like refugees to my apartment, while Ava and I came face to face with Vic's ride, a black Range Rover sport luxury SUV.

I'm not a car guy, but this thing was shiny.

Ava let out a low whistle.

"Damn, Bishop. I think I know why Jackie left you for him."

I glared at Ava as I stalked to the driver's seat as she slid into the passenger side.

"No answer from Dave or Nero," she announced as I gunned the engine.

"Here," I said and reached for her phone. A moment later, I'd logged into the website and activated the app.

Ava fiddled with the phone for a bit, then smiled.

"Got him," she announced, then held up the phone and synched the GPS with the maps application. "We can officially say we've had a bad night now. Let's take it out on some unlucky motherfuckers."

"That's my girl," I said, grinning evilly as the Land Rover's tires devoured the distance between us and our friends.

The GPS led us across the Mississippi and into Algiers, and then through most of the village on the far side of the river, following a series of turns onto increasingly smaller roads toward the eastern portion of what can only vaguely be considered New Orleans. It's a place where most of the built-up and pricey bed and breakfasts and tributes to the jazz greats give way to more modest, single-level homes with faded siding and overgrown front yards.

Trees and heavy growth lined the narrow, cracked asphalt streets, whose sole illumination on this cloudy evening was our headlights stabbing out into the night. After the lights, sounds, and feel of the Nawlins, being out here on the edge of the bayou felt like we'd entered another world, a hostile alien landscape. Malice hung thick in the night air, making the drive tense. My anxiety over leaving Dave, Nero, and Nat because of Chase threatening Mary was high. Either Ava felt the same, or she'd picked up on my worry and claimed some of it for her own.

Our last set of turns took us along a small road separated from the Mississippi by a wide field and a hill and ended at a fence line of what appeared to be a warehouse. The chainlink fence surrounded the property, its gate closed and likely locked. I pulled off onto the grass, a hundred yards out, then killed the engine. The headlights vanished, leaving only the dim moonlight glowing through the misty night air to see by.

"The place isn't lit up, so either Dave and Nero are here and hiding, or they've been grabbed."

We started forward, whispering to one another.

"And no real way to find out before we go in," Ava paused, looking down at her clothes: A club dress that had been cut away from one shoulder and black heels. Ava shook her head. "I really should have thought to ask for a change of clothes. Not my best 'sneaking ensemble'."

"We were a bit distracted," I replied.

"Blood loss: The great equalizer," she agreed, then gestured toward me. "Your shirt's not exactly any sort of fresh either, Bishop. Seems someone had the bad grace to bleed all over you at some point."

"I don't think there was any malice intended."

"You never know. Some people are nefarious with that sort of thing. Spite bleeding. I'm pretty sure it's a thing."

"I'm almost positive it's not."

"Suit yourself. Be gullible," she replied, maintaining a straight face before focusing her eyes back down the lane again. "Looks like the fencing runs all the way around the property."

"Not like there are any other roads all the way out here anyway. They only need to worry about the one."

I paused, narrowing my eyes, and looked for signs. Anything out of the ordinary. Auras. Loose energy. Anything. I came up blank. It was as mundane as a light industrial zone could be. A small cluster of trees was the only thing between the fenceline and the warehouse parking lot.

"Okay. I'm going to assume Dave and Nero are in there someplace, and they're not grabbed."

"Makes sense. That way, we don't do anything that screws up what they've got going on."

"Exactly. We move in and hope they'll be along to help if we need it."

"If we need it? I like your optimism, Bishop. The way our luck has been going, it's gonna be when not if."

Grimacing, I replied. "Last chance to back out."

Turning to look at me, Ava pursed her lips and eloquently lifted one eyebrow.

"I'll take that as a no," I observed to no one. Pausing, I leaned down and picked up two handfuls of dirt. Cupping it in my hands, I breathed heavily, whispering words from a long-forgotten tongue into the soil before shoving it into my pockets.

Looking up, I saw Ava watching me, waiting patiently.

"What? You're just jealous because you never took the time to learn how to make magic dirt. There's nothing wrong with some quick and dirty magic."

"Dirty?" she asked, looking from the dirt on my hands and back to my eyes. "You should be *ashamed* of yourself. First, the dad khakis, then dad jokes? How're the forces of darkness going to manage to tremble in your presence if you've turned into a giant dork, Bishop?"

I opened my mouth to object, then snapped it shut and shrugged. "I make it work. Let's do this."

With a groan, Ava followed.

We arrived at the front gate without apparent detection. It was a ten-foot-tall chain link fence, topped with razor wire that ran completely around the perimeter. The road continued along on the other side, snaking slightly to the right, where it emptied into a parking lot that surrounded a large, multistory warehouse. It was by far the largest structure we'd seen for miles.

"Suspicious," I commented. Ava just looked at me, shrugging. "The roads back here are too small for trucks to use regularly. Too beat up. And the building is ten times larger than anything else around here. It just doesn't make any sense, which feeds straight into our theory that they're not on the up and up."

"We were still looking to prove that?" she asked incredulously. "I was fully on board that train when the GPS led us here."

"It's always good to have proof."

"Why do we need proof? We have a bunch of stuff that would never stand up in any court. Because you used magic to find the place, to begin with."

I glared at her, then muttered under my breath as I checked the lock on the gate. Just as secure as I expected it to be, so I smiled at Ava.

"Hey, you feeling butch?" I asked. "I could finagle the lock, but it might set off some alarms if they've got a willworker in there, and after what Nero saw? I feel like there's *probably* a willworker in there."

Ava sighed, then stared at the lock for a moment. Her petite hands took it delicately, one on the body, the other on the clasp, then she pulled the thing apart with straightforward brute force. Holding the pieces up, one in each hand, she smirked, then dropped them.

I slid the gate open quietly, then closed it behind us as we padded up the lane toward the warehouse proper. The night was cooling rapidly, causing ground fog to roll off the river, blanketing the turf with wispy tendrils that swirled lazily as we moved through them, leaving a gauzy trail behind us. As the small asphalt trail led us around the copse of trees that blocked a direct view of the entire structure, we saw the parking lot, filled with a couple dozen plain white box trucks and work vans.

Ava grunted, and I nodded in response.

"And that's how they're moving around the city so easily," Ava whispered. "Nothing to see there. You can grab pretty much any kid at any time and vanish into traffic with no one the wiser."

"There," I said, pointing out the black SUV parked up against the building. "There's the car that took Nat."

We paused, taking a long moment to look around, as I concentrated, pushing my senses out as far as I could, hoping to detect something that would tell us anything. There wasn't much.

"There's a slight buzzing from the building like they've got some sort of spell effect going on."

"Or they're building to one," Ava suggested, worry evident on her face.

"Yeah, that's a good point. Let's go get our girl."

We moved forward, staying low as we reached the vans and cars, just in case any of them still had occupants. We wove our way through the formation and up against the wall of the warehouse itself, still without seeing any sign of trouble. Which was a concern in and of itself.

"For an evil, human sacrificing cult, I'm a bit disappointed. I expected a bit more. This is just lazy," Ava commented, looking around and smirking.

I wasn't so sure. Something felt off. I just couldn't quite place my finger on it.

"Be careful. This has all been way too easy so far, and I don't like that we haven't seen Dave or Nero yet."

Her smirk faded. Looking out into the night and around the parking lot, she nodded.

"Point," she agreed. "Chances are they're inside."

"Yup. Which means we go in, too."

"It's a trap. *Again*. You know that, right?"

"Oh, absolutely. No doubt in my mind. I don't know what kind of trap, but it's most definitely a trap."

Ava paused, looking at the door, then at me.

"Would we be dumber if we didn't know it was a trap and went in anyway, or is our approach of going in with our eyes open on it being a trap but ignoring that information just catastrophically dumber?"

"I think our approach is at least fifty percent more stupid."

She rolled her eyes, then forced a smile. "I'm excited about this plan. Let's do it!"

"Time to be heroes."

"Idiots. We're being idiots," she whispered.

"Same thing," I replied.

The door into the warehouse was distressingly unlocked, but we entered anyway. We were all in at this point, and there was no reason to pretend otherwise. The interior was dimly lit, with small circular fluorescent light bulbs hanging from the ceiling high above, casting their weak, flickering light vaguely out into the dusty expanse of the warehouse's innards. The structure's main floor was laid out in a grid, with massive shelves holding a variety of crates and boxes that reached nearly from floor to ceiling. The aisles that ran north and south were wide enough for four people to walk abreast, while those intersecting every twenty yards or so, running east and west, were wide enough for one. I had to assume there were some bigger ones further in, but I couldn't see them from where we stood.

Ava wrinkled her nose within moments of entering, causing a look of confusion on my face until the smell reached me as well.

"Smells like--" I started.

"Death," she finished.

I reached out to take her hand and give it a squeeze. She looked down, then up at me and forced a smile but didn't make a move to let go. I looked down, confused.

"So we don't get separated," she whispered.

Again, I nodded in reply. Made sense.

We started forward, me leading, the warmth of her hand in mine, re-assuring. We worked our way to the south along one of the large aisles until we encountered a smaller one, then ducked in there. The shelves were around six feet wide, giving us enough room to peek around corners before making turns, but so far, the warehouse had proven to be frustratingly empty. I was becoming worried this might not be a trap.

That we were too late.

As we moved toward the southern side of the building, I noticed the light getting marginally brighter and began to slow my pace. Ava squeezed my hand, drawing a glance from me.

"Voices," she whispered.

Holding my breath, I closed my eyes and listened hard. Murmurs, but yes. Voices. Rhythmic. Possibly chanting. Not good.

I squeezed her hand twice and started forward faster, ignoring the need for stealth completely. We built speed until we ran, Ava with her shoes in her right hand, all the while the chanting rang droned on. The hairs on the back of my neck began to stand up, soon followed by the ones on my arms. Power was building.

"Bishop," Ava's voice carried a note of warning.

I skidded to an abrupt halt, but what Ava had heard came around the corner we'd just passed: a guard armed with a shotgun.

She turned, preparing to commit some form of unspeakable violence. Usually, I'd be on board with this, especially given the current choices, but I didn't think we could afford the noise, so my hand snaked into my pocket, grabbing a small handful of the dirt. I tossed it over her shoulder and directly into his face.

The guard gasped as it made contact, then went stock still, eyes glazing over and body rigid.

Ava's shoe-carrying hand stopped just short of smashing into his throat.

"What the fuck?" she asked.

"Midnight Soil," I whispered.

"Night soil? Like...manure?"

"No, midnight soil. Old voodoo spell. Puts the person who inhales it into a deep trance. Supposed to help make it easier for the loa to skin ride them."

Ava grunted, and we ghosted up to the end of the aisle and saw two groups: the first was the same trio of men from the club standing with their backs to us, with Nat cuffed to a large wooden post in front of them. She glared defiantly at the three of them, then called out.

"Don't worry, Evangeline, I'm gonna get us both out of this. Then I'm gonna take turns biting each and every one of my friends *who said they'd fucking be here.*"

The second group was a circle of robed figures chanting as they surrounded a single figure in the center. Evangeline Grey, daughter to Papa Ivé, looked up groggily at the sound of her name, swaying slightly. The dark-skinned girl was wearing a nightgown and had her hands tied to the altar she rested on.

The sound of flesh striking flesh brought my attention back to Nat, who's head now lolled to the side with a bright splash of blood staining her teeth where one of the goons had slapped her.

"I get that one," Ava announced. "He's mine." She moved without further prelude or warning, darting quickly forward, bent low and sticking to the shadowy fringes of the light as much as she could. The large man who struck Nat had no idea he was a dead man until he saw Ava, his head having been forcibly rotated 180 degrees, so it was now facing directly back out over his shoulder blades. He made a loud gurgling noise, then a louder one still as Ava palmed his face and slammed it forcibly into the concrete floor, crushing his skull as the pair of men with him raised their voices in shock and alarm.

I didn't blame them. What they'd just witnessed was grotesque, but I didn't have time to lose in either shock or admiration of Ava's handi-work. It was one or the other. I'm not sure how I feel about not knowing which. Instead, I was in motion as well, charging the used car salesman and tackling him to the ground just as his mouth opened. I sandwiched his body between the cement floor and my shoulder, driving the wind from his lungs and maintaining a position of strength on top of him so I could rain punches down on his little weasel face.

Or that was the plan.

The big man next to him was inexplicably not fighting with Ava and instead grabbed a double handful of my hair and tossed me like a ragdoll off of his apparent boss. I felt my back impact one of the shelving units, which were not nearly as soft or pillow-like as I had hoped they might be while I was mid-flight. Now it was my turn to gasp for breath as I pulled myself up to my feet while the wall of muscle, bad breath, and Gym Bro Body Spray stalked toward me full of bad intentions.

Glancing over his shoulder, I saw that Ava had moved to free Nat but had to step forward to stem a tide of new arrivals that were attempting to enter the area through a door on the other side of the pole that had held our friend.

Fine...I guess that would do.

An inhuman roar split the air above me and to the left, drawing my and Mr. Body Spray's attention.

It was Dave. Sort of.

My friend and bartender had called on his birthright, transforming from the large but amiable man I knew so well into a horror. Nearly nine feet tall and black as pitch, chitinous armor with short, rough hairs covering his hide. Each of his four arms ended in a large, hooked claw. He was literally the stuff of nightmares made flesh and launched himself off of the shelving unit, smashing into the mass of charging cultists with unnerving fury.

Ava's style left me conflicted. Dave's did not. Where the violence she perpetrated was compact, graceful, and almost artistic, his onslaught was savage, visceral, brutal, and bloody.

I spied Nero moving toward Nat as Mr. Body Spray refocused on me. I shouted to him. "The girl! No, not her! Evangeline! In the circle!"

Nero changed course; baseball bat gripped in his hands.

Where the hell had he found a bat?

The question was interrupted as a fist the size of a canned ham made contact with my gut, lifting me off the ground and back into the shelves, just as I'd planned.

I mean, it hurt, and I really *wasn't* ready for it, but I had a plan.

The beginnings of a plan. Part of one. Okay. I was in trouble.

Mr. Body Spray picked me back up, which allowed me to jump slightly, driving my head up under his chin. It's an old trick that's served me well in many situations and will put even the biggest human opponent back on his heels.

Sunglasses askew, Body Spray looked silently down at me with cold, dead eyes.

Literally, cold dead eyes. He was undead. A walking corpse.

Sonofa-

His hands darted forward, wrapping around my throat and hoisting me off my feet. The mixed smell of the body spray and the sickly-sweet smell of decay intermingled, trapping me in their miasma. I pounded on his arms, neck, and head in a mild panic as my blood and oxygen flow were cut off, kicking feebly at his midsection for good measure.

That's right, Bishop. Kick the dead guy in the nuts. That'll do it for ya.

I struggled against impending panic. Fighting to draw in enough breath, I forced my throat and lungs, and mouth to form a word as my palms shot forward over his eyes.

"I-"

Nothing. The pressure on my throat was nearly unbearable.

Focusing, pushing, I tried again.

"I-g-"

Things were going grey. It was just around the edges of my vision, but it was there. No more time for games, Bishop. You don't do this. You're a dead man. Killed by some hopped-up minion who's already dead. What the hell sort of way is that to go out?

"*Ignem!*" I finally croaked, then saw the flame erupt from my hands and lance through the thing's eyes.

It dropped me, howling like an air raid siren as the holy fire did its work, purifying the unclean, removing its taint, and saving my ass. I greedily gulped at the air as I lay, shaking my head and trying to regain what semblance of wits I had remaining.

*Chapter
Sixteen*

The room swam as I lay on my back, the air having been driven savagely from my lungs after the undead thing dropped me. The smell of burning flesh intermingled with the coppery tinge of blood in the air (either Ava or Dave's handiwork) served as an urgent reminder that lying on my back wasn't the best defensive stance under the current circumstances.

Now, if only my body would cooperate and actually move the way I was telling it to.

With a supreme act of will, I brought myself upright, leaning heavily against the shelving that had bludgeoned me seconds earlier. Or a lifetime ago. It was hard to tell.

My eyes took in the chaotic scene in front of me, parsing the carnival of chaos into digestible, understandable chunks: Ava striding forward like an angry goddess, lashing out with hands and elbows, feet and knees at any of the cultists who had the misfortune to end up within reach of her. Her movements looked delicate as she moved forward: a woman performing an intricate dance that resulted in broken bones and smashed skulls.

The other side of the mass of cultists roiled and reeled as the monstrous form of Dave tore through them. There was nothing dance-like about his motions. Each one was brutally efficient and intended to inflict the maximum amount of injury. No one in their right mind stood against Dave when he called on his LeBlanc blood. Not if they wanted to live to see the next dawn.

He had me worried. I knew how dangerous this form could be for him. The longer he was in it, the harder it was to come out the other side and retain who and what he was. He could lose himself to his family. To the monster. He was taking a horrible risk for us, and we all knew it—him most of all.

But what choice did he have? Without him, we'd have been overrun immediately.

Nero had Evangeline, while Nat swung a baseball bat at the robed figures who surrounded her like she was trying out for the Dodgers. Two lay on the ground, and the others seemed to think better of seeing if a third would fare any better.

Something was itching at the back of my head. A thought that wouldn't quite form, it was like trying to grasp smoke, but— I shook my head. There was no time to sit around woolgathering. The longer Dave remained like this, the more danger he was in. We needed to leave, and the sooner, the better.

"Nero! Nat! Grab the kid and get out the door! North side! Ava, show 'em the way!" All three immediately broke off from what they were doing,

Ava dashing forward, her shoes long since forgotten (possibly) or embedded in the body of some unlucky sap who had run afoul of her (more likely). Without pausing or breaking stride, she grabbed Evangeline's hand in hers and hurried toward the door we'd entered through, Nat and Nero close behind.

"Dave! Me and you are the rearguards! Let's keep 'em off everyone's backs!"

I started to move to follow, only fully turning once I saw that Dave had disengaged moved in my direction.

He was still in there. For now.

And so, we ran.

The flight through the warehouse was as tense a time as I can recall in my life. The knot of Ava, Evangeline, Nat, and Nero was ten yards ahead, give or take, with Dave and me coming up behind, pausing from time to time to discourage pursuit. I knocked things off the shelves when we cut into the smaller aisles, attempting to trip up the cultists. Dave's methods were far more direct.

Every shadow that crossed our path had the potential to be something awful. Every turn we made screamed in my mind that it would be a trap. But, somehow, the shadows remained shadows, and the trap's jaws never snapped shut. And so, we ran on.

I heard the door to the outside slam open as Ava ushered everyone through, waiting until I arrived before shouting, "I'll get them to the car. Can you get Dave?"

"Go!" I urged.

Dave sprung through the open door with a snarl a heartbeat later, and I slammed it behind him. I dearly wished I had my full bag of tricks, but I'd left it in Nero's car and simply hadn't had time to go back for it when Chase interrupted our evening. I had nothing to bar a door with.

As I stared at the door, I felt Dave's eyes on me. His increasingly malevolent, hungry eyes.

I swallowed hard, vividly remembering where I'd found him. His cannibal family. What I'd helped him leave behind.

I met my friend's eyes and smiled.

"Okay, Dave. Time to come back to us. The danger's passed. Enough. We can do it."

The clacking, hissing noise that escaped the monstrous jaws in front of me seemed to disagree.

I shook my head, refusing to show any fear. Dave didn't deserve that. Not when he'd risked so much for us.

"No, I refuse to accept that, Dave. You've been under for way longer. Remember when we were out in the bayou? At your family's plantation? If you hadn't come through back then, I'd have ended up in the dinner pot. Ava too."

The clacking hiss again. This time, Dave lurched forward, lifting a barbed appendage, but pausing at the top of his swing when I held his eyes, unflinching.

"I know you're still in there, Dave, and I know that no matter what, you'd never hurt me. No matter how things look. No matter what the situation is, I know you. I know your heart. I know your soul, and I need that back way more than I need some sort of barbed horror right now. So, come back. Bring me back, my friend."

The creature's red eyes began to fade, replaced by Dave's mismatched blue and brown ones. The body became fluid, sloughing off the hairy, chitinous outer layer in unappetizing piles, leaving a very slimy, very naked Dave.

He immediately collapsed to his hands and knees.

—or would have if I hadn't stepped in to catch him.

"Asphalt's hell on your knees, big guy," I told him, helping him to his feet.

He shook his head, tears in his eyes. "Almost didn't make it back this time, boss."

I smiled. "Almost is for wimps, but we're not outta this yet, man. There were a lot of those fuckers in there, and you and Ava didn't manage to kill anywhere near all of 'em."

He shook his head.

"Almost went after you, Bishop. I was—"

"In control. I never had any doubt that I was safe," I reassured him as I began to lead him away from the door and toward the car. I could hear voices coming from the other side. It sounded like we were out of time.

He grunted in disgust, allowing himself to lean heavily on me. Dave was not a small man by any stretch, and I wasn't in the best of shape at this point either, so I ended up leaning on him nearly as much as he leaned on me. As friends do.

We wound our way through the maze of vans and cars back toward the front gate as voices exited the building and flashlights began to scan the parking lot.

Multiple gunshots rang out into the night, hitting something, but not us.

We continued on. Side by side and step by step. Neither willing to leave the other, but both aware that we weren't going to make it the way things were.

A fact that Ava apparently realized as well, as Victor's SUV roared up long before we got through the gate, with our succubus savior behind the wheel.

"You boys look like shit. Get in."

Dave nearly wept as I helped load him into the far back and closed the door, then I practically collapsed into the front seat as Ava peeled out to the sound of more gunfire behind us.

Looking into the center row seat, Evangeline Grey was sandwiched between Nat and Nero, sobbing quietly onto Nat's shoulder.

We'd done it. We'd accomplished the impossible: In less than two days, we'd found Ivé's daughter. So why did I feel like I was missing something obvious?

Aside from the part where we had to get her to him alive. That was obvious and presented its own challenge as the fleet of cars, trucks, and vans that had occupied the parking lot we'd just left seemed to be streaming up the single-lane road behind us en masse.

I shook my head and turned around with a grunt, closing my eyes for a moment and taking a deep breath before moving over to speak quietly to Ava.

"Do you feel like that was at least fifty percent too easy?"

"Are you out of your fucking mind?" she hissed back. "In no one's world would that fit any description of the word 'easy,' Bishop. I know I gave you shit for not thinking and not having your head in the game, but this level of paranoia is a bit much, even for you. We got the girl; now we've gotta dodge these gun-toting assholes and get her back to her Daddy without any of us taking a bullet. I think the degree of difficulty is plenty high, thanks."

I sat back, looking at the side mirror to see the fleet behind us struggling to make up ground on the tricked-out Range Rover and its pilot with her supernaturally enhanced reflexes.

Maybe Ava was right. Maybe I was looking for something else to go wrong just out of pure orneriness, or maybe even habit. I nodded and put my hand on her bare leg, just above the knee, giving it a reassuring squeeze.

That drew a glance from her, first at my hand, then up at my face. A smile spread to the right side of her lips before she reached down, giving my hand a squeeze. Letting go, she went back to the trivial job of keeping us alive and ahead of the mass of human trafficking cultists that seemed intent on murdering us for stealing the high-value Evangeline Grey.

Y'know, priorities. Fragile male egos can wait. Sometimes. If only briefly.

The Land Rover's tires greedily devoured the road as we flew at a break-neck pace down the small lane, sprinting toward the relative safety of New Orleans proper. Ava's eyes remained locked on the road in front of us, so I took the job of keeping an eye on the pursuit.

Trees blurred by in the darkness, indistinct shadows filled with sinister omens, briefly illuminated by our headlights before fading back into their posts, nocturnal sentries observing the passage of time around them.

At the speed we passed by, we wouldn't even appear as a blip.

"Some of 'em are peeling off," I warned Ava.

She muttered a curse.

"Why's that bad?" Nat called up from the back seat, Evangeline's face still buried in her shoulder.

"Because it probably means they're trying some other back roads to get in front of us," Ava replied through gritted teeth.

I nodded.

"They know this area better than we do. They may have shortcuts they can use to get ahead of us, set up some sort of roadblock or ambush," I added, glaring at the cars behind us. "Think it's worth leaving the GPS route?" I asked, looking to Ava.

She shook her head. "I don't know Algiers. I'm as likely as not to get turned around and end up in the exact situation we're trying to avoid. Better to just get through as fast as we can."

"S-Some of—" Evangeline started, then trailed off.

"What's that?" I asked, turning quickly to her.

Something about my question, my demeanor, or my face seemed to be the opposite of what she was hoping for because she went pale and hid her face in Nat's shoulder again, which drew glares from Nat, Nero, and Dave in the back seat.

"It's okay. He's one of the mostly good guys," Nat reassured the younger girl. "What were you trying to say?"

After a long moment where the silence hung heavily in the car, her voice reemerged, barely above a whisper.

"Some of those people are police. I-I saw their uniforms when they came in."

Her news hit everyone in the car, drawing a series of curses, expletives, and assorted statements of frustration.

Only Nero remained quiet, simply shrugging and nodding. "It makes sense," he said. "They wouldn't be able to stay under The Man's radar without someone working some juju on the inside for 'em. Hard enough for them to dodge the spooky sorta attention. Only the fact they grabbed the wrong person made anyone on that side take any sort of notice. People disappearing in New Orleans isn't exactly new. Having cops help it along? God knows how long this was going on or how long it would have kept going."

I sat in silence, considering Nero's words, then nodded. "They don't exactly seem like this is a new thing for them. They've got organization, facilities, and a lot of manpower. Cults like that don't just spring up overnight. Evangeline, do you know why they wanted you and the other runaways?"

The girl shook her head.

"N-n-no. They only s-s-said they had...plans for me. The other people they brought in they—"

She trailed off, unable or unwilling to say what happened to the rest. Not that she needed to. Everyone in the car knew the score on that front.

Nat reached up, pulling the girl's head back down onto her shoulder and stroking her hair while I leaned forward and started looking closely at the map provided by the GPS.

The options weren't great. There was a maze of residential streets that any left-hand turn would take us down, which would then dump us onto route 428, a sort of highway interspersed with traffic lights, supermarkets, and other commercial buildings. Ending up there provided far too many easy opportunities for the pursuit to catch us. It was also the only option that would take us back to the Crescent City Connection and across the Mississippi.

Relaying the information to Ava, I got a terse nod in reply, then she cut the wheel hard to the left. Tires squealed as the Land Rover made the hard turn, tilting dangerously as it did. We tore down the side street, Ava's eyes locked on the road ahead while mine scanned behind us and to the left for headlights and found far too many for comfort.

"They're cutting down the other side streets," I warned.

"I know. I told you they would, remember?" she replied.

"Still a bunch behind us," I added.

"I know that too," Ava said.

"The lights—"

"Are gonna fuck us. I know."

I fell silent, frantically searching my brain for anything that I could do, then sat bolt upright in the seat. It was a long shot, but it was something.

"Does anyone have a marker?" I called back.

Four pairs of eyes stared at me in confusion.

"A marker. Something that'll show up if I draw on the side of the car!"

"Lipstick?" Nat asked

I nodded frantically, and she reached into her cleavage and produced a tube of lipstick, and received a frown of disapproval from me.

"What? Every girl uses our boobs for storage, Bishop. Grow up. You had me keep the penny in there."

"She's not wrong," Ava added with a smirk.

I looked to Dave and Nero for support, but neither seemed ready to engage, so I gave it up for a lost cause and rolled down the passenger window.

"Dave, I need a brace," I announced before leaning out.

Dave scooted up from the far back, and I felt his massive hand grab my leg as my waist hit the door's ledge. The wind whipped savagely at my face and hair, stinging my eyes to the point of uselessness. Sure. Why make things easy?

Closing my eyes, I got to work, drawing ancient sigils of power and concealment on the outside of the car, trying to keep the lines true as the Land Rover's suspension continued its deathmatch against the lackadaisically paved roads of Algiers. Trees whipped by. Parked cars passed far too close to my head for comfort, and I was drawing this thing blind and upside down.

What could possibly go wrong?

I felt the lipstick circle nearing completion, took a deep breath, then bit the shit out of the skin next to my thumbnail, drawing a small trickle of blood and a gasp of pain from me. I smeared it into the empty spot, then traced over with the lipstick to complete the mystic circuit.

One down.

"We're gonna need to shift," I announced, and then the great game of in-car Twister began. Nat slithered over the center seats and into the back, with Evangeline catching on and following suit a moment later. Dave slid over to where the two girls had been moments before, and I slid between the two front seats and took Dave's spot.

Rolling down the window, I looked to Dave, who smiled and nodded at me.

"I got you," he said.

Out I went for round two.

The moment my body was clear of the car, I heard a crack and felt something rush by my head a split second later. Our pursuers had gotten close enough that they were shooting.

"Fucking *perfect*!" I shouted over the wind as I got to work, drawing the next of the necessary symbols on the side of the car. Another series of cracks, this time resulting in a large graze in the car's paint, right where my hand had been braced moments before.

"When we get out of this, I'm gonna take away that gun, and I'm gonna stuff it into a *really* uncomfortable place, you little bastard," I muttered under my breath. After either a short eternity or the longest three minutes of my life, I smeared more blood and pulled myself inside. "Two down," I announced, then shifted and switched spots with Dave, hanging out another window and repeating the process. The crack of gunshots was becoming more and more frequent, and as I shifted back into the front seat, the rear window exploded in a shower of glass as one of the cultists' volleys nearly found their mark.

Nero and Nat flattened in the back, pulling a now screaming Evangeline down with them. Ava bit off a curse then swerved as another volley of bullets screamed past the SUV.

"I know you need to get my door, Bishop, but I can't shift, and you can't climb out there like this. Whatever you had up your sleeve is gonna have to stay there! We've got a traffic light in about 90 seconds!"

Traffic light? Fuuuuuuuck.

"Okay. Hit the cruise control, roll down the window, and shove the seat all the way back," I barked, leaning over her and starting the process at the same time Ava did as I asked. I leaned out, closing my eyes and hanging upside down, frantically scrawling the sigils. As I rounded the first curve, I started to slip out of the car, my eyes going wide and my hands scrabbling for purchase, only to feel Ava's hand grab my thigh, pinning it to the door.

And holding me in. How I managed to hang on to the lipstick, I had no idea.

"Sixty seconds!" Ava's voice called from inside.

Focus, Bishop. Follow the pattern. Block out everything else.

"Forty-Five!"

Okay, maybe not go totally zen.

The sigil was nearing completion. It wasn't nearly as neat as the others, but it was what I could manage under the circumstances.

"Thirty seconds Bishop, move your ass!"

Focus, Bishop.

The last round. Inscribe the runes. Power it with blood. Close the circle.

Say the words.

Done.

I jerked myself back into the SUV, shouting, "Got it!" as I did.

Ava's feet could no longer reach the pedals, but she reached between her legs to adjust the seat, then Dave shoved from the back, propelling her forward and bringing her foot back into contact with the brake. She slammed down hard, serenading everyone around us with the sound of squealing tires as we laid down a track to the beginning of the intersection.

Then we stopped with our nose just shy of the onrushing traffic on the highway in front of us.

Chapter Seventeen

The car was dead silent, the engine's light purr the only sound any of us could hear as we all held our breath at the same time. Nero was the first to exhale loudly, then call from the back.

"They're gonna be on us before this traffic lets us through! We gotta get out!"

"No!" I shouted, holding out a hand behind me. "No. Stay in the car. Quiet. We've got a—camouflage. Sorta."

"Camouflage?" Dave asked.

"Sorta," Ava added, latching onto the more pertinent word.

I nodded.

"Sorta. The sigils will make us easy to overlook. Uninteresting."

A pickup truck pulled up just behind us, its bed filled with men holding rifles. Their eyes moved to the SUV, then slid off, looking further down the road, straight ahead, and both to the right and left. Nero smiled broadly.

"OhthankyoubabyJesus. I thought we were dead," he whispered.

"Don't thank him just yet," I muttered.

"Easy to overlook? Uninteresting? In a car? In New Orleans? We're gonna die, Bishop. You didn't really think this through," Ava replied.

"It was all I had."

"I know," she replied with a sigh, leaning forward. "But between the other drivers not realizing we exist, and the cultists, we're not in for an easy commute."

"I-I'm sorry," Evangeline whispered from the back. "This is my fault. If it wasn't for me, none of you would be involved in this. I just—I didn't mean for anything like this to happen."

"Pssh," Ava hissed. "I got shot tonight before I ever set eyes on you, kiddo."

"She did. By a priest," I added. "If it makes things better, I think he might have been aiming for me."

"Not a chance, egomaniac. I was clearly the primary target." Ava replied.

"Just a narcissistic martyr. Don't you pay one bit of attention to the crazy woman? He was gunning for me." I retorted.

"I...what?" Evangeline asked, confused.

"You get used to it after a while, sweetie," Nat reassured her. "Bishop and Ava think they're really clever."

"And they love the sound of their own voices," Nero added.

"Almost as much as they like to hear the sound of the other one's voice," Dave added with a smile.

"Hey!" I objected.

Ava contributed by turning back and glaring at Dave in particular until the glow from the light turned from red to green. She inched the car forward, now mindful of the other traffic, which, just as predicted, showed complete indifference to whether they were going to crash into us or not. We just weren't interesting enough not to crash into, you see.

Ava played her game of cat and mouse with the other traffic, yanking the wheel to the side or slamming the brakes at the last minute to avoid an incalculable number of collisions, and while she did, a clear pattern began to emerge.

"That's the fifth patrol car out with its floodlight on in the last ten minutes," Nero announced.

He was correct. Whatever contacts the traffickers had in NOPD, they'd called them in.

"No way to tell if these guys are part of the group, or if those guys just called in some sort of BOLO on this car."

"Why does that matter?" Evangeline asked.

"Because if it's just cops doing their jobs, Bishop will be less likely to take 'em on directly," Nat replied. "He has a thing against getting normies involved in our squabbles. Some sort of paternalism or something."

"Pragmatism," I corrected her.

"Why is that pragmatic?" Evangeline asked, frowning.

"Because there are around seven billion people in this world, and the vast majority of them have no idea The Gloaming exists. They walk in the daylight, and the sort of darkness that we live in never touches their lives. When something they don't understand *does* attract their attention, they have one reaction: they destroy it.

"There's a reason the leadership of the supernatural creatures agreed to Council of Trent: The Inquisition worked, after a fashion. It killed a lot of innocent people. Far more than it found actual witches, vampires, or werewolves, but it still found some, and it killed them. In Salem, during their witch trial hysteria, they caught and killed an actual willworker. Now, pause to think about how people would react today if they found out about nightmare creatures living among them and preying on them. With the access to weapons and technology that people have. With the level of paranoia about anything "other." Really think about it for a minute. Blood would run in the streets. The loss of life would be horrific. Cities would become abattoirs, and not with just the blood of the supernaturals. Humanity's batting average on actually killing its target during these orgies is pretty piss poor. Something like a thousand regular people for one supernatural person or creature they manage to kill. So, yeah. Bishop avoids involving regular people in what we do so we can all stay safer," I growled.

I also avoided dealing with cops with anything other than kid gloves because they complicated the shit out of your life the second things got rough. All the clout in the world, all the influence you can bring to bear, none of it means shit if a beat cop spots you and puts a three-shot spread into your chest because they want you for hurting or killing one of their fellow boys in blue. In situations like that, cops shoot first and ask questions later, and I'd prefer to stay out of their crosshairs.

But there's no real need to go into that for the rest of them. One bout of awful news at a time is plenty.

I'd trailed off just as the latest of the patrol cars rolled by, its light shining directly into the windows of the SUV as Ava deftly avoided the latest near-miss with a soft curse.

"Jason?" she said.

Uh oh. First name meant things were serious.

"I'm not sure we're gonna make it this way. With the way the patrols are rolling, the next logical step is a checkpoint or roadblock," she said, whispering to me.

"Do you think they've got the pull for that?"

She shrugged. "It's not just that. The spell was brilliant. Saved our lives, probably, but it's gonna get us trapped in a fender bender at this rate. We're like fish in a barrel out here."

I nodded. "I can remove it."

She shook her head.

"We'd be made in less than five minutes. Then we're in an even worse spot than before. They're in front and behind us now, and they've brought in the police."

"How much do you want to bet we're currently wanted for kidnapping Evangeline Grey?" I asked her.

Ava shook her head. "Sucker bet."

We drove in silence for a moment while we thought things through.

"Guys?" Nat called from behind us. "If we need to go someplace and need someone not to find us, why not be invisible in a way that won't get us killed?"

"I can't do that, Nat. There are limits to what I can—"

"Yeah, yeah, we know, Bishop. I'm talking about something simpler. Let's call an Airport Shuttle out to Louie Armstrong, then hop a cab back to the Quarter? Shuttles are everywhere, and no one pays a bit of attention to them."

"They're invisible," Dave agreed.

"That's genius, baby girl," Nero added.

I nodded in agreement. "You may have just saved our lives, Nat."

"Somebody had to," she replied with a smile. "Now, if one of you who wasn't held hostage by murdery cultists could loan me a cell phone, I'll make it happen."

Ava pulled into the parking lot of a church just off of the highway, killing the engine and leaning back in the driver's seat with a loud sigh.

Turning toward the back, I watched Nat work on Nero's phone, the soft glow of the screen casting light up onto the young woman's face, then looked over at Dave as he watched her as well, noting the tenderness and the note of awe at what she was doing. She noticed him watching and gave him a gentle smile in return.

I smiled. Not my business, but I wished them nothing but the best.

A gentle shove from Ava reminded me how little of my business it was.

"Let them be," she mouthed. All I could do was shrug and smile in reply.

"Okay, we're golden. A shuttle is on the way, and Ubers and cabs are always lined up by the dozen at the airport. We just have to sit for the next hour or so, then we should be on our way," Nat announced, her face beaming.

"We might just pull this off yet," Nero remarked.

My eyes stayed on the darkened streets outside and the patrol cars that still cruised along them like hungry sharks searching for their next meal. Two more passed by in the next fifteen minutes, both illuminating us with their spotlights. Neither so much as pausing as they continued on their courses.

It looked like we were in the clear, so why did the feeling in the pit of my stomach keep telling me that I was missing something? That things were way worse than I was giving them credit for?

The intervening hour passed by in tense anticipation as we waited for the airport shuttle's arrival.

Fifteen minutes was spent scrounging together something that would preserve Dave's modesty. Thankfully, Vic was the 'be prepared' Boy Scout type, so we found a blanket that could wrap around Dave's waist to serve as a kilt. Mostly.

For the balance of the time, we waited, often in silence. Five more police cruisers rolled by, as did four different truckloads of cultists and one highly suspicious-looking Chevy Suburban with its windows blacked out.

But none stopped. None noticed us. The sigils held. I'd have lost a lot of money betting against that outcome.

When it seemed inevitable that one of us would crack, the blue Airport Shuttle van pulled into the church parking lot without any obvious complications. Nat slid out of the Land Rover and talked briefly with the driver, then waved everyone else over. Heart in my throat, I watched as our little group entered the van one at a time, with me bringing up the rear.

I held my breath as I exited the sanctuary offered by Victor's car and felt a pang of guilt at leaving it in this condition across the river from its owner. A very brief pang of guilt.

Okay, I felt like I should feel guilty about it, and that's nearly the same thing, right? It's the thought that counts, but in the moment, the emotion I could register wasn't guilt. It was relief: we might just live through this after all.

Sitting in the far back of the shuttle, I closed my eyes and leaned my head against the window, listening to the noise of the city as we traversed Algiers, then crossed the Crescent City Connector over the Mississippi. The cool glass against my sweat-covered skin was soothing, helping bring me down from the constant state of near-panic, anxiety, and general adrenaline-induced fervor I'd operated under for the past several hours. And as that invulnerability faded, the aches and pains started to make their presence known. My neck and throat were raw and angry, vividly recalling their run-in with the undead monster that had tried to choke me to death. My back more than ached, making comfort next to impossible. I could feel at least two places that were sore to the touch. It's possible that being tossed like a ragdoll left me with a collection of cracked ribs. My right hip and arm both hurt from where I'd fallen on them after being thrown into the shelving units, and I still felt light-headed.

Because, why not?

After far too short a time, I opened my eyes, taking in my surroundings and trying to regain my sense of equilibrium. Our driver was doing a credible job of ignoring us, a talent that locals had perfected when it came to the tourists that regularly descended on the Big Easy. I don't know what Nat had told him, but whatever it was, it worked.

For her part, Nat was sitting quietly next to Evangeline, comforting the younger girl. I guess as the person closest to her own age, Ivé's daughter had gravitated to the charismatic Filipino girl, who was mother-henning the hell out of her. Nat was proving to anyone who doubted her that she wasn't a lost kid and was more than capable of pulling her weight.

Evangeline clung to her like a shipwreck survivor clings to driftwood. Nero had his eyes closed. At first glance, you might think he was sleeping, but as I looked closer and concentrated, examining the aura surrounding him, I could see that wasn't the case. Nero was using his gift and was projecting out into the wide world, looking for information or just hoping to give us a warning if something awful was on the way. He was doing what he could, in his own, quiet way, to make sure everyone was as safe as he could make them.

Because that's what he does.

Looking to Dave, my friend's eyes were downcast. His hands were balled up in his lap, and he sat with his shoulders hunched. I didn't know if he was anguished over the lives he'd taken tonight or that he'd come so close to adding me to that count.

My heart ached for him. I wanted to tell him it was okay. I was okay. We were okay. But he obviously wasn't, and there was no way for me to get him to okay. It was a trip he'd need to make on his own. This wasn't about me.

Ava sat next to me. I could feel the warmth of her thigh against mine. She was looking down at her bare feet with mild frustration. I followed her gaze and nodded: her pedicure had been ruined. Looking back up, I tried to suppress a smile and mostly succeeded, which means I partially failed.

Ava did not fail to notice my expression.

"Why are you grinning at me like some sort of jackass?" she asked, her brow wrinkled and a half-formed smile on her lips.

"No reason. Just been a long day."

"It's not over yet, Bishop," she reminded me.

I nodded, sighing. "Yeah. And so far, the hits have just kept coming," I commented, my eyes shifting to the bandage on her shoulder.

"Hey," she said, her hand cupping my chin and moving my face up to re-establish eye contact. "I'm here because I want to be. Because it's where I belong. No regrets, Bishop. No matter what."

I smiled sadly. "No regrets," I agreed.

She gave me a nod, then sighed.

"Besides, not even we could end up in a situation so fucked up that we get killed returning the kid, right?"

I just stared at her.

"Did you just ask, 'what's the worst that could happen?' Did you honestly just say that?"

She smiled, shaking her head.

"Nope. It only counts if you say the actual words, so you did."

I groaned, staring at her in horror.

"We are so fucked," I muttered.

We offloaded at Louis Armstrong International Airport, instructing the shuttle to drop us off at the arrivals area as opposed to departures. Given the state of dress of some of our group, the lack of shoes, and Dave's lack of shirt or pants, it seemed like a wise approach to limit our exposure to regular people.

Some things will attract attention, even in a city as strange as New Orleans. We were a motley enough assortment that airport security kept a close eye on us, but seemed content to let us load into one of the Union Taxi minivans that idled at the curb. We got in, gave the driver our destination, and were off once again.

It was about half an hour from the airport to the Lower 9th, where Papa Ivé held sway, most of it on the interstate. Buildings whizzed by, and I started to gain confidence; this would finish without any further complications. That we'd be able to return the girl, stop the bloodshed before it got started, head off the Order and their extermination crusade, and save Mary from whatever consequences they had in mind for her all in one fell swoop. The van transitioned from the interstate and onto the neighborhood roads in the 9th, and I started to breathe even easier.

We were in Ivé's territory now. You'd have to be insane to come here while acting in opposition to him. His people were out on the streets, intermingled with regular people, just going about their business, only distinguishable because of the hoodoo bags around their necks or the symbols of power tattooed or branded into their bodies.

As my sense of calm increased, Evangeline's grip on her own was slowly degrading. Each time we passed one of Ivé's people, she looked away, one time going so far as to flinch.

"It'll be okay. Your dad's really worried about you," Nat reassured her, earning a sad smile from Evangeline.

"I'm just sorry I caused so much trouble," she said quietly.

I opened my mouth to reply when the cab came to a gentle stop in front of Papa Ivé's storefront. Shifting forward to settle up with the driver, everyone else exited the van. I followed suit, closing the door behind me, then turned and came face to face with a dozen of Ivé's people, arrayed on his lawn with their weapons drawn.

"Not exactly the welcome I'd expect you to give your boss's kid," I observed a bit more loudly than necessary.

The man in front of the group smirked. "Ain't no tricks gonna work this time, dawg. I'm ready for your ass."

I frowned, looking down at his bandaged hand, then up at the hatred in his eyes, directed specifically at me.

"Oh...hi, Floyd,"

"Fuck you, Bishop."

Nat shook her head. "You do have a way with people," she told me, then stepped toward Floyd with a smile on her lips.

"Look, your boss is gonna want to see us. Recognize her?" she asked, pointing to where Evangeline stood, obscured by Dave's massive chest.

Floyd's eyes went wide.

"Aw shit! I didn't...I thought... fuck! Let 'em through! Let 'em through, goddammit!"

"Pleasure doing business with you," I said through a smile.

Floyd's sullen look of hate-filled anger was all the thanks I needed as we walked by, entering through the front door.

The man himself stood in the center of the room, eyes wide and mouth agape as he stared at his daughter. Evangeline sobbed behind her hands, whispering, "I'm so sorry."

And then she was enveloped in his arms. He was no longer a fearsome voodoo witch doctor. Gone were the trappings of power, replaced by a father who was just happy to have his little girl back home.

I swallowed down the lump that formed in my throat and waited.

It had been clear in the street in front of Jackie and Victor's house that he hadn't ever expected to see her again. Not alive. This moment was important to him. It was stealing something back from a vicious and uncaring world. Pushing back the soul-crushing despair that even the strongest and most powerful among us could feel, and I'd be damned if I took that away from anyone.

Plus, he might turn me into a toad. So, there was that.

They both clung to one another, neither of their eyes dry. It was Ivé who finally took half a step back. "Have you eaten?" he asked, his voice thick.

Evangeline shook her head.

"We have etouffee in the pot on the stove. You should have a bowl. Get settled back in while I talk to these fine people who have returned you to me."

Evangeline smiled, sniffling, then moved to the back of the house and toward the kitchen, disappearing behind the beaded curtain.

"Where?" he asked.

I shook my head.

"Ivé, there's something strange about all of this," I objected.

"Who and where?"

The words didn't leave any doubt as to who was speaking. This was no longer the relieved father. This was once again Papa Ivé: Voodoo King of New Orleans. The direct physical and spiritual descendant of the great Marie Laveau and one of the most accomplished, powerful, and dangerous will workers in the world.

Nat and Nero took half a step back. Ava and Dave took half a step forward.

I remained rooted to the spot.

"I'm not doing this, Ivé," I told him. "We just went through hell to bring her back to you, and we're not going to indiscriminately rain hell down on these people. There were too many questions about that place. About what they were doing. Questions that need answering. We won't get any sort of answers if you reduce them all to ash with a thought. I asked you for time to find your daughter. I'm asking for the same thing now: give me time. This isn't over."

Ivé glared at me, his eyes wide and nostrils flaring in barely contained rage. I could feel Ava and Dave at my back, one on each shoulder, each as tense as a drawn bowstring. Finally, Ivé gave the slightest of nods, defusing the potentially explosive situation.

"You brought her back to me, charlatan. Whatever I think of your methods, whatever I think of your skills, you did what no one else could. I am in your debt for that, and so I will give you what you ask."

I nodded.

"Can we sit?"

The request took Ivé off guard, his eyes narrowing, but he nodded.

"Come back to the parlor," he instructed, turning and walking through the curtain.

"...said the spider to the fly," Nat whispered, which earned an elbow to her ribs from Nero, who went wide-eyed at the statement.

Taking a breath, I followed Ivé back to his parlor, finding it exactly as I left it. Its eerie lighting gave it an otherworldly feel, highlighting the skull-like appearance of Ivé's face, his pronounced cheekbones becoming even more so, and the dark recesses of his brow ridge swallowing his eyes.

"Now, what do we need to speak on?" Ivé asked, leaning back in his chair. "What is important enough that upon returning my daughter to me, you ask me not to be by her side?"

I swallowed, wincing at the pain. He was right; this wasn't a great time, but then again, when was?

"I'll try to be brief. The people who were holding Evangeline, they were skilled. They had logistics, a large membership, supplies, and facilities. They had a warding circle set up around her that was being actively manned at all times."

"How many in the circle?" he asked, his eyes flashing as he leaned forward.

"Thirteen," Nat answered. "But they're down two."

Ivé nodded. "Continue."

"They had supernatural help other than that. A pair of undead. I've never seen anything like them before. Big. Bigger than Dave. With filmy blue eyes. They smelled of rot but moved independently. Not like a zombie where the master has to control every little thing."

Ivé nodded.

"It sounds as if you encountered a revenant."

"I'm not familiar with those."

"Few are. Spirits of the dead, forcibly returned to a living body, bound to the will of their masters. They are intelligent, and can act independently, and require immense power to create. If you saw two of these, then there's someone supernatural behind it. A skilled someone. If you find them, you likely find the source of this organization."

He paused, then continued. "The warding circle was a witch's coven. They can have any number of members, but only thirteen can ever take part in a single spell. They're how the loa were fooled into thinking my Evangeline was dead."

I nodded. Recalling the face of the smaller man who had been flanked by them. It all lined up, but something was still itching at the back of my head.

"Dead, not lost?"

Ivé shook his head.

"They were quite certain, but witches can twist even the loa's perceptions. Acting in concert, their arts can turn aside even someone of my talents, it seems."

"So, it seems."

I looked to the rest of the group.

"Does anyone else have anything for Ivé?"

Blank looks and shakes of the head were all I got in response, so I turned to the man and nodded, coming to my feet with a grimace.

"Bishop, Ms. Dufrense, Mr. LeBlanc, Ms. Jenkins, Mr. Frye: you have all done me a great service today, and not one I am likely to forget any time soon. You have my thanks, and I am in your debt. If there is anything me or mine can do for you that is within my power, it will be done."

He solemnly took each of our hands in turn, making eye contact and shaking.

"Now, please, allow me to spend time with my daughter. We have been apart for too long."

Ivé's debt apparently involved arranging cars to take us all home.

Each of us said our goodbyes, and plans were made to gather at Bishop's Crossing the next day. Hugs were exchanged, and Nero got in touch with his boyfriend Aaron to let him know he was coming home. I watched each of them drive off with a mixture of gratitude, pride, and sadness. Having them back around me again was like stepping back into a warm bath after being out in the cold. It was comforting, and I craved more.

As I stood there with Dave by my side, waiting for our turn, I felt the same dull ache in my chest. Ever since I cut everyone off, I'd been lonely. Dave was great. He'd helped a lot. Staved off the worst of it, but there were times when the Crossing was hopping, filled to the brim with people, and I still felt more isolated and alone than I can possibly describe.

Some people just fill in the empty parts of you. They spackle over your cracks and hide the fact that you're shattered, if only for a moment. That's what these people were to me. I don't know if that's what normal people would call 'family,' but it's the closest word I can find for it in any language I'm familiar with.

As the car pulled up next to Dave and me, I smiled at him.

"Let's go home."

Chapter
Nineteen

I once again fought my way out of a deep sleep, clawing my way toward the surface, toward consciousness. I was once again vaguely aware that my mouth felt and tasted like the bathroom floor of a dive bar. I swallowed and instantly regretted it, pain lancing through my throat.

Gotcha. Different day.

Cracking my right eye open, the bright light poured in from my bedroom window and sent an unpleasant electric jolt straight into my brain, eliciting a groan. Consciousness had brought with it a stark reminder of the punishment I'd endured the last twenty-four hours.

I looked down at myself and shook my head. I'd fallen asleep in my clothes, bloodstains and all. Definitely gonna need to change the sheets after this one. I crawled out of bed and stumbled to the bathroom, moving on autopilot through my regular morning routine.

On my way, I noticed a piece of paper on the nightstand with my name on it in Jackie's familiar scrawl. *We stayed a bit, but Chase knows where you live so we're heading to a hotel. Stay safe.*

Half an hour later, I had showered, changed, forced some water down my ravaged throat, and brushed my teeth. I pulled on a white button-up shirt, some blue jeans, and my black combat boots, then stomped my way downstairs to the bar.

Dave was already there, also looking much improved from the previous night. And clothed. He was sitting at a table with Ava and Nero, a plate of beignets between them. Glancing at my watch, I noted that it wasn't even noon yet. Impressive for a crowd without a morning person in the lot.

I slumped into a chair, and moments later, a cup of mystery liquid was placed in front of me. I smelled it and fought back a gag. I glanced up and saw Nat's smiling face as she slid around and took the remaining chair.

"Dave's family recipe. We were wondering when you'd rise from the dead," Nat commented.

"I was ready to try a seance," Nero added.

Ava rolled her eyes, taking a bite of the pastry in front of her, then sipping at her cup. "Not all of us. Some people can contain their excitement."

"Excitement over what?" I croaked in reply. "Job's done. Don't get me wrong, I'm grateful as hell and more than willing to hang out, but we finished things up."

"Boss," Dave started, shaking his head and just looking at me.

"We heard your questions for Ivé last night, Bishop," Nero added.

"And I saw the way you were acting ever since we grabbed the girl. I know that look. Something's bugging you. You know something, so what is it?" Nat demanded.

I looked around at each of them, finally settling on Ava, who shrugged.

"You think something's off about this whole thing. We're just waiting for you to decide to admit it so we can get to work. The rest of us figured this was more efficient than waiting for you to blunder your way into it."

I stared at her, then nodded.

"Well, it doesn't add up. First: Nero's vision and the loa both saw Evangeline dead, not lost. Not taken. Dead. It was only afterward that Nero saw the coven's spell."

"Ivé said a strong enough coven could warp perceptions," Nero said slowly.

"Did it feel like magical interference to you? You've done this for long enough that you know what it feels like, and you never said a word about it. The loa wouldn't. That's not how they operate. But you? You might know. Might recognize it. Did you?"

Nero sat silently for a moment, then shook his head. "Sugar, I wish it did. But not a bit. That girl felt dead to me."

I nodded.

"Second, it was too easy to get her out. There were no guards that were any place that made any sense. We got into the building like it was open to the public, then got out again without nearly as much trouble as we should have. With all of the guns, we saw going by in those trucks, with all of the people that were involved, including cops? That place should have been buttoned up like a bank vault. Instead, it was more lightly guarded than your average flea market. No way should there just have been a lock guarding the gate, for starters."

Nat nodded. "They didn't seem to care if anyone got in. I just assumed they thought no one knew where they were."

I shrugged, shaking my head, and took a sip of my tea, wincing as I swallowed.

"Maybe. But the entire time I was in there, I had a headache that made it hard to concentrate. Felt dizzy. Like something was trying to mess with my head. We know one of them was a willworker and that they had at least one active coven of witches. So, what didn't we see? What else was going on? If they sacrificed every one of those street kids they grabbed, that means they've either got some sort of massive store of energy saved up or—-"

"Or they've used it," interrupted Ava.

I nodded. "Or they've used it," I agreed. "If they used it, what did they use it for?"

Everyone at the table looked at one another. None of us had an answer.

"Right. Getting Evangeline back to Ivé stopped the immediate crisis: The vampires and his people aren't going to war. Ivé won't push after them, and Conrad's people aren't quite to the point they're willing to be first in line to confront the wizard. That should mean the Order won't step in and do something draconian, but—"

I trailed off, shaking my head.

"But," Dave agreed.

"I can put the word out to the community in the city. Find out if anyone knows, suspects, or has felt anything," Nat offered.

"I'll ask some of my people, too," Ava chimed in.

Nero took a breath and nodded. "I'll start looking around with my gift. I uncovered where she was; maybe I can find out something more about the people associated with her."

"I'll stop down to the permitting office and see if I can find out anything about the property that we were at last night. Might lead to something. Probably not," Dave offered.

"And I'll break out my tool chest to see what sort of ritualistic trouble I can get into," I added. "Between the lot of us, we might just be able to find the other shoe before it drops."

"Do you think that's gonna happen?" Nat asked.

"Not if we do our jobs. Otherwise? The other shoe always drops," Ava said with a shake of her head.

The day passed, the skies cleared into a bright blue with a few fluffy clouds high in the sky, and the five of us wandered in and out of the building. We split time between my apartment and the bar area, depending on people's mood and drawn by the allure of fresh air. My new phone arrived, so I put in a brief call to Jackie and Mary to touch base and promised to visit the next day, followed by a call to Raimond to update him on a job completed.

The rest of the day, we worked, ate, talked, and planned.

Eventually, the sky traded its robin's egg hue for a darker tone, and the flickering gaslights of the French Quarter sparked to life, pushing back against the darkness in their unique way. The crowds grew thicker as revelers resurfaced to take part in the true New Orleans pastime: drinking.

Our little group sat back and people-watched, forcibly putting troubles and worries out of our minds for the moment.

"I think I know that guy," Nat commented, squinting at a young African American man who was dancing at the far end of the bar. My bar has neither band nor background music.

"You know everyone, sweetie," Nero observed.

"The one dancing to no music?" I asked. "Of course you do."

Nat stuck her tongue out at me. "No, I know him. He's...Marcus! The guy Ivé's kid was so hot for. Strange that he'd come to your bar, Bishop."

"Yeah," Dave rumbled, coming slowly to his feet.

I put a hand on his forearm.

"It isn't a thing yet," I told him, bringing my focus to bear on the young man. "No reason to make it one."

"I think it's already a thing. We just don't know what *kind* of thing. Yet," Dave corrected.

The sea of bodies between Marcus and our group parted for the briefest of moments, allowing the young man to get a good look at us, and more importantly, for me to get a good look at him. What I saw was a potential problem.

"Marcus isn't exactly Marcus anymore," I said. "Marcus is a vampire. A baby one. By the look of the aura around him, not more than a couple of months."

"Hasn't Evangeline been seen with him in the last couple of months?" Ava asked, frowning.

Nat nodded slowly. "Yeah, she has."

"See? Now it's a thing," Dave growled.

"I hate it when it becomes a thing," Nero groaned.

"Fine. It's a thing," I admitted. "Let's go ask him some questions, preferably someplace a bit more private."

"You mean the street? 'Cause he's leaving," Nat announced.

Shit.

The five of us came to our feet in unison and followed him out.

Now, we've established previously that following someone in the French Quarter isn't the easiest thing in the world to do. That's part of why I created the tracking spell we used with Nat. Tracking a vampire, who grew up in the area, through the French Quarter's crowded streets is like trying to find a venomous snake in a pile of hay. Not only is it a pain in the ass and next to impossible, but if you do it badly, you could also very well end up dead. Even baby vampires are dangerous as hell.

Marcus expertly wove his way through the tourists, making the wise decision to make the turn and beeline straight for Bourbon Street, clearly counting on the crowds to brush us off. He didn't account for the fact that we'd done this and done it as a team. We fanned out, two on each side of the sidewalk, and one in the street behind him, keeping one another in sight at all times.

Some of Marcus's technique was good. He didn't look over his shoulder to indicate that he knew he was being followed, but his body language and pace screamed that he was a man (vampire) looking to avoid someone behind him. Sloppy. I almost felt offended.

He nearly made his break clean as he briefly lost himself in a walking tour crossing Bourbon, but Nat kept her eye on the prize and re-oriented us. He made a play as if he would turn right onto Orleans Street, but swerved back onto Bourbon, then ducked into the jazz pub on the other side of the street.

Once inside, Dave and Nero stayed by the two front doors while Ava, Nat, and I moved into the bar. Walking through while the band was playing felt like we were swimming upstream against the constant torrent of sound. It was practically a physical presence. I started to worry that he'd somehow given us the slip after all and started frantically scanning the crowd until I felt Nat tug on my arm. She was pointing to the corner, where he was talking to a girl.

We moved toward the pair just in time to see the girl turn and spot us.

She looked just like Evangeline Grey.

But not quite. This wasn't the girl we'd saved yesterday. There was something different. Something off.

From the stage, the band finished their set, and the lack of sonic assault caused me to stagger for a moment. The girl smiled.

I looked at her closely, taking in her complexion, her eyes, the way she stood, how she moved, her smile, then my eyes widened.

"Oh God," I whispered, my heart dropping into the pit of my stomach. "She's a vampire."

Chapter Twenty

Ava and Nat both stared in shock, as unprepared to see Evangeline here as I was. "This is bad," Ava said, showing a talent for understatement.

"Maybe not?" offered Nat.

I swallowed, wincing slightly. I hurried over the leaned forward, telling the pair, "The two of you need to come with us. Right now."

They looked at each other, then me, and nodded.

It was a silent walk to the front of the bar. The pair of freshly-minted vampires kept shooting furtive glances at us, then at each other, but the only sounds we made were footfalls on floorboards. As we reached the front, Dave looked shocked at Evangeline's presence, and Nero's eyes went almost comically wide, but seeing the expression on our faces, both held their questions.

We marched en masse back to Bishop's Crossing, the cadence of feet upon asphalt replacing the bar's floorboards. Upon reaching Bishop's Crossing, I headed straight upstairs, waving off the wards and showing the pair of bloodsuckers in ahead of me. They sat next to each other on the couch, their knees touching and looking for all the world like a couple of overly pale young people in over their heads.

Everyone else settled around them, their faces wearing expressions of varying severity.

I gathered my wits, then looked at Marcus.

"You came here for me to find you, didn't you?"

He swallowed, then looked down, then nodded. Evangeline sat, still, hands folded in her lap, and her eyes downcast.

"Yeah. I didn't want to just walk in with Evie. I didn't know how you'd react."

I nodded.

"Why did you think we'd react badly? You heard about what happened yesterday?" Ava asked.

He nodded again.

"Yeah, the whole city's been buzzing about it. I've had Evie hiding at my place this whole time. No one knows that we ran away together."

"Together?" Nero asked.

He nodded, then nudged the girl next to him.

"Tell 'em, babe."

Evangeline...Evie...swallowed then took a deep and completely unnecessary breath.

"My dad isn't the most...open person in the world. He's old. Way older than he looks, and a lot of his ideas aren't from this century. He's real old fashioned, and he wanted more for me than I wanted. I've known Marcus here for years. I...we...I love him."

She paused, reaching over to take both of his hands in hers and gaze into his eyes.

I groaned inwardly but managed to keep a poker face. Seventeen-year-old love drove kids to do some really stupid shit, and it seemed that Ivé's daughter was no exception. She'd decided that her and Marcus's love was forever, so when he got turned, she decided to join him.

"That's...great, sweetie," Nat said, a rictus smile plastered on her face. "But won't your dad be sorta mad? He's not like regular dads; his 'mad' can end with tidal waves and plagues of locusts."

Evie's face fell.

"Yeah. I told him that I loved Marcus, that we were going to be together. That's when he sent him away. Banished him from the Ninth. Said that some street kid wasn't good enough for me. He told all of the guards he sent with me when I went dancing that if Marcus came anywhere near me, they should shoot him."

Marcus nodded.

"I'm not good enough for her, but I love Evie, and Evie loves me, so I swore that I'd find a way to make it work. Before I left, I slipped her a burner phone, so we could keep in touch; then, I tracked down some of the vampire nests we used to monitor. I found a guy coming out and took him down, just like Papa taught me."

"Jesus," Nero groaned. "You pissed off Papa Ivé and Conrad? Forget about forever, honey. You're gonna be lucky to live out the month."

"I'm not scared of them," Marcus objected.

"Then you're stupid," I added. "Both of them terrify me. They terrify everyone in this room, and they should terrify you. They're dangerous as hell, especially when crossed, and you crossed the shit out of both of them."

"I didn't kill the vampire! I just kept him locked up till he agreed to my terms. He was gonna make me a vampire and then teach me enough to survive. Once I was good, I let him go."

"And the first thing he did was tell Conrad what you did," Ava told him flatly, shaking her head.

He shrugged.

"Conrad hasn't done shit. Went to ground once he tried to kill Bishop and failed."

"You know about that too, huh?" I asked, grimacing slightly.

"Everyone knows about that. It's one of the big stories floating around right now: how you came out of retirement, and the first thing you did was walk into his office, into something you knew was a trap, then walked out with Ava on your arm."

"Excuse me?" Ava interjected, her left eyebrow arching dangerously.

Marcus shrugged; Evie seemed clueless. Everyone else in the room avoided eye contact, finding something engrossing on either the floor or ceiling.

"That's what the story is."

"I drag his ass three-quarters dead out of an elevator, haul him to the hospital, and I get to be the arm candy. Of all the—" she sputtered, then took a breath, shook her head. "Please, continue."

Marcus looked dubious but began once again.

"Well, once I had what I needed, I called the special burner. Told Evie it was time. That we could be together."

Evangeline came to life. Well. She became more animated. She was still very much undead.

"He did - It was so romantic! I waited until everyone was sleeping, then I snuck out. Marcus was waiting for me, and we ran away through the night, hand in hand."

Nat and Ava exchanged a look that expressed a level of disgust I can only aspire to. Nero's eyes rolled so hard I was afraid he was having a stroke. Dave looked like he was going to swallow Marcus whole.

"You nearly burned the city down over this," the big man rumbled.

"We never wanted to hurt anyone; we just wanted to be together. Needed to be together!" Marcus objected.

I pinched the bridge of my nose, trying to think.

"Okay, so you're not the one we rescued last night, which means whoever it was, they've been with your dad, inside of his defenses for over twenty-four hours. I don't know who or what she is, but we have to assume she has something that can subdue him," I said.

"The sacrifices," Ava said. "They probably used them to transform someone into Evangeline's likeness."

"But the disappearances have been going on for months," objected Nat. "That would mean—oh, God."

"That they've been planning this for a really long time," Dave finished.

"And they know exactly what they're doing. Sugar?" Nero said, looking to Marcus. "This isn't gonna feel great, and I'm really sorry, but we're short on time, and we need answers. Now."

"Wha—GAH!" Marcus replied.

His question was interrupted by Nero reaching out and laying a hand on Marcus's temple, then establishing a psychic connection. Nero's eyes closed. Marcus's eyes rolled up into his head like a slot machine.

"What are you doing to him?" Evie demanded, half coming to her feet.

I held up a hand. "Getting answers. Your boy-thing will be fine. Nero's a pro."

This was an aspect of Nero's gift that he rarely used. It was intrusive. It was draining. It was scary as hell for the person on the receiving end. Nero's mind was simply too strong to resist, and it forced its way into memories. At this point, he would be moving through Marcus's mind like he was reading a newspaper, scanning what he wanted, and examining what he needed.

Blood started trickling from Nero's ears and nose, but still, he persisted.

"He wasn't exactly tampered with," he said, his voice low and thick with strain. "But the short guy from the warehouse has met with him a few times. He pushed him to run away with the woman he loved. Pulled the strings from behind the scenes."

Nero's eyes flickered open, and he sagged. Thankfully, Dave was there to catch him. Nero looked up gratefully, nodding.

Marcus reeled back against the couch with Evie fretting over him.

"I'm getting sick of this mystery, man," I growled.

"You and me both," agreed Nat.

Evangeline held Marcus close to her and glared at Nero before turning to the rest of us. "Look," she spat. "We came to you because we know you can get things done, and you don't work for anyone. You're your own people. That's all we want! We want the chance to live our lives without someone else telling us we're wrong! We may seem like kids to you, but we're not stupid. We know the risks! We know what's at stake! What we've done! I just...I can't let me following my heart be something that hurts my dad! Please. You've got to help him!"

Fuck.

I looked around the room at the expressions on my friends' faces. Each of them watching me. Waiting to see what I would say. What I, no, what *we* would do.

Finally, I looked to Ava, who's brown eyes locked onto mine. They narrowed, ever so slightly, then she gave the slightest of nods.

Yeah. That's sorta what I figured too.

I sighed, then slowly nodded.

"Yeah. I think we do."

Chapter
Twenty-One

Potentially going up against Papa Ivé, the people who had arranged the body double, and whatever the hell else was going to be standing in the way was incredibly risky. Ava, Dave, Nero, and Nat were ready to ride or die with me. Marcus and Evie both expressed their willingness to help with the cause.

All of that was great, but I was damned well going to go in better prepared for a fight than I had been previously. That meant cracking open the arsenal in the back room.

I entered with one of my black backpacks slung over my shoulder and immediately started loading it with the essentials: blessed crucifix, bells, mirror, salt, holy water, pry bar, pepper, wolfsbane, lighter fluid, Zippo lighter, multitool, blessed knuckle-dusters created with silver and cold iron. To cover all the bases.

I grabbed one of my banana kukri knives, the wards I'd placed on it years ago glinting maliciously in the light. Sheathing it, I tucked it into the small of my back, then pulled down the peacoat with the protective rites woven into the fabric. It wouldn't stop a bullet, but it might negate enough impact to keep me alive. Looking around, I grabbed the remaining Midnight Soil I'd made at the warehouse. You never know. And, last but not least, a .38 revolver, which I put into my peacoat's pocket.

Magic is great and all, but sometimes the straightforward ways work best.

The team followed behind, each moving toward items they knew well from previous nights on the front lines.

Ava scooped up a handful of rings and began sliding them onto her fingers. They had a variety of uses: some stored kinetic energy, which boosted the impact of strikes, others offered a sort of protection from a variety of attacks, while still others would work in concert to enhance her natural speed. She loved those things. The day we pulled them out of a sunken riverboat was one of her favorites.

Dave moved over to his trusty oversized pry bar. It had runes etched into the metal that matched those on my blade. He slapped it into the palm of his hand three times, a smile coming back to his face, then pulled on a leather vest, whose surface seemed to writhe if you weren't looking at it directly. One of the few family heirlooms he took with him when he left.

Nero pulled a bandolier of holy water ampules, easily thrown and fragile enough to shatter on contact, along with a shotgun and extra shells, pulling on a duster to allow for some concealment. For all that he was an eccentric psychic, he had a practical side.

Nat found her baseball bat. Unlike normal ones, this one had a bunch of nails driven through the head, each made from different metals and infused with a variety of rites designed to allow it to affect nearly anything likely to appear in this dimension, and quite a few things that weren't. She added a small crystal necklace that glowed slightly the moment it made contact with her.

Marcus and Evie stood in the doorway, barred entry by the wards, their eyes wide and mouths agape as we all took turns checking each other over, just as we had dozens of times before.

It was time. We moved out of the bar and onto the street.

"But how are we going to get there?" Evie asked. "There's seven of us, and I don't see a car."

"I've got a car that'll work," Ava told her. "I put in a call. It's on the way."

"On the way?" Marcus asked.

Ava nodded, her eyes squinting as she looked down the street.

"Sweeties, Ava, here's what you call 'connected.' To be connected, you need to help people. Do favors. She generally doesn't need her big ol' SUV here in the Quarter, so she loans it out to friends. Deal is, if she calls, they come runnin'," Nero offered.

"And she called," Ava added, not looking away. "ETA's three minutes."

"So, what's the plan?" Marcus asked. The young vampire was filled with nervous energy, smelling the increased adrenaline in the blood of everyone around him.

"We go to Ivé's," I said simply.

"And?"

"And that's it. We don't know enough to make a plan beyond that. We need to know what these people are up to if we want to stop them. Till we know that we can't make a plan."

"You can't go up against something that could do this without more than a 'go get him'!" Marcus exclaimed.

"Boy," Dave rumbled. "We got this. You follow along and do what you're told, and you might just come out of this alive."

"Well, no more dead than you already are," Nat added, with an apologetic smile and shrug.

Marcus opened his mouth to retort when a large, pearl white Cadillac Escalade pulled up to the curb. The door swung open to reveal someone that had to be a male model. The guy was dressed to the nines in a tailored black suit with a deep red silk shirt (top button undone, naturally). He slithered out and sauntered over to Ava, a bemused expression on his face.

"This is what you stand me up for? Trick or treating?" he asked. He had a slight British accent because, of course, he did. Also looked like he was an inch or two taller than me.

"Not now, Ivan. I need my car. We need my car. It's going to be dangerous tonight. I'd get indoors and stay there."

He brushed Ava's cheek with his right index finger, his smirk unchanging.

"You know how I love danger, love. Bring me along. I'm sure you can find some—" He looked her up and down, then quirked an eyebrow. "use for me?" he finished with a wide smile.

I hated him on general principle and felt my fists clenching as I imagined how satisfying burning the smarmy grin off of his face would be. A little angel fire wouldn't be the worst thing in the world, would it?

"I don't have time right now, Ivan. I'll call you later," Ava said, though she didn't remove the finger from her face.

He shrugged, which seemed to somehow involve his hips, then handed her the keys with a bow.

"I will be all aflutter with antici—"

And he paused.

After a second, Nat yelled, "—PATION!'

He smiled at her, shooting a wink, and I died a bit inside.

"Precisely, my lovely."

Now it was Dave's turn to growl.

"Happy hunting to one and all. I shall absent myself from your endeavors," he announced, placing his hands into his pockets and strolling off into the night, presumably in search of a cab.

Nero looked hard at Ava, quirking an eyebrow. Nat stared blatantly at Ivan's ass as he left.

Ava shrugged. "Old flame. We keep in touch, but we don't really have time to talk about my love life right now, do we?"

Yes. Yes, I think we do.

"No, of course not. Let's load up, people," I said out loud as I slid into the passenger seat.

I needed to focus. Whatever group this was, they had gotten inside of Ivé's defenses by capitalizing on Evangeline's infatuation with Marcus and her subsequent flight from home. They'd shown they had a ton of power at their disposal and the ability to apply it in unexpected ways. They'd played us by having us be the bag men for delivering faux-Evangeline to Ivé. I didn't have time to twist myself into knots over how Ivan looked at Ava. Or vice versa.

I had enough trouble with getting Jackie back. The whole situation with Ava was a distraction. She knew that. She pointed it out forcefully yesterday when she tossed me across the room. I didn't disagree with her on any of that. On what she said, on how she reacted. It was deserved.

But now this? Why did—

No. Clear head. Eye on the prize.

"Hang on. Tonight's probably gonna hurt," I warned everyone in the back of the car, then looked at Ava and nodded.

Apparently, in more ways than one.

Ava expertly pulled onto the street, moving the massive car into the flow of traffic, and making a beeline for Ivé's domain in the Lower Ninth

Ward. If it felt like a different world from the Quarter during the day, adding darkness to the equation brought out an even more sinister feeling. Unfriendly eyes watched the car glide by in the night, just as aware as we were that we were unwelcome interlopers.

Miraculously, we arrived at Ivé's without incident.

There were no cars out front—no trucks around the corner, and no one on the porch.

"We're too late," Nat moaned.

"Not yet," I muttered, throwing my door open and striding up to the front door. "IVÉ! WE NEED A WORD!"

My voice echoed in the humid night air, disturbing the wary silence that pervaded the area.

"IVÉ!" I shouted, moving straight up the porch and hammering on the front door with the flat of my fist.

"Damn, Bishop! You tired o' livin?" a voice asked from around the corner.

"I don't have time for games, Scrabble," I growled, concentrating hard, then squinting at the house and shaking my head at the web of interlocked spells that served as security, each more deadly than the one before it. "Where's Ivé. It's vital."

"No doubt, no doubt. . . but Papa's offsite, con man. He wasn't willing to let matters lie when his little girl started tellin' him what those guys that had her did. Sick fuckers. She offered to show him the place they were holdin' her. So he can get his pound o' flesh. Him an' the gang took off a couple hours ago."

I closed my eyes.

"Fuck, fuck, *fuck*," I said, building in volume before turning on my heel and stalking back to the car. "Thanks, Scrabble, you may have just saved his life."

Scrabble blinked, then tilted his head. "Any chance y'all could put that in writing?" he called as I closed the door behind me.

"The Algiers warehouse," I said.

"From last night?" Nero asked.

"Of course," Ava muttered with a shake of her head. "With all of the power that was floating around in the air, there's no way they were finished with it."

"No," I agreed. "I'm not sure what they're doing, but they're doing something."

"What if the power was the setup?" Nat asked.

I turned to face her. "How do you mean?"

"I dunno. What if, like, the power you felt was the setup. Like they were priming a pump? And they need more power to get the thing moving."

I frowned, considering, thinking back to the feel of the place as we were leaving. How the pressure built over time. How it built every time, someone died. How my head felt like it was stuffed with cotton and crammed into a vice.

"Oh no," I whispered. "Nat's right. It could be a gate. It's just not juiced up enough yet."

"Juiced up by what?" Marcus asked from the far back.

"Human sacrifice. Every one of those cultists we killed last night helped power it a bit more. Helped to get it ready. Once your would-be father-in-law shows up, he's gonna rain down some Old Testament-style vengeance on the people he thinks took his little girl. A whole shit ton of people are going to die, all at the same time... and I'm guessing that these are going to be made up of willing sacrifices almost in their entirety," I said.

"That'll blow the door open to anywhere," Ava replied, her lips pursed. "With that much power, they could bring through just about anything."

"It needs a host," Dave observed. "Some things from the outside, even if they're as familiar as a demon, need a host if they're gonna stay in this world for long."

"And they've got a massively powerful willworker right in front of the door as it opens," I pointed out. "Ivé's the intended host. He's gotta be."

"Would it work? Can something from the outside actually possess Papa Ivé?" Nat asked, her voice filled with awe.

"Yeah. Things from the Outside are on a whole different level," Ava replied with a sigh. "Nothing in this world could resist them, short of a fae lord or a dragon, and we're fresh out of those."

Nero shuddered. "So we're lookin' at trying to put a stop to a righteously indignant father, who's out to avenge wrongs done to his little girl at the hands of a bunch of cultists that are looking to get killed for their cause, which will then turn loose some sort of tentacled horror to possess Ivé, giving it the perfect vessel to...to what?"

"I don't know. Nothing good," I replied. "Also, the tentacles aren't guaranteed."

An uneasy silence descended over the car as we navigated the streets of New Orleans and crossed the Mississippi for what felt like the hundredth time in two days.

The gates blocking the parking lot of the cult's warehouse were hanging askew as we drove up, wires jutting up like rib bones from some twisted monster laid low and left to rot. Ava brought the car to an idle, and I lowered my window, listening closely.

"I hear a fire, I think," I said, pausing. "But no people. Guess we go in."

Ava drove up the lane to the parking lot we'd traversed the night before and encountered the remnants of a warzone. The parking lot looked like a toddler's playset after the diminutive owner had thrown a tantrum. Cars were flipped over and lying on their sides or roofs, several still crackling with fire, the nauseating smell of the burnt rubber overwhelming all other odors. It was destruction on a level we hadn't seen since the levees burst.

Ava parked her car well away from the wreckage. We opened the doors and spilled out, fanning out in a rough semi-circle facing the building.

"Okay," I began. "Ivé's gotta be in there with a lot of his crew, plus a bunch of cultists that are looking to die. Every life taken, every drop of blood spilled, gives power to the ritual they're performing. We can't give 'em what they want. We need to get in there and stop Ivé, no matter what happens. Any questions?"

"So, what the fuck are we supposed to do, use harsh language to stop 'em?" barked Marcus as Evie shrunk behind him. "And why the fuck are you guys going in loaded for bear if you're not supposed to be killing anybody?"

I gritted my teeth and took a deep breath. "We're going in armed for bear because if it's them or us, I'd rather it was them. If it's too much, you and Evie can stay out here and make sure nothing happens to the car. That's our way out, and there's a real good chance we'll need to leave in a hurry," I replied.

We really didn't have time for 'on the job training' right now with two vampires whose fangs had barely come in. But here they were, the cause of it all, smack in the middle of things. What could possibly go wrong?

Fine, I *definitely* said it this time.

Marcus puffed up his chest to reply when Evie squeezed his arm. He looked back at her, then grimaced, and nodded.

"Yeah. I think - I think that's a good plan, Bishop. We'll keep an eye on the car."

I nodded. "Good man. Girl. Vampire. Anyone else?"

The four sets of eyes that were looking back at me were ready. It had been a while, but we'd been down this road before.

"Stay together. Stay safe. Now, let's go be stupid," I said.

We strode toward the same door we'd used before, with me in the lead, Dave and Ava behind me, and Nero and Nat behind them. The door we'd entered was shattered, and a poor sap who had been too close when it exploded was just inside. His face looked like it had been worked over by a cheese grater. The flesh that was left resembled ground beef more than anything recognizable as human.

Glancing down, I stepped over him. Nothing to be done at this point.

The moment we were inside, the familiar, coppery scent of fresh blood overwhelmed the burning rubber smell from the parking lot. At the same time, the power infusing the air hammered into my skull, making concentration a challenge. I staggered at its unexpected intensity and felt Ava and Dave's hands fall, one on each arm, as they steadied me. I smiled slightly without turning, then started forward again.

We rounded the first corner and came face to face with a nightmare. Ivé's work. The three cultists that lay gurgling on the floor had literally been turned inside out. Organs twitched, and the bare eyeballs staring up at us moved. Their jaws flexed.

"My God. They're still alive," whispered Nat in horror.

"At least--they're not fueling the ritual," I replied, my voice catching. I swallowed, fighting off a wave of revulsion.

"Yet," Ava added. "We need to pick up the pace, Bishop."

I nodded and did just that. Given what we'd seen of the layout the day before, we all knew where shit was going down, so we ran quickly and quietly in a direct line for the place where we'd found Nat and the fake Evangeline.

As we rounded another turn and made it into the main aisle, I could hear Ivé's voice thundering from ahead. Whatever was happening hadn't ended yet. We might still have time.

I started to run faster, sprinting ahead with the rest of them on my heels. I was so intent on making time that I missed the sigils on the floor.

The moment I crossed them, they flared to life, and instead of running into the middle of the confrontation between Ivé and the cult, I ran straight into my nightmare.

The warehouse was gone, and I was alone.

Reaching up, I could feel the collar around my throat. I saw the black shirt, black pants, and black shoes from my seminary days. I pulled at it, hoping to loosen its choking pressure around my throat, to allow myself to breathe a bit. No, the symbolism wasn't lost on me.

My chest was burning. Air came in ragged gasps, which made sense. I'd run here, after all.

I looked around my childhood home, feeling for all the world like I'd seen this before. Not the room, but the scene. Everything seemed so horribly, comfortingly familiar. Like it had happened before. Like I'd done this before. Like it was inevitable.

I smelled that terrible, sickly coppery odor as I burst into the foyer and heard the voice chanting from the study. My father's voice.

I heard a gasp as metal bit into flesh. Then again. And again. And again.

I saw my father's eyes, filled with regret regarding me.

"Jason, I'm sorry you had to see this," my father repeated for the thousandth time. "But this is for you, son. It's all for you."

"Jason. Please..." my sister whispered, pleading. "Help...me...don't let him...I'm scared..."

I saw Catherine's pleading eyes as blood welled from her mouth, her hand reached out for me, trembling. I saw my mother's body lying on the floor like a discarded puppet. Limbs askew and unmoving.

"It was a mistake to ask you to look away. I know that now," my father explained. "You're stronger than that. I always knew you were stronger than that. You're my son. I'm just so sorry it had to happen this way."

Something was wrong. This wasn't how it happened. I tried to fight through, to find the right memory. To find the nightmare that I'd lived through so many times before, but I couldn't. It wasn't there.

I looked up at my father. Edward Bishop. He was older than I'd remembered him. Older than he was when Katrina collapsed the house, killing him.

I couldn't help it. I had to respond.

"Happen what way?" I demanded. "You killed them. You slaughtered them. Like they were livestock."

"Livestock? Jason, I loved your mother and your sister. More than anything in the world aside from you. That's why their sacrifice was so important. A sacrifice without loss has no power. It nearly broke me to do what I did to both of them."

"What you did?" I spat back. "You killed your family!"

"Yes. Yes, I did. That's my burden. My terrible, terrible burden."

"Don't give that shit to me. You're a psychopath. They begged you, Dad. Begged!"

"And I wept when I took their lives. The torture was the worst part. Their souls had to be made ready for the transition to the nether realms."

I felt sick to my stomach.

"Nether realms? You sent them to Hell?!?"

Edward Bishop nodded solemnly. It was everything I'd feared. Everything in my worst thoughts and nightmares. They were being tormented for all eternity, and it was my fault.

"That was one of their requirements. To bring about a deluge, the likes of which hadn't been seen since the days of Noah, both your mother and sister needed to be gifted to Hell. But I was weak. At the last minute, I couldn't send your mother, so only New Orleans drowned. Your crucible was unfinished. You were never given the gift I intended."

"Crucible? Gift? You killed them both, and the deluge killed thousands. How is that supposed to help me?" I asked, confused. Something was very wrong. This...I shook my head and shrugged; my backpack slid off of my shoulder. I slowly reached inside and felt my hand close around the handle of the silver bell inside. This wasn't how it happened.

"Of course, Jason. I love you. More than anything and all of this has always been for you." Edward replied. "You have power in you, Jason. Potential. The same sort of power I do, but you've never been one to embrace it. You've always tried to find tricks. Shortcuts. Loopholes. Instead of embracing what is within you, you looked for ways to outsmart your problems. Instead of accepting your greatness, you sought to live a pedestrian life. You were going to be a priest. Live in the service of others," he said. "After that, you drank away your life, taking on cast-offs and collecting bits of true power like a supernatural magpie, never accepting that you didn't need any of it."

He snorted, staring into my eyes.

"Then you were willing to give it all up for the very definition of mediocrity: domestic bliss with a completely ordinary wife and child. I couldn't let that happen. Not to you, Jason. You deserve more. I promised you more! So I arranged this. All of it. To finally give you a challenge that you couldn't avoid. To provide you an obstacle so great that you have no choice but to embrace the greatness inside of you. To accept your power!" he pronounced.

"You're insane," I whispered.

"Is a father's love insane? Is wanting what's best for my son insane? If that's the case, then yes, I'm insane. Call me any name you want. Hate me. My job as your father is to prepare you. To give you the opportunity to be the best version of you that you can be! When Belial comes forth from the

Pit and inhabits this heathen's body, you'll have no choice but to rise to the occasion or witness Armageddon!" he replied.

I closed my eyes, ignoring the sights and smells of my home, ignoring the bodies of my mother and my sister. Ignoring the insanity pouring from the thing pretending it was my father. I pulled the bell out of the backpack and rang it for the first time. Its peal was loud and true, and as it rang, I recited the words of unmaking, some of the first pieces of ritual magic I'd ever discovered. Words to remove enchantments and spells. Words to free the mind.

"*No!*" the thing wearing my father's face cried out.

I rang the bell a second time, repeating the words.

The sound moved away from me like a ripple in a pond, and as it washed over features from my home, it wiped them away, like the tide taking a sandcastle at the beach. My mother's body. My sister's body. The library. The altar.

I rang the bell a third time, repeating the words once again.

Where previously I'd been alone, the waves washed over empty places and showed that all of us were still here.

Ava was struggling to her feet, her own eyes red with tears after whatever nightmare of her own she'd encountered. Dave was on one knee, breathing heavily and staring at his hands in horror, a low growl escaping from somewhere deep in his chest. Nero was on his knees, his hands over his ears and his eyes closed. Normally slicked-back hair had straggling bits sticking up everywhere, and as his eyes opened, he took a long, shuddering breath. Nat was fetal on the ground, rocking back and forth, quietly chanting "no...please no..." before a film cleared from her eyes, and she looked around, startling into a seated position, then slowly coming to her feet, her eyes hard. Papa Ivé appeared as the peal spread further, splayed out on the same sort of stone altar my sister had been, but still alive.

The peal washed over my father.

Edward Bishop remained.

"I wish you hadn't done that, Jason."

I stared at him, mouth agape.

The Edward Bishop who stood before me wasn't the fixture of New Orleans high society who had vanished thirteen years ago. That man had been filled with vitality and charisma. He was the center of every conversation, a consummate politician even if he never had any political inclinations.

The shell of him that stood in front of me was a madman. A funhouse mirror reflection of the man I knew as my father. This man was smaller and wrinkled, with eyes that burned with a fervent zeal that only the clinically insane can truly possess. His once silver-grey hair had gone stark white and longer. His previously athletic frame had withered over the years, leaving him gaunt and scrawny.

I'd always thought my father's gaze was intense. I'd seen the rich and powerful shrink under its intensity. Seeing those eyes stare out at me from this face as he stood over Ivé, just as he had stood over his own daughter, my sister Catherine, those thirteen years ago, brought everything crashing down.

"You're dead. This isn't possible."

"Oh, I'm afraid it is, my boy. I'm afraid it is. Belial was - disappointed with me after I failed to live up to my end of our agreement. As Katrina struck the city, he pulled me out of this world and into his. I was a living human soul in hell, with his servants rending my flesh and making it whole over and over. For a decade. I was broken, remade, and broken again at the foot of his throne," he said.

"I begged him for another chance. Begged him to return me so I might serve him, but even after all that time, I only told him a partial truth: I did indeed have a vision for what could happen, but that vision always remained on you, my son. I would provide you the challenge you always needed to become what you were always intended to be. For the past three years, I've moved in the shadows of the city. Made contacts. Created my network. Mr. Marrane was instrumental in it, but so much more was just finding like-minded people. People that understood the need for sacrifice. People that could see the sickness in our world."

Mr. Marrane? I needed to put a pin in that for now and keep him talking. Ava was trying to creep around on his left, while Dave slipped to the right. Nero and Nat had fanned out slightly behind me, each angling for a way to take the old man out before he could bring the knife down on Ivé. Nero slowly pulled one of the ampules of holy water out and balanced it in his hand. Smart man.

"What I was intended to be? You're gibbering like a lunatic, old man. I've walked my path, and it's led me here, where I'm going to put a stop to this. Back away from Ivé. Give up, and I'll see if we can get The Order to go easy on you. Maybe a nice cell someplace where they can try to undo the damage you've done to yourself?"

"The Order," he spat. "Children running around playing at being police for things they can't possibly comprehend. Do you think dedication to their little god is going to save them? Do you think it's going to save you? Your potential ordination was a joke. I had to put a stop to it before you made a terrible mistake. My sacrifice was the only answer to that."

I felt queasy as my father continued his diatribe. The facts were incontrovertible. He was telling me he'd killed my mother and sister, sent my sister's soul to Hell, and he'd done it because of me. To live up to something in me that just wasn't there. Something his fevered imagination had seen.

Talk about projecting.

I held up my hands, trying to keep him calm(ish). "Look, Dad. I don't want to hurt you," I lied, pacing to my left, bringing his gaze with me and away from both Ava and Nero.

He opened his mouth to respond, but Nero had seen his chance. He threw a perfect strike with the ampule. It hit my father in the center of his chest and shattered, spraying holy water all over him.

From someone that had been dragged down to hell and lived as one of its denizens for a decade, I expected burning. Screaming. Dissolving.

We got laughter.

Edward looked down at his chest, then up at Nero, and laughed, throwing back his head in a full-throated roar. He reached down and wiped the wet place on his shirt with his left hand, then made a dismissive gesture with his right that sent Nero careening through the air and smashing back into the unyielding bookshelves.

"Now," Edward said, his voice calm.

The room erupted into violence.

Cultists poured out of the doors, came charging down aisles, like ants defending their hive.

"**_NO!_**" Dave roared, charging Edward with the prybar cocked.

"This is what I mean, Jason. You surround yourself with mediocrity. With pathetic examples of the supernatural world," Edward commented as Dave closed with him. My father sighed, then gestured at my friend. Dave's roar turned into a howl of agony, and the big man went down, curled up around his stomach, clutching at it in pain.

Ava's clandestine approach to Edward was interrupted by an influx of cultists. She was attempting to hold them off as the howling fanatics swarmed. In a smaller, thinner space, it might have worked; she probably would have stemmed the tide. But the wide pathways allowed too many to attack her at once. They began to surround her, their blows finding their mark more and more often.

I knew it was a distraction. I knew the real problem was my father and that I needed to stop him.

But I heard her scream in pain, and I snapped.

I vaguely saw Nat charging toward my father, her spiked bat ready, as I rushed forward, slipping my specialty brass knuckles onto my left hand and pulling out the long, banana-bladed kukri blade with my right. I ignored the warning I'd given everyone about not spilling blood as I waded into them, lashing out with fist and blade, slashing, punching, kicking, and throwing them as I attempted to unwind the knot of humanity that had formed around Ava.

The cultists didn't seem interested in simply dying. This group was armed with clubs and knives, and I could feel the impact of both. Only the sigils on my peacoat saved me from deep puncture wounds as one cultist or another slid behind me, attempting to end my interference. But finally, after what seemed like hours (but was probably closer to thirty seconds), I broke through to Ava. She'd fought her way to a wall to limit the number of sides she had to defend, and as I savagely punched the back of the man's head in front of me, she whirled, her hand moving toward my throat.

The world seemed to freeze as our eyes locked, her brown eyes wide, her pale skin smeared with blood, some hers, some not. She was gulping air, and there were scratches on her face. Her hand stopped scant inches from my windpipe.

"***Enough***!" Edward's voice rang out over the room.

The cultists immediately stopped. I broke eye contact with Ava and looked over toward my father. I wished I hadn't.

Power from the new crop of sacrifices hung visibly in the air above his head, swirling in an accelerating vortex. The small, weasel-faced man from the night before was just behind him, sporting a black eye, a scorch mark on his white shirt, and a set of scratches on his cheek. Unfortunately, he also had Nat kneeling in front of him.

She had some sort of glowing red collar around her throat that led back to weasel-face's right hand. Her eyes were closed, and her jaw was set. She was in pain and preparing for worse.

I grimaced then took a quick look around.

Nero was on the ground, out.

Dave was writhing on the floor behind my father. Whatever had been done to him, it looked bad.

"None of the parlor tricks will work on me, Jason. I've had years to study what you do. What you've done. What you know. What your little band of groupies knows. It's over. Ms. Jenkins here will be the last piece. A person of power that will be used to tear open the walls of reality and allow Belial himself to take possession of this vessel."

"He'll destroy everything," Ava said. "Everything. You. Your son. *Everything*."

Edward nodded.

"Your friend understands. Yes. Yes, he will. Unless someone stops him. Unless *you* stop him, Jason."

Nat opened her eyes and looked at me, a single tear running down her cheek; then she shook her head.

I gritted my teeth.

"You're out of your damned mind. Even Ivé, with his full bag of tricks and centuries of training, couldn't do that! Think for a minute. You can still stop. Still walk away. You don't have to do this!"

"No, but I will. For you."

"*NO!*"

Somehow, Dave had gotten to his feet despite the pain and lunged for Edward. The big guy had propelled himself straight at him, but the old man seemed ready. Without so much as a glance, he held up a hand and caught Dave in midair.

"Predictable. As I said, I know all of you. None of your abilities will work on me. Not the tricks you carry. Not the petty schemes you play at. Now, Jason. Come here. Stand next to me and witness Belial's birth into this world and look into the eyes of your enemy."

I swallowed, then started forward. I wasn't going to let him sacrifice Nat. No matter what.

Ava clutched my upper arm, and I looked at her.

"Jason..." she whispered, shaking her head.

I forced a smile. Then nodded.

She forced a smile in return, swallowed, then slowly nodded back, releasing my arm.

She knew.

Taking a deep breath, I walked slowly forward, dropping my weapons and putting my hands in my pockets. This was a single-use plan: if this was all for me, then I had to take me out of the equation. That would remove the need that Edward had for me to become something more. For me to prove myself. For him to finish the ritual and kill everyone.

My right hand closed around the .38 in my pocket.

I'd have one chance at this. I couldn't miss my shot. Right before they killed Nat.

Pull.

Place gun under chin.

Fire.

No more Bishop.

It wasn't a great plan. It wasn't even a good plan, but it was what I had.

I stopped in front of Nat and took a deep breath.

"Hey, kiddo,"

She opened her eyes.

"Didn't think I'd go out this way, Bishop. I mean, always sorta figured it'd be with you or because of you...or both...but...not like this."

"Yeah. I'm sorry, Nat. I'm sorry for everything."

She sniffled, then looked up at me. "You know what? I didn't think I'd say it, and I didn't think I'd mean it, but I wouldn't have traded a second of it, Bishop. Not for anything."

"Me either," I replied, then frowned.

My hand had brushed against the Midnight Dirt in my left pocket, and an idea started to form.

I still had another option.

"Nat. No matter what, just have faith. Pray like you mean it."

"That's rich, coming from you."

"Jason, it's time," my father instructed.

It was. Now or never.

I pulled my left hand out of my peacoat and tossed a fistful of the dirt into weasel-face's eyes. He'd been expecting any number of actions on my part, but apparently, that wasn't one of them. His eyes went wide, then he stood stock still, pulled into the same fugue state as the cultist from last night.

The glowing leash vanished from around Nat's neck, and the kid went flat as I pulled my right hand and the .38 revolver out of my pocket and pointed it at my father.

"WHAT?"

The flat cracks of gunshots echoed in the warehouse as I fired at him, emptying all six shots in rapid succession.

Edward Bishop had studied me. He knew all about the Angelic Flame. He knew about the equipment I carried. He'd prepared for it. My parlor tricks and dodges wouldn't work on him.

Bullets aren't my style, but bullets aren't a parlor trick. Bullets are cold lead and physics. Bullets are the personification of the potential for deadly violence, and bullets were something my father simply hadn't considered.

He staggered back away from the altar with his eyes wide. Three of the bullets had struck him in his torso, and red blossoms began to appear on the white shirt, spreading more quickly in the spot Nero had hit with his holy water balloon a few minutes earlier.

My father looked down at his chest in shock, then up at me, confusion spreading on his face before he staggered back and slumped to the ground.

"What...how...why?" he asked.

I was going to answer. I really was. You don't get a chance to do movie-level drama all that often, but there were other things to worry about. The cultists stood in shocked silence for a heartbeat after he fell, right up until he asked me why and then the vortex above his head started to spread. The willworker who'd held it together was gone, so the energy needed an outlet.

Purple bolts of lightning began to arc out of the swirling mass, and when one lanced a cultist, the rest decided this wasn't the way they had intended to die. They broke and scattered.

It was pandemonium, with people running in every direction while I tried to locate *my* people.

Ava had worked her way over to Nero and had hoisted him up over her shoulder.

Nat was up and moving toward Ivé, which left Dave for me.

I ran over to the big man and helped him to his feet. His skin was covered in sweat, and his legs were rubbery, so he leaned heavily on me. Dave has a lot of heavy to lean with, so it was a challenge.

"Over here!" I called out, trying to gather everyone.

Nat was first, with Ivé leaning on her. The voodoo king of New Orleans looked like he'd been drugged. His eyes wouldn't focus, and he stumbled frequently.

"My daughter. Where is...my daughter..." he slurred.

"Oh, we've got a hell of a surprise for you," Nat muttered.

Ava was over with Nero next. Our psychic had been revived but had a nasty bump that was probably going to leave a knot on the side of his head.

We ran.

As we ran, the lightning was quickly turning the entire warehouse into a blasted hellscape. Bolts of eldritch energy lashed out indiscriminately. The six of us tried to find our way out across the sea of cultists who were no longer interested in continuing my father's work now that he'd fallen. There was no sign of the faux-Evangeline, and we'd left weasel-face standing, comatose, back by the altar.

All in all, it hadn't been a banner day for the cultists.

"Stay low!" I warned everyone, giving extra attention to both Ivé and Dave, since both men were freakishly tall, even hunched over. "No, lower than that! Unless you really want to see what happens when one of those bolts rewrites your fundamental nature!"

"Is that what they do?" Nero asked as Ava he and Ava leaned on one another.

I shrugged. "No clue, but it sounds about right, doesn't it? Why risk it? Stay low!"

We rounded corner after corner, but each turn offered the same view: a rapidly darkening warehouse, gathering gloom only interrupted by all too frequent lightning strikes.

"I don't know how long this place is going to hold together," I warned, looking at our injured. "Running is probably a better plan than this high-speed stumble."

"If your people can make it, I can make it, charlatan," Ivé replied, his voice hoarse and barely above a whisper.

"Yeah, yeah. You're a badass, Ivé, we know. Dave, Ava, Nero? You guys up for a little jog?"

Ava grunted. Dave gave a thumbs up. Nero groaned. "You're gonna be the death of me, sugar—but yeah. I can run."

I fought off the urge to point out that the death of him was precisely what I was trying to avoid and instead herded everyone forward, bringing up the rear and hoping for the best. We'd made this run last night, under different circumstances. It was still tense. Still chaotic, but a different flavor of tense and chaotic. That sort of distinction is important.

Our pace picked up. The stench of ozone was thick in the air as we moved closer to the exit, with the strikes becoming more frequent the closer to the edges we moved. Finally, we stopped twenty yards from the exit, staring at a near-constant barrage of lightning strikes surrounding the door.

"How the fuck are we supposed to get through that?" Nero wailed, gesturing at the shooting gallery in front of us.

Nat narrowed her eyes and looked around, then smiled.

"Dave, can you knock over some of these shelving thingies? That one. That one. That one," she said, pointing out three in succession.

"Clever girl," Ava purred approvingly.

I nodded, smiling. "Good job, Nat."

Nero blinked, then glared, then shook his head, then winced.

"*Why?*" he demanded.

"The shelves will form a bridge. If Mr. LeBlanc pushes them, so they lay against the far wall, they'll form a sort of umbrella for everyone to move through. The energy will strike them instead of us," Ivé offered, the slightest hint of a smile on his face. "As they said: very smart."

Nat preened as Dave got to work, knocking down the units just as requested. They slammed loudly against the walls, and their contents poured out, smashing onto the ground in the walkways, promising treacherous footing as we went.

But it was far better than being par-broiled.

Each of us got on our hands and knees and started crawling forward in a single file line.

"Don't touch the metal!" I called out as Nat started forward. She raised an eyebrow at me and then vanished into the tunnel.

One by one, they went through until only Ava, and I were left.

She stood silently, looking not at the tunnel but at me. Finally, I tilted my head.

"What's wrong?"

She started to shake her head, then stopped and set her jaw.

"Don't you ever fucking do that again," she said, her voice quiet.

"Do what?"

"Don't play dumb with me, Bishop. We both know what your plan was back there. With your father. Don't you ever do that again."

I paused, looking at her for a moment, then I shook my head.

"I can't promise that, Ava. I wish I could, but I can't."

"You have some sort of goddamned death wish?"

"Far from it. I want to live. I wanted all of us to live, but I couldn't think of anything else that got everyone else out. Anything else that could have stopped my father from finishing the ritual. Anything that would stop him from summoning a monster like Belial here into New Orleans. Anything that would keep Mary from having to live through that. In that situation? No, I'll make that call every time, if that's what it takes. I can't promise anything else."

She looked at me for a beat, then shook her head.

"I'd have been the one to tell your daughter, Bishop. I'd be the one that would have to tell your little girl that her daddy isn't coming home. Did you think about that for even one second?"

I looked her in the eyes for a moment, then gave a very brief nod.

"Yeah. Yeah, I did. I didn't see another way out."

Ava swallowed. "Work with me on one next time, okay? For all that you're a jackass sometimes, the world's a better place with you in it. And for some reason, that little girl of yours loves the shit out of you. Don't you dare leave her before it's your time."

Ava held my gaze for another beat, then, satisfied she'd made her point, started her own trip through the tunnel. I gave her a five-count, then followed. I fully expected some sort of supernatural horror to lunge after me, grabbing my ankle and forcing me into a hair-raising life or death battle while my friends wondered what had happened to me, but thankfully, that proved to be a simple bit of paranoia on my part. All six of us made it out the door and to the outside, safe and sound.

The atmosphere outside of the warehouse was a stark contrast to the inside. The ambient energy loose inside of the building had raised the temperature to the point that all of us were sweating, but the cool, humid October night air had a bit of a bite, raising goosebumps on each of us as we cleared the door.

"They told me you would explain, Bishop. So now explain: where is my daughter? Where is Evangeline? She was with me when we entered the warehouse, but something—something happened. We were separated."

Ivé shook his head.

"Okay, Ivé. I need you to remain calm."

"Why do I need to remain calm?" he asked, his voice taking a dangerous edge to it.

"See, that's exactly what I'm talking about you not doing," I admonished him.

"Bishop, has telling someone to 'calm down' ever worked?" Nero asked.

"No," Ava and Nat answered in unison, both of them looking irritated and crossing their arms over their chests.

Shit.

"Okay, it's like this: The girl we brought back wasn't actually your daughter," I said.

"Yes, she was. I'd recognize Evangeline anywhere," Ivé replied.

"She couldn't be. We found Evangeline the next day," I said.

"No, my daughter was with me," Ivé insisted.

"I'm afraid not," Ava added. "We were all there when Bishop found the first girl. And we were there when we were led to your actual daughter."

Ivé's expression darkened. His brow knitted.

"Ignoring the fact that you were duped—" he started.

"So were you!" Nat objected.

Ivé shot her a glare, which brought Dave to step in front of her.

"Ignoring that. I will find this imposter and deal with her later. But you, you then found my actual daughter - tonight?"

"We did," I said, pausing.

"What's wrong? What's happened to my Evangeline?" Ivé demanded. My hesitation didn't seem to be improving his mood.

Almost on cue, Evangeline Grey stepped around an overturned van to our right. Ivé's gaze fell upon her, and a smile started to appear on his face and then vanished.

"No..." he gasped.

"Yeah," I said.

"Who?" he asked, his voice trembling with rage. "Who did this to my child?"

"I did this, Daddy," Evangeline said. "I did this. I ran away. No one took me. No one forced me to do anything. I'm...I'm in love."

The look on Ivé's face was one of barely contained violence, probably because the violence he wanted to perform currently had no viable target. Sensing death on the horizon, I chose to remain quiet in order not to become said target.

"With whom?" he asked, his voice dangerous.

"No, Daddy. I won't do that. I won't let you do that. Not to him. Not to me. Not to you. You'd regret it. Eventually."

"I can assure you. I would not." Ivé said.

"Killing the man I love? Losing me forever? Yeah, you would. I'm still your little girl, Daddy. I'm still your Evie," she took a step forward, her eyes pleading.

Ivé looked at her, the rage fading from his face, replaced by hurt. By confusion. The anger was still there but tempered. Lessened.

"But you will change, child. The Curse does not lay lightly upon its victims, and make no mistake: you are a victim. It will degrade you as time goes on. Strip you of your humanity. Make you more and more into the beast that The Curse stirs. You can feel it even now, with all of the blood in the air. You can hear the blood calling to you, can you not?"

Evie stood quietly, her eyes downcast.

Ivé sighed. "And you've almost certainly fed recently. This is what it feels like now. The Hunger *will* get worse. It will become all-encompassing. It will push you to sate it, no matter the cost. It will take what is you at the core of who you are and twist it. That is the true cost of vampirism. Not the need to drink blood and avoid the sun. The way it makes them slowly fade away before the eyes of those they love."

Tears stood out in Ivé's eyes. Red started to rim Evie's as well.

"We can fight it, Daddy. Together."

"We'll fight it, child. We'll lose, but we'll fight, all the same. I love you, Evangeline. I love you with all of my heart. With all of my soul. If it meant stopping this from happening to you, I would renounce my power in an instant. I would give all I am to stop it, but that's beyond even my power." Ivé said.

Evie nodded, sniffling, and then was unexpectedly engulfed in an embrace from her father.

The pair clung to one another, holding each other close, each crying their own tears as they did.

I looked from them to our group and gestured to the car.

"C'mon. Some things are better without an audience," I whispered. It was clear we were no longer needed here.

We passed Marcus on the way to the car and gave him a quick update. He decided to give them some space but refused our offer of a ride back to the Quarter. All for the best, really. Touching reunion or not, he was definitely on Ivé's shit list, and I'd rather not be nearby, just in case a stray bolt of lightning happens to find its mark.

The ride home was a quiet relief. I had a lot to unpack about what had happened. My father had come back like a slasher movie villain and very nearly destroyed either the world or the city, all for some sort of crazed idea about what I should be.

I'd fallen back into my old patterns and was up to my neck in the Crescent City's supernatural world and couldn't even pretend I was upset about it. Jackie was engaged to Victor, and now both of them knew about the work I did, the world I lived in. Mary had worked a really damned complicated spell at eight.

As Ava navigated the path back home, I rested my head against the cool glass for the second night in a row. It felt good after so many close calls. Calming. I sat quietly while Ava dropped off the others: first Nero at his apartment, then Nat and Dave at hers.

I quirked an eyebrow at them as they left the car, but Nat glared at me, while Dave simply shrugged.

"Mind your own damned business, boss."

I smiled in reply, and the two of them vanished up the stairs.

"So," Ava said, looking over at me with a smirk. "It's down to you, and it's down to me."

I nodded. "I should check on Mary, Vic, and Jackie," I replied. "Make sure the kid's okay. They might still be at the hotel, but let's swing by the house first, just in case."

Ava nodded as her smile faded. "Yeah. I'm guessing all of that father/daughter drama had to set off some odd feelings in you. We'll be there in two shakes."

The Escalade glided through the night as my mind worked on the events of the last few days. My stomach was unsettled, and I had a headache. Probably from stress, and almost certainly aggravated by watching what Ivé had gone through with Evie.

Teenagers, am I right?

I stole a furtive glance at Ava, who was busily attending to traffic, holding a death grip on the steering wheel. I forced down the urge to smile. She'd nearly been killed helping me. But in spite of it all, she was still here.

My reverie was interrupted as we pulled up to the house.

"You coming in?" I asked as I opened the door.

"No, like you said, some things are better left without an audience," she replied.

"Mary will be heartbroken."

There was a long pause. She opened her mouth to say something but paused. Then again. Then a third time with the same results. Finally, her shoulders slumped slightly, and she sighed. "Fine. I'm in to say thank you to Miss Mary for saving my life; then I'm out. You can do your weird fawning reunion thing without me."

Ouch.

"Deal," I replied. The two of us walked up to the front door, and I knocked, only to have it swing open under the impact of my light touch.

Frowning, I crept inside with Ava behind me, my eyes immediately locking on the baby doll transfixed to the wall leading up the stairs, a knife driven through its throat, and a note attached to the front.

"Come to the Cathedral with your demonic whore, or I kill all three and leave their bodies in your bar in pieces."

My heart plummeted in my chest. I couldn't breathe. The room spun.

"Oh, God, Bishop. He's got them," Ava gasped.

My head filled with static. Noise. "He has them," echoed over and over in mind. It drowned everything else out.

"BISHOP!"

Ava's voice snapped my attention back.

"He has Mary and Jackie, Bishop. You've got to go get her. Them. We have to get them."

I stared numbly, then turned, walking toward her car.

We had to go get them. This had to stop. No matter the cost.

The Garden District was deathly silent as the Escalade flew down its back roads. The shrubbery around us was once again a dark blur as we raced the three miles from Victor's house to St. Louis Cathedral.

"They'll be fine, Bishop," Ava reassured me. "Chase is a zealot, but it's not them he wants. It's you and me. He won't do anything to jeopardize that."

I shook my head in reply. "You can't predict crazy, Ava, and don't think for one second the man isn't. Dangerous but crazy. I lost my bag back at the warehouse, so I don't have so much as a rabbit's foot, and that man's a trained killer."

"You've got a pretty decent body, count yourself," she replied.

I grimaced, fighting to clear the static out of my head as she made turn after turn. As we took the corner onto Royal, Ava pulled the wheel to the left and put the two driver's side wheels up onto the curb, and we came to a screeching halt about a block away from the Cathedral. The car was still rocking. We both exited, ran toward the front of the building, then came to a skidding halt when we saw Raimond standing outside.

"Raimond..." I said carefully as my former seminary mate's eyes met mine.

"Father Chase arrived a few hours ago with your daughter, her mother, and stepfather. They're in St. Anthony's Garden. Behind you," he blurted, pointing back the way we'd come.

I stared at him for a moment, fighting the urge to punch him in his pious face as Ava stood just behind me and to my right. Swallowing, I asked a simple question.

"Why? Why, Raimond? How could you help him?"

"Help him?" Raimond asked incredulously. "I've been trying to stop him. He swears that if anyone other than you or Ms. Dufrense enters, the girl's mother dies. He's heavily armed and completely unwilling to listen to reason. The man's unhinged."

Gritting my teeth to hold in the anger, I hissed back. "You promised me the Order would owe me a favor, Raimond. This seems like a far fucking cry from a favor. That lunatic has my little girl."

"I know," he replied miserably. "I can call in a team to neutralize him, but..."

"But they'd go scorched earth," Ava finished for him.

Raimond looked over at her. "As the lady says."

I took a deep breath and looked to our left. The wrought iron gate and bushes hid St. Anthony's Garden from easy view from the street but did nothing to block sound. Chase was right there, armed and waiting.

Listening to everything we said. Raimond followed my sightline toward the Garden and gave the briefest of nods.

He knew as well.

"Around the back?"

He nodded again.

Taking a deep breath, I walked toward the Royal Street gate into the Garden with Ava at my side and Raimond trailing behind.

"You can't go in there," I whispered. "It's sanctified ground. It could kill you."

"I know the risks," she replied noncommittally. "We're getting Mary away from that asshole, no matter what."

Arriving at the gate, I paused, turning to her.

"You getting yourself killed isn't gonna help anything, Ava. If anything happens to me, promise me—"

"You're coming out of this, Bishop. Same as you always do. You're not gonna bring everyone back together just to bow out on us. You can't do that. Not to Mary. Not to Nero, not to Nat," she paused for a long moment, then locked her eyes onto mine and added, "Not to me."

I stared at her, then swallowed.

"I'll do my best."

The gate was unlocked, a fact I'd missed in my rush to the front of the cathedral moments before. I pushed on the black-painted metal and winced as it shrieked in protest.

"*Daddy!*" Mary's voice rang out of the darkness near where the garden backed against the Cathedral.

I winced at the fear in her voice—the desperation. My baby girl was terrified. She huddled against Jackie, who held her tight. Victor was on the ground in front of them. He looked unconscious. Probably tried to put up a fight.

He was lucky Chase didn't kill him.

"You came, after all, Mr. Bishop. I was beginning to have my doubts. You wouldn't be the first to abandon his family for the temptations of the flesh the servants of Hell offer."

And this was the self-righteous motherfucker who was responsible.

Chase stood in front of the statue of Jesus that dominated the middle of the lawn, a wicked-looking blade, and pistol on his belt, and a long gun slung across his back. His smirk sickened me. He glanced over my shoulder, and the smile widened, making the nausea worse.

"And you've brought the demon whore herself. Excellent. I'll make this easy for you: You give me the demon, I'll let your little dysfunctional family walk away. It's the sort of offer The Order doesn't make twice, Mr. Bishop."

"Mary? Jackie? Just stay back. It's gonna be okay," I tried to reassure them, tasting the lie on my lips.

"You can't give him Miss Ava, Daddy!" Mary declared.

I smiled at Mary before settling my hate-filled gaze back on Chase. "Not even an option. You know better than to think I'd entertain handing anyone over to a piece of shit like you."

"I do," he agreed. "But now I can proceed with a clear conscience. You had your chance to repent. To cast off the succubus, but you chose to remain her willing thrall. To allow her influence to remain upon your child. What kind of father are you?"

"The kind that's about to kick your ass," I replied.

He made a show of removing his weapons belt and unslung his rifle, placing them in a pile at the foot of the statue of Christ. Gotta love the symbolism, right?

I slowly removed my peacoat, holding it loosely in my left hand, and started toward him.

"In a way, it's almost sad, Mr. Bishop. If it weren't for the tragedy you suffered during seminary, you and I would have been friends," Chase said as he watched me approach.

"You're already planning to kill me. Do you really need to insult me too?" I asked him as I continued forward.

Chase shifted his stance, presenting his side to me and going up on the balls of his feet. The man was a trained fighter—a killer. I'm a guy with a bad temper and a history of scrapping. It's not that he's out of my league. It's that we're not even playing the same sport.

Just outside of his arm's reach, I tossed the peacoat straight into his face and charged.

I may as well have told him what I was going to do, as effective as it was. He saw me coming before the coat even made contact, slid slightly to the side, and stepped forward as I threw what I hoped was going to be an effective haymaker. It wasn't.

He landed a pair of open-handed strikes on my ribs, just under my outstretched arm, driving the breath from my lungs. I swung with my left hand, only to have my arm met with a two-handed block, which he followed with a pivoting elbow strike that landed hard in my gut.

"Jason!"

Ava's voice rang out from behind me as I gasped and staggered back, but he was right on top of me. His foot lashed out in a front kick that sent me sprawling in the dirt.

"It's not an insult, Mr. Bishop. You have heart; I'll grant you that. You're strong-willed, and you're willing to fight, even die, for your misguided beliefs. If you'd received the proper training, you might even have been a half-decent fighter. But you didn't. You left. You fell into debauchery and allowed yourself to be seduced by the servants of Hell. Even now, she calls to you. Maintaining her hold on you. How are you the only one that can't see it?" Chase said. The bastard wasn't even breathing hard.

"You don't have to do this, Harlan," Father Raimond called out. "Bishop brought his group back together in service to the cause! Stop this insanity!"

"Insanity? You're the one who went outside of protocols, Brother. You knew that I could never stand idly by and watch someone who knows so many of our secrets fall under the influence of someone like her!"

He looked up, pointing angrily at Ava, and I smiled. I kicked out hard, and my foot connected solidly with the front of his right knee. Father Chase howled in pain and joined me on the ground, but I was already rolling to my left, coming to my feet.

"I've never seen somebody take a hate to Ava quite as hard as you have. Did she turn you down or something, Chase?" I said.

Chase snarled and lunged back to his feet. I scrambled away, carefully keeping an eye on him as I did so. He was limping, but not nearly as severely as I'd hoped. Reaching down, I picked up my coat once again.

Chase was angry, not thinking. He stepped closer and threw a punch that I stepped into, trapping his left arm under my right. I threw a couple of quick punches to his face, then wrapped the coat around his head before throwing a bunch more. I felt the impact, and it felt good to finally lash out after everything that had happened over the past three days. After everything Chase had said and done.

The good feeling didn't last long as he shoved me off and tore the coat away from his face. Seeing a chance, I charged in again, trying to bury my shoulder into his gut and bear him down to the ground.

I realized my mistake as soon as I felt his arms wrap around me.

His right knee, the one that I kicked earlier, came up hard into my stomach. It slammed home repeatedly, moving like a piston as he held me. The air was savagely driven from my lungs, and I struggled to draw breath. I fought to free myself, punching ineffectually at him, but Chase's back was corded muscle. I would have had as much luck hitting the cathedral wall.

My legs went rubbery, and I gasped for air. Chase shifted his grip, grabbing my hair and bringing an elbow down between my shoulder blades. I fell to my knees, only held up by his grip, then received a knee to the face that sent me back to the ground, seeing stars, and tasting blood in my mouth.

I struggled, trying in vain to come to my feet, to do anything, but there was nothing left. My body wouldn't listen.

"You fought bravely, Mr. Bishop, but this isn't a movie. The plucky underdog doesn't win, and there's no cavalry to save you." Chase sneered.

"Don't bet on that, asshole," Ava snarled from behind him.

I dimly saw Chase turn in shock to come face to face with Ava. Her eyes blazed with fury, and her face was anger personified as she uppercutted Chase off his feet, sending him three feet up and five feet back. He landed with a loud thud and a gasp.

Smoke boiled up from the ground around Ava as she stalked forward, her hands balled into fists.

"You wanted the 'demon whore', well, you've got her," she spat.

Chase rolled to his feet, coming to his hands and knees, only to get punted hard by the object of his hatred. He rolled away from her after the impact, but now it was his turn to gasp for breath.

"You've shot me, you've threatened the people I care about, and you've gone out of your way to make my life a living hell, and for what? I'm associating with people that you don't think I should. Fuck you, you misogynistic piece of shit!" she raved. "You don't get to tell me who I can be around. Who I care about! No one gets to tell me that. I make my own choices!"

She reared back to kick him once again, but this time, Chase was ready. His foot snaked out and swept her plant leg out from under her, sending her crashing to the ground. The sanctified ground.

Ava screamed in agony as a sizzling noise erupted wherever she touched the grass. Smoke poured around her as her eyes closed and her face contorted. I still couldn't stand, try as I might. I wanted desperately to get up, to help her, but all I could do was crawl, knowing I'd never reach her in time.

Chase smiled and came to his feet.

"Sacrificing yourself for Mr. Bishop? An odd ploy, Ms. Dufrense. I don't understand, but no matter," he commented as he reached into his pocket and removed a rosary. He wrapped it around his right hand, reared back, and punched Ava full in the face.

She screamed as he hit her, the rosary doing far more damage than mere flesh and bone would have.

"NO, HARLAN!" Raimond's voice cut through as Chase moved to strike her again. The other member of The Order stood right next to him, his face a mask of outrage. "You won't. If she's as debauched as you say, she couldn't have entered this holy place at all."

"Look at her! Look at how it rejects her."

"But she's alive! Just as she lived after you pierced her with the blessed ammunition. There is something at work here."

Chase regarded Father Raimond for a moment, then lashed out with a foot, kicking him hard under the chin. Raimond's head snapped back, his eyes rolling up in his head as he fell to the turf, unconscious.

"No. It's a trick. Mr. Bishop is famous for his tricks. No more! You'll see, Raimond. You'll all see."

He moved to strike her again, ignoring the soft sobs of agony escaping Ava's clenched jaw, but a high-pitched shriek stopped him. Mary sprinted between them, throwing herself on Ava and trying to protect her with her small, frail body.

"*No*! I won't let you hurt my Daddy or Miss Ava anymore!"

Chase looked at Mary, his face twisting in hatred at this small thing that stopped him from his good work, denying him his prey.

"I give you to the count of five, child. Move, or I **will** hurt you," he said flatly.

"*No!*" I called out.

"M-mary...run, sweetie," Ava whispers.

"One."

"I can do things!"

"Two."

"Daddy showed me. I'll stop you!"

"Mary, run!" I begged as I crawled forward.

"Three."

"I'll be okay. Go," Ava pleaded, trying to push the girl away. Mary squirmed her way back, trying to stay between Ava and Chase.

"Four."

"Please, God, don't hurt her," I cried.

"Five, you bastard," Jackie snarled.

Everyone's eyes jumped to her at the foot of the Christ statue, holding Chase's gun and sighting down the barrel directly at him. A split second later, the gun barked, and Chase careened backward, struck in the shoulder.

The former soldier struggled backward, but he'd lost track of where I'd crawled to and came within my reach. I wrapped my arm around his throat and pulled back, squeezing with everything I had left. I closed my eyes, vaguely aware of Mary and Jackie's voices urging Ava up. Of their voices trailing toward the street. Of the strangled wheezing escaping from Chase. Of the feeble impacts of his arm as he tried to free himself.

I pulled harder, bearing down with all my might, with every fiber of my hatred, fear, and anxiety. I thought about my father coming back. I thought about how I killed him. I thought about nearly dying at the hands of vampires. I thought about the powerless feeling I had as Ava had laid on the floor next to me, grievously wounded by Chase's bullet. I thought about the terror I felt when I was convinced that Chase was going to kill Mary.

The arm stopped moving. I considered for a moment, then finally released the chokehold and opened my eyes. Taking a deep breath, I staggered gingerly to my feet.

Seventy-eighth time is the charm, right?

Mary, Jackie, and Ava were in the street, with Ava leaning heavily on Mary. Jackie looked up and saw me. Tears stood out in her eyes. Brushing her arm across face, she ran toward me.

I blinked, confused as she threw her arms around me.

"Oh, God, Jason! I was so worried!"

Before I knew it, her lips were on mine, kissing me with a hungry intensity that threatened to drown everything else out.

This was what I'd wanted for the past four years: Jackie wanting me back. Seeing that I'd changed and choosing me over everyone else. Everything else. Her arms were on my back, pulling me closer to her. Clinging to me like a life vest.

Needing me.

But something wasn't right.

This is what I *had wanted*, but it didn't feel like what I *wanted now*.

She kissed me harder, her breath coming in little gasps, but I pulled back and slowly pushed her away. Before I could say anything, she looked up at me and smiled.

"Let's get out of here. You, me, and Mary. We'll get into the car and get the hell out of this city. Away from this nuthouse. Just the three of us. Someplace we can all be safe. Start over."

"I—I can't," I whispered.

She looked up at me in confusion.

"Can't? Jason, if this is about Victor—"

Victor! I looked back into the garden, to where Victor, Chase, and Raimond all laid, unconscious.

"It's not. It's—" I searched for the words, then sighed. "Look. Jackie. Everything you said about us before, everything you said about me before, it was right. I didn't know what I wanted, and I created some sort of sketch of you in my head. A version of you that doesn't exist. One that would spackle over all of the dings and dents inside of me and make me feel whole. But that's not you. That's not fair to you, it's not fair to me, and it's not fair to Mary. Doing what you're asking, it seems like a dream come true, but at the end of the dream, we'd wake up to nearly the same situation that you walked out on four years ago."

Jackie looked up at me, surprise morphing into disappointment on her face. "But you said you still loved me," she whispered. "And then what you just did—"

"Is what I do. Really think about it. About you and me. What's different now?"

Jackie stared up at me, conflicting thoughts and emotions warring on her face. Finally, she took a deep, shuddering breath and nodded. "I-I'm sorry."

"Almost dying does funny things to you," I agreed, looking over my shoulder to see Mary standing on the sidewalk alone. Jackie's gaze followed my own, and she nudged my arm.

"I want you. I need you. Go get her, tiger." she said

"Huh?"

"Ava, you moron. She left. After all of the shit you two went through. After all of the things that you did to save each other, she just left. That's not a coincidence, you idiot. I'm sorry if kissing you messed things up for you."

"There's nothing between us," I protested. "We're just friends."

"You *are* an idiot, and you're lying to yourself," she replied. "And you don't have time for that right now. Go. Me and Mary will wake up Victor and the priest that tried to help us."

I frowned, then nodded, taking off my belt. I quickly fashioned restraints to use on Chase and tied his hands behind his back, looping them through the wrought iron gate surrounding the garden.

"Go!" Jackie urged.

Finally, I nodded and hurried toward the gate.

My head felt like it was stuffed with cotton. Thoughts were coming slowly and garbled. The world spun as I moved through it, but I pushed on, ignoring the almost certain concussion that clouded my thinking. I reached my daughter, who smiled up at me.

"Miss Ava said she had to go when she saw you and Mommy kissing. She went that way, then turned that way," she said, pointing left toward St. Peters Street, then to the right. I nodded and kissed her on the head. "Hurry, Daddy," she urged.

Even the French Quarter has to sleep at some point, and it was the dead of the night as I rushed down the street and followed Mary's directions. Hurry, she'd said. An all-out run was beyond me, but a fast stumbling walk seemed like it was just my speed. Thirty seconds on St. Peters, and I could see Ava's form ahead. She was walking slowly, hugging her midsection as she went. It looked like she was crying.

My heart sank as I quickened my pace.

I had no idea what I was going to say or do when I caught up to her. Only that I needed to. I needed to catch up to her and make the crying stop as much as I had ever needed anything in my entire life. I needed it like a drowning man needed air.

I was twenty feet behind her, and I could hear her sobs.

Fifteen.

"Ava!"

I called her name, and she startled, turning to look back. When she saw it was me, she quickly wiped her eyes with her right hand, leaving her left, cradling her stomach.

I opened my mouth—but couldn't think of what to say.

"I—are you hurt?" I blurted out.

"Hurt?" she asked, laughing through a sob and pursing her lips to hold back tears. "Go back, Bishop. Go back to your family reunion. I'm a big girl. I'll be okay."

I shook my head and walked forward.

"I thought that's where I was supposed to be too, but it turns out I was wrong," I said.

"I didn't think the great Jason Bishop admitted that out loud where people could hear it," she said.

"I've been wrong about so damned many things, Ava, and I was *definitely* wrong about me and Jackie."

Ava sniffed and tilted her head. "Come again?"

"She was right. I was wrong. We'd never work, not in a healthy way," I admitted.

"I just saw her expressing a very different opinion with her tongue, Bishop. Get back there before you screw this up," she pleaded, her eyes moist.

"I'm trying to undo one screw up, not create a new one," I explained. "Ava, I—I think I love you."

She stared at me for a heartbeat. Then another. Then a third before letting out a bitter laugh.

"How the hell am I supposed to respond to that?" she whispered.

"How 'bout that you think you love me too?" I asked.

She shook her head, her expression miserable.

"I wish I could, Jason. I really, really wish I could, but you're betting on the wrong horse. I'm a demon, remember? A succubus. We don't love people. We use them. Trap them. We can't love. It's not in our nature. I'm sorry, but I—I think you're looking for something that just isn't there. Again."

"Bullshit. I know you, Ava Dufrense. I know you better than I know myself. I've seen the way you care for Nat. For Nero. For Dave—"

"That's different. Those are—" she stammered.

"Bullshit. I know you care about them. They're your family. You may have started out as someone else. Something else, but where you ended up is right here. They've changed you as much as you've changed them. Hell, as much as we've all changed each other."

She closed her eyes and shrugged.

"Fine, I care about them. That's not the same thing as—" she said.

"Love? What do you call love, Ava? Is it risking your life to help someone? Nearly getting killed repeatedly over the course of three days. Is it entering sanctified ground when you knew it could kill you to save that person? His kid? Ava, you were caring before, but tonight you were the textbook definition of selfless. I hate to break it to you, but that's not something actual demons are capable of. That sort of behavior takes more."

She opened her eyes, frightened, but with a glimmer of hope.

"I—I don't—"

"I do," I continued, stepping forward and wrapping my arms around her.

"Why?" she asked, looking up at me. "You say you love me. Fine. It's a terrible idea, but fine. Why? Why would you love me?"

I shrugged. "Because we make sense. The last few days, with all of this craziness going on, you're the first person I think about when I wake up—"

"One of those days you'd just had a blood transfusion from me. That might have factored in," she replied, resting her hands on my chest and staring between them.

"You're the last person I want to see before I go to sleep. I love catching the whiffs of vanilla that linger after you leave a room, and you make me want to be better. Not to prove something to you. Just to be better for you," I said.

She looked up.

"I—I don't know how to be what you're going to want me to be. I don't think I can be who you need me to be," she whispered, her eyes on mine.

"I don't know what I want you to be either, and I've got no idea who I need you to be, other than you. We're both gonna need to figure this shit out as we go along. We'll probably both fuck up," I said.

"You're almost certainly going to. Epically," she agreed.

I didn't have a great reply, so I went with my gut and kissed her.

Luckily, she kissed me back.

It wasn't the hungry, desperate kiss I'd shared with Jackie earlier. Ava was tentative at first. Not certain that she was doing the right thing, but willing to test the waters. She was unsure of what she was doing. What we were doing, but I felt her arms wrap around me after a moment, holding me tight as she increased the intensity of her kiss, losing herself in the moment.

It was the sort of kiss you want to stay inside of as long as you can. To savor. We stood in the middle of St. Peters Street, our arms around each other, ignoring the world.

I breathed in the heady scent of Ava, ignoring my mashed, bloody nose, just as she seemed to be ignoring the burns and bruises she'd picked up over the past two nights. We held onto one another, afraid to let go. Afraid to lose what we'd just found. I'd questioned everything in my life for the past thirteen years. I'd picked at each and every decision, second-guessed everything I'd done, and analyzed everything.

But not this. This felt right, and I wanted this moment with her to last forever.

The kiss lasted an eternity but was over far too soon.

Swallowing, she looked up at me and offered the slightest hint of a smile.

"Let's go home."

She wrapped her arm in mine, laid her head on my shoulder, and we did.

The End